WHAT THE LADY WANTS

EMMA ORCHARD

Boldwood

First published in Great Britain in 2024 by Boldwood Books Ltd.

Copyright © Emma Orchard, 2024

Cover Artwork and Design by Rachel Lawston

A CIP catalogue record for this book is available from the British Library.

Paperback ISBN 978-1-83561-064-0

Large Print ISBN 978-1-83561-063-3

Hardback ISBN 978-1-83561-062-6

Ebook ISBN 978-1-83561-065-7

Kindle ISBN 978-1-83561-066-4

Audio CD ISBN 978-1-83561-057-2

MP3 CD ISBN 978-1-83561-058-9

Digital audio download ISBN 978-1-83561-059-6

Boldwood Books Ltd
23 Bowerdean Street
London SW6 3TN
www.boldwoodbooks.com

To all the librarians, booksellers and book bloggers who work hard to get people reading. Where would we be without you?

PROLOGUE

AUTUMN 1816, THE DUCHESS OF NORTHRIDING'S BALL

Number one

Isabella was excited, arriving in Grosvenor Square and climbing the steps to enter the mansion between rows of tall footmen in black and silver livery. It had been dark for hours, and flickering torches struck gleams of light from the jewels and costly gold lace that adorned the Duchess's distinguished guests, and from their avid eyes. The air of anticipation was almost palpable.

Isabella was sure, though, that her internal turmoil must be of quite a different order from the emotions of the other guests. They were there to dance, to observe and to gossip, perhaps to flirt; she had so much more at stake. But that was a dangerous way to think, and liable to make her panic. She was all too aware of her growing agitation and told herself sternly and silently that she must suppress it. She had made a plan, and she was about to set about its execution, that was all. She scanned the crowd eagerly but surreptitiously for him, conversing with her companions and greeting acquaintances in a mechanical sort of way, and paying very little attention to her opulent surroundings, familiar as they were. She'd spent part of her honeymoon in this impressive mansion, not so very long ago.

Isabella – or, to give her the proper title, Lady Ashby Mauleverer – was not yet twenty-two, but she was a widow. Her husband, Lord Ashby, second son of the Eighth Duke of Northriding and brother of the Ninth, had died at Waterloo. Had died in her arms the day after the battle, in fact, and the shock of his death and the horrifying manner of it had caused Isabella to enter a dark time, a period lasting a year or more which she preferred not to remember, certainly not to dwell on. She had recovered, though, with the support of her family and the most modern and humane medical aid, and one of the things that had helped her to do so was a private resolution she had made: to take control of her life. That was the purpose of her plan. After a long time in which she had not even been able to decide whether to rise or stay in bed, what to wear, what to eat or how to spend the day, she would be in charge. If her plan worked, completely in charge.

She had been discharged from her doctor's care in the summer, and now it was autumn. Against the wishes of her parents, who persisted in seeing her as fragile and probably always would, she had come to London to stay with her sister-in-law, Lady Blanche FitzHenry, and tonight she was attending a grand ball at Mauleverer House, which her brother-in-law Gabriel and his bride Georgiana were giving to celebrate their marriage a couple of months ago. This was the perfect occasion to set her scheme in motion because she was confident that not a single one of the guests present tonight would be looking at her or noticing what she did. She had been something of a novelty in a small way when she had first emerged into London society: a young and quite well-off widow – her jointure was ample, and would not cease if she remarried – undeniably well-connected, and not unattractive, she supposed. Ash had found her beautiful, had told her so a thousand times – no, she would not think about Ash now, she must not. But she had attended many parties and other events over the last few weeks, had done nothing at all to provoke any comment, yet, and any interest that the sensation-loving ladies and gentlemen of the haut ton had been disposed to show in her had waned.

She – and every other topic of gossip that summer and autumn – had been eclipsed by the far more fascinating subject of Gabriel and Georgiana and the thrilling, scandalous circumstances of their recent union. This suited Isabella very well, and she felt herself to be as good as invisible in the crowded silver and white ballroom, which was already full almost to the point of discomfort with loudly chattering persons dressed in the very height of fashion. Lady Jersey was close by, conversing with Lady Sefton in the genteel sort of shriek that was necessary to make oneself heard above the din. Isabella was truly surrounded by the very cream of the polite world – it seemed that even those who had been absent from London this autumn had returned for this most intriguing of events, and there was a hum of expectation as the music struck up.

The newly married Duke and Duchess took to the floor and opened the dancing, both of them dark and glamorous and endlessly fascinating, their love for each other written plainly on their faces, and Isabella's hand was, as she had hoped, solicited for her first set by Captain Leo Winterton.

He was tall, broad-shouldered, handsome; he also looked nothing at all like Ash. The first part wasn't terribly important, or shouldn't be, but the second part was. Isabella was aware that the execution of her plan would surely remind her of her husband, and she was resigned to the inevitability of that. There was no need to make things worse by choosing a man who resembled Ash in any

way. Lord Ashby had been tall, like all his family, but he had also
been dark, his black hair prematurely streaked with silver, his eyes
a striking shade of silver too. His older brother the Duke resembled
him greatly, and in the early stages of her bereavement, Isabella
had found it hard to look at Gabriel, and especially to see little
quirks of expression, little mannerisms, that the brothers had
shared. She had reason to be proud that she had been able to put
all that behind her now and meet Gabriel with composure – she
had just done so, not half an hour since – but it would be foolish to
tempt fate by choosing a tall, dark, grey-eyed man to help her
execute her scheme.

Captain Leo Winterton was by contrast fair, as fair as she was,
and his eyes were a clear blue, his complexion tanned by his years
at sea. He seemed sunny-natured, of a cheerful, light-hearted
disposition, and again this was unlike Ash, who had been intense,
serious, though never humourless. The two men were perhaps
similar in height and build, but in casting her eyes over her possibilities (this was a different list; Isabella was quite addicted to lists),
she had discovered in herself a natural preference for a tall man,
and she could not see any harm in indulging it. Although there was
no possibility of what she planned leading to anything lasting, it
was most necessary that she found the man attractive. And she did.
She was prepared to admit as much to herself, though of course to
nobody else. Hence, perhaps, her excitement tonight.

He smiled down at her as they danced, and they conversed of
nothing in particular, but in a comfortable, easy fashion. They had
only recently become acquainted, during the past few weeks of
Isabella's stay in London, and they were in a sense related, if only
distantly and by marriage, since Captain Winterton was Georgiana's first cousin, and Georgiana was now Isabella's sister-in-law
and Gabriel's new Duchess. There was a certain safety, she thought,
in choosing someone who was in some sense a member of the

family and therefore unlikely, if it turned out that he greatly disap- proved of her scheme, to spread dangerous gossip. Isabella did not much care if she became the subject of society murmurs once her plan was successful, not on her own account, as she did not intend to stay in London beyond this short visit, but she had no desire to embarrass Ash's sister Blanche, who had been nothing but good to her. And if her parents came to hear of it, which she devoutly hoped they never would, she knew it would hurt them, and heaven knows they had been hurt and worried enough already since her bereavement.

When the set ended, she cast down her eyes and said, 'I feel a little unwell – the heat of the room... Would you escort me some- where cooler, sir?'

The Captain was instantly all solicitude, and she felt a little guilty. 'You do look pale, ma'am. Can I fetch my cousin or Lady Blanche...?'

'No!' she blurted out, alarmed. That would not suit her purposes at all. And then, in gentler tones, 'If you could give me your arm and take me out into the garden for a moment... It's just beyond the end of the entrance hall, on the right, through the furthest door. I do not want to make a fuss or attract unwelcome attention, and I should hate to spoil the party for anyone.' This much was true.

Isabella knew the house well, and soon they had pushed through the press of people; in a moment or two they were outside. If she'd really been unwell, she'd probably have swooned long since in the heat and the crowd, but luckily she wasn't. It was indeed much cooler out here, which was no great surprise given that it was October, and Captain Winterton was about to express concern that it might be too cold for a lady's delicate constitution after the heat inside, she thought, when she forestalled him by melting into his arms. She did this by essentially flinging herself at his chest and putting her gloved hands upon it to cling to him – it was a little awkward since he was not in the least expecting it. As chests went, it really was agreeably broad and firmly muscled, she noticed in passing as she clung.

He was taken aback. The courtyard garden was not well-lit, illuminated as it was only by the light that spilt out from the ballroom windows that overlooked it, but she could see an expression of puzzlement upon his handsome features. He did not appear disgusted by her proximity, but he was surprised by it, certainly. 'You are unwell, ma'am,' he said, 'I cannot think you mean…'

But his strong arms came around her, as if by instinct – perhaps he thought she would fall if he did not support her, and in that instant, she thought perhaps she might – and she looked up at him and said, 'I am perfectly well. I am sorry for deceiving you, but I could not think of any other way of ensuring that we should be alone. I was hoping, you see, that you might kiss me.'

'You… were?'

'Yes,' she said. He was still holding her, which was good, but he wasn't kissing her, which was excessively disappointing. 'I thought you wanted to, but I fear I was mistaken.'

'Oh no,' he said, and she thought she saw a ghost of a smile cross his face. 'No, you weren't mistaken.' And he bent his head, and his lips found hers.

He was very gentle at first, but it was pleasant, it was more than pleasant, and when she opened her mouth a little in encouragement, he was not slow to respond. His lips were warm and soft and his breath was sweet. He smelled good, he felt good. He held her tightly in the shadows, though his hands did not explore her body, and he kissed her very thoroughly, and she kissed him back with great enthusiasm, and only a tiny little corner of her brain thought, Ash will no longer be the last man I kissed, or the only man I ever kissed. But that was part of the point, so she repressed the fugitive thought, and gave herself up to the sensual enjoyment of the moment and the comfort of being held in a strong embrace after so long.

When at last he drew away from her a little, but only a little, she looked up at him and was glad to see that his eyes were dark with desire and his face soft with pleasure and a sort of wonder.

'Lady Ashby, Isabella...' he said, his voice low and drugged with sensation. It was rather thrilling to think that she had had this effect on him, especially since she found herself not unaffected too. 'I did not intend or expect...'

'I know you didn't,' she said, and she was surprised to hear her voice emerge as a sensual sort of sigh, almost a moan. This would never do. 'I know you didn't,' she repeated more firmly. It was important to be business-like, to keep her head, to take control. 'But I did.'

'I realise that now,' he said, his ready humour warming his voice. 'Did you – I apologise if this is too strong a word, but I am in a sorry state of confusion and can think of no better – did you bring me here with the intention of seducing me, ma'am?'

'No! Well, yes, I suppose so,' she conceded in a spirit of fair-mindedness. 'But you liked kissing me, didn't you? It wasn't in any way disagreeable to you?' She knew he'd liked it; his body had betrayed exactly how much, but she thought it best not to mention that just now. It would be crude, unladylike, and although Ash had not objected to a little plain speaking in such matters, her experience did not extend beyond him and she could not tell if Captain Winterton might feel the same or not. If her plan worked, she would find out. She could not suppress a delicious little shudder at the thought.

He was still holding her close, his hands about her waist, and her arms, it seemed, had crept up around his neck, and were still there. It was a little awkward now, but it hardly seemed the moment to remove them. 'It was very far from being disagreeable,' he said. 'It was rather wonderful, in fact. I hope you liked it too...?'

'Oh yes,' she said a little breathlessly. 'I liked it very much. I thought I would, and I was glad to be right. Because I have a proposition to put to you, sir. I have a list.'

1

AUTUMN 1816, A FEW WEEKS EARLIER

He'd seen her at last. Met her again, when he had least expected it. Leo was presented to Lady Ashby directly after his arrival in London, and he feared he'd gaped at her in sad confusion for a long moment before he gathered his scattered wits and greeted her, but if his reaction had been odd, it seemed nobody had noticed. She certainly hadn't. If she had the slightest recollection of ever having laid eyes on him before, let alone been introduced, dancing together, she showed no sign of it, so in common courtesy, he had no option but to do the same and greet her as a stranger.

Good God, he discovered now to his astonishment that she was a sort of connection of his – her late husband, whom he remembered perfectly well, had been the younger brother of the rather intimidating Duke of Northriding, who was now married to Leo's own madcap cousin Georgiana.

Setting aside this unexpected family connection, there was not the least reason why he should be surprised to see her – it wasn't impossible or even unlikely, after all, that a young lady once encountered in society in Brussels just before Waterloo, when the city had been full of British soldiers of high rank and their families, should be met again eighteen months later in London. It might even be considered inevitable, the world of the haut ton being so small and he in some sense a part of it now.

Leo had tried, over the last year or more, to tell himself that he had no hope or expectation of ever setting eyes on her again. He'd known that it would be both wrong and useless to wish to do so, because she was happily married, and he was not the sort of man who pursued a married woman or pined after her like a mooncalf. He'd never done such a thing in his life and he had no intention of starting now. If he had dreamed of her – when he had – he had told himself sternly that he had no business permitting himself such a shocking liberty.

Their acquaintance had been so very brief, barely deserving the name, though he could not deny that it had assumed a greater importance in his mind, both at the time and afterwards. He'd been at a loose end during the summer of 1815, his ship *Paris* undergoing long-overdue repairs in the naval dockyards, and an unusual spirit of restlessness had seized him. Bonaparte had escaped from Elba and was rallying his scattered legions for what must surely be his final throw of the dice; Britain and its allies were assembling to meet him. It seemed tame to sit at home when such momentous events were unfolding just across the Channel. His estate was in good order, and his widowed mother was spending the summer at some seaside resort with his orphaned young cousins. He felt a little guilty leaving her to it, but all at once it was unbearable for a man of spirit to spend his precious free time bear-leading three wild young cubs and attempting to keep them out of mischief when he could be witnessing history in the making.

He'd crossed to the Continent almost on impulse on a crowded packet-boat and found cramped lodgings in a Brussels inn, then, along with the rest of Europe, he waited to see what would happen, with Bonaparte in Paris making his plans and the Allied armies gathering here, a scant two hundred miles away.

He'd not expected the summer to consist chiefly of balls, picnics and parties rather than military alarums, but so it had proved, at least at first. There was a sort of hectic excitement in the air, a sense of imminent danger that gave spice to the most ordinary of events, and Leo found himself caught up in it. Though he had no intimate friends in the town, he'd introductions aplenty, as half his naval shipmates seemed to have brothers or cousins serving in Wellington's army. They were welcoming and friendly, albeit very ready to mock a member of the senior service and call him all sorts of unflattering names, but since they were about to risk their lives in battle and he currently wasn't, he could hardly argue and must smile at their roasting and retaliate in kind, calling them Hyde Park soldiers. Friendship, even intimacy, seemed to blossom quickly here, as the normal rules of society had not broken down, but certainly had eased. And this was how he found himself dancing, one warm summer evening, with a young lady with dark blonde hair and big brown eyes. He didn't know her name, and he'd go bail she didn't know his. It was most unusual, even irregular. But in this time and place it didn't seem to matter.

He'd been presented to her in a scrambling sort of fashion by one of his new military friends, but the young lieutenant was slightly foxed already and besides the large inn's assembly room was crowded and very noisy, so that he hadn't caught the casual words properly. Lady A something – Lady Anne? Lady Alice? A woman of high rank, then, the daughter of a nobleman, but she didn't seem like it, putting on no die-away airs but only smiling at him in an open, friendly way as he bowed over her hand.

The scraping of fiddles resolved itself into an actual tune, a country dance, and the sets formed up in somewhat chaotic fash-ion. There was little room to turn and step, it was not at all convenient, but most of the dancers were young and in giddy, infectious high spirits, and they were smiling as they made their way up and down, trying and not always succeeding to avoid bumping into others. Nobody seemed to mind. Soon he was laughing at the sheer ridiculousness of it, and so was his partner. She had a lovely laugh, free and unaffected – enchanting.

And she was lovely, all in blue, her hair shining in the candle-light. She wasn't delicate and willowy and disturbingly fragile-seeming like many of the other young ladies he'd danced with here, nor was she elegant and remote; she was real. She was short, voluptuous, all soft womanly curves. Her hair was a rich honey-blonde, long and straight, worn braided around her head, and even as he danced he experienced a sudden strong forbidden desire to undo the braids, shake it free, run his fingers through its silkiness, then bury his face in it. He imagined it would smell wonderful, and he'd love to have a chance to find out. Her eyes were a deep brown, very large and expressive, and it seemed to him that she looked at the world with a frank, level gaze that he was beginning to find enormously appealing. They spoke a little, breathlessly, as they whirled, and she did not chatter or flirt or giggle shrilly but was direct, matter-of-fact, her face flushed with honest enjoyment. It was a brief moment, and he couldn't fool himself, then or later, that they'd established any sort of special connection – but how he'd have liked to. He'd not previously been aware of loneliness among so many people, but now oddly he was.

The set had barely finished when another fellow claimed her hand in a possessive fashion, a tall, dark man in the gold-laced uniform of a crack cavalry regiment. She knew him well, clearly, and didn't seem to resent his presumption; with a brief apologetic smile at Leo, she allowed herself to be whirled away into the next dance. He was left standing, feeling a little foolish, arms empty, suddenly bereft, and stabbed by a sharp pang of jealousy as ridiculous as it was unwelcome.

He'd hoped to dance with her again – one of the new waltzes would have been perfect – but although he'd looked for her for the rest of the evening he hadn't found her. He could only presume that she'd left; no doubt she had other invitations aplenty. He'd tried to ask his friend Lieutenant Paterson who she was, but the inebriated young idiot had just shrugged and said he couldn't recall introducing Leo to anybody at all.

Leo had seen her again, though. He hadn't passed the last year and more thinking wistfully about a woman he'd danced with once and never set eyes on after; he wasn't quite as bad as that. He spent a great deal of time over the next few days joining the fashionable afternoon promenade in the crowded streets and extensive park of the town, or sitting at outdoor cafes watching the colourful throng pass by, and eventually his perseverance was rewarded. Suddenly, with a little leap of the heart, he saw her in an open carriage, shielding herself with a lacy parasol and accompanied by an older couple who must surely be her parents, so greatly did the lady resemble her in form, feature and colouring.

Daylight did Lady A no disservice. She was every bit as attractive as he'd thought, and as he stood by the roadside, quite close to her barouche, she turned her head and saw him. Could he flatter himself that she blushed just a little? He couldn't be sure. But she smiled at him in recognition, as warm and open as she'd been before, and he smiled too and bowed to her. They were close enough that they could have greeted each other, and he was about to speak. But then the obstruction in traffic that had permitted this tiny, insignificant encounter cleared, and the carriage had moved on before he could utter a word.

It had been the second week in June by then, and the hourglass was running down on the hectic gaiety of the city. But there'd been another impromptu assembly at the same inn just before the end, and this time Lieutenant Paterson was sober and alert – all sorts of rumours were swirling around to the effect that battle might be joined very soon, and every man of Wellington's army must be ready for it – so that when Leo saw the young lady enter with her parents, he was able to say with what he hoped was sufficient carelessness, 'Paterson, that's the girl you presented me to a few nights ago, but I never caught her name, though I danced and conversed with her. It's cursed awkward, I see her everywhere and she plainly recognises me, but I cannot speak a word to her – could you be a good fellow and tell me who she is?'

Paterson craned his neck and then whistled. 'The tall beauty with the red hair and painted toenails? Well, I see you navy dogs have dangerous tastes! That's the notorious—'

'No, you clod-pole, not her! The shorter woman with the blonde braided hair, in the gold silk.' The gold silk that clung quite charmingly to her frame, Leo couldn't help but notice.

'Oh, I see her now. You mean that plump little dab of a thing?' he said casually. 'That's Isabella Richmond – I grew up with her in Harrogate, you know. She pushed me in a pond once, can't recall why.'

'I thought you called her Lady Something,' said Leo with exaggerated patience.

'Of course I did. She's Lady Ashby Mauleverer now – married to Northriding's brother, you know, this past twelvemonth. Quite the love match. Don't see her pushing *him* in ponds.'

'Married...' said Leo dazedly. It hadn't so much as occurred to him that she could be, though now he didn't know why he'd been so blind. She'd been wearing gloves, of course, so her wedding ring hadn't been visible, and if there had been subtle clues in the way she was dressed to indicate her status and her unavailability, he'd missed them. Perhaps he'd wanted to miss them.

And as he watched he saw that the tall, dark cavalry officer he'd seen with her before was present now too, right at her side, smiling down at her warmly, intimately, and she was smiling up at him with what he could not help but recognise as love written on her sweet face. They looked happy, they were happy, and he felt like an idiot.

Three days later, he now knew, the man was dead and cold, along with so many others on the fields of Quatre Bras, Ligny and Waterloo. His regiment had fought with outstanding bravery and suffered appalling losses, Lord Ashby among them.

Leo had seen those wounded men and would never forget the awful sight, cavalry and infantry and artillerymen, hundreds upon hundreds of them. He had helped carry them into inns and private houses so that they could be cared for, had fetched and carried for the nurses and the surgeons. He'd done what little he could to help, even if that had meant just gripping a frightened boy's hand in futile reassurance and talking to him as he died in agony, screaming pitifully for his mama, or, more mercifully, slipped into a sleep from which he never awoke. He'd had similar experiences at sea, of course – had lost close friends – but the sheer scale of this, not to mention the incongruous domestic setting, was new and horrifying.

Leo hadn't known that at the time, of course, that Lady Ashby's husband had been one of those poor fellows. How could he? He had never seen the notice of one man's death among so many others, and now that he had the information he wasn't sure what to do with it. She was free, but it seemed entirely wrong to be glad of it.

2

Leo Winterton was twenty-seven years old and had spent almost half of his life in the navy, but the wars were over at last, thank God, and he was done with it all. He had passed the wet, cold summer of 1816 teaching his wild young cousins how to sail, but now they were at school – God help the school and its poor unsuspecting teachers – and he was at a loose end. His older cousin and close friend Hal, Lord Irlam, aware of his lack of purpose, had invited him to come and stay with him and his wife Cassandra at their grand mansion in Town, and, for want of anything better to do, he had agreed, and here he was.

He had little experience of polite society – whatever the navy had been, it hadn't been that – and after taking ship so young this was his first real taste of London parties and London life. Somewhat to his surprise, he had found himself in demand in a modest sort of a way. He was well-born and well-connected enough, though he was no aristocrat, and somehow word had got round that he had taken several valuable prizes during the late wars with France, and had won by his exertions a respectable fortune to add to the modest sum and small Hampshire estate his father had left him. Various young ladies had looked up at him with melting eyes and invited him to share his fascinating reminiscences of life at sea with them – these offers he had politely declined. He had no taste for puffing off his own consequence, and he didn't think any of these refined damsels were really interested in what it was like to go into battle, the sights, the sounds, the smells... No.

But it was undeniably pleasant to be clean, healthy, well-fed and well-dressed, with nobody firing cannon at him or attempting to put a period to his life in any other manner, and to take a good-looking young woman in his arms and twirl about the dance floor in exhilarating motion. The waltz was now danced everywhere, and it was an innovation greatly to his liking. It was pleasant too to ride in the park on one of Hal's excellent horses, and to sit at ease in Hal's club and take a glass or two of good wine with one of his Corinthian friends, or to while away a few hours in pugilistic exercise at Gentleman Jackson's saloon, where Hal was a regular and favoured visitor.

He found, also, that he enjoyed Cassandra's company, and this was new. He had been back at sea when his cousin had married her last autumn, so he had only made her acquaintance quite recently, and he liked her enormously. She and Hal were plainly very well-suited and very happy, and perhaps inevitably the sight of them together made a man think of settling down. He'd never thought about marriage before – as a naval ensign, lieutenant and then commander it had not crossed his mind, he'd been too young, and when, a little older, he had gained his own ship and really begun to make his way in the world, he had been too occupied to dwell on such things. It had seemed unwise to cherish dreams that might never be realised when a French cannonball or a wickedly sharp falling spar or heavy piece of timber could at any moment have cut him down, knocked him overboard, crushed or maimed him.

But here he was, whole and more or less undamaged, unlike so many, and he felt for the first time in his life the pleasure of refined feminine society, as he sat in Cassandra's parlour and took tea with her. He was not in the least in love with her, but she was friendly, sympathetic, quick-witted, as well as undeniably attractive to look upon, and he could perfectly understand why his cousin had fallen for her so quickly and completely. He was not a savage; he had spent time with his mother, of course, while on leave, but he realised now that he was not closely acquainted with very many *young* ladies at all, and none who were not his relations by blood. This was an omission that should be rectified, he felt, and London was the place to do it. If he cherished a memory of a girl in blue laughing up at him, one warm night in Brussels, he'd pushed it away. It had, after all, been nothing more than a fantasy.

And then he set eyes on Lady Ashby again so unexpectedly. It hurt just a little to see that she had no memory at all of him, but when he realised that her husband had fallen at Waterloo – had been recovered from the battlefield horribly wounded and died in her arms – he understood why it should be so, after all that she had suffered, and could not think to blame her for it. The last thing he wanted to do was remind her of that time, which had ended in such tragedy for her. And so he said nothing. Having not mentioned it at first, of course, it was now too late to raise the matter as their intimacy increased.

The connection between the families meant that they were often in each other's company as the weeks passed; if he'd wanted to avoid her, which he didn't at all, he'd hardly have found it possible. They made up pleasant family parties and attended the theatre, the opera and many private events. It was very odd indeed to think of Georgie the tearaway as Her Grace the Duchess, married to a reformed rake with a terrible reputation, but they seemed ridiculously happy, just like Hal and Cassandra. Everybody was married and everybody was happy. Nobody was single and lonely and a little sad, going to sleep and waking up in a cold, empty bed, apart from him. And, dare he imagine, her? Leo felt that fate, or providence, or one of those Greek deities they'd bored on about endlessly at school, was practically yelling at him, irritated by his obtuseness, *See these other fellows? This could be you, sapskull!* Could it, really? Could the past be overcome so easily? Slowly, cautiously, Leo began to hope that it might.

He'd thought at first that Lady Ashby, widow of a duke's younger son as he now knew her to be, must be far above his touch, but on talking to her he'd found to his delight that this was not the case at all. As he grew to know her better he discovered that she came, in fact, from a background much like his own: her parents had a small estate just outside Harrogate, and like him she was an only child, having lost several siblings in infancy. She told him with a frankness that touched his heart that she had met Lord Ashby, a major in the Seventh Hussars, when he had been recuperating in the spa town of Harrogate from wounds taken around the time of Toulouse, and thus her connection with a grand ducal house was only by marriage rather than by blood. This was heartening, as it was not entirely dissimilar to his own relationship with the Pendlebury family; his father had been a solid country gentleman of unremarkable fortune and his mother was a country lady, whose late sister had happened to marry very well, becoming Countess of Irlam. He believed with some confidence that he need not fear that she, Lady Ashby – Isabella – her parents, nor anybody in her family would think him presumptuous in aspiring to her hand.

He did aspire to it, he realised as the weeks passed and their acquaintance deepened. But he resolved to take things slowly. It would be foolish to rush matters, and he must be patient. It was not just a question of respecting her grief, though that was responsibility enough. He understood from things that Isabella herself had said – for it seemed to him that deception or concealment were entirely foreign to her nature – that she had been most unwell after her husband had died, and lost in a sort of fog of unhappiness for a long time, from which she had only now emerged. He detected in himself a desire to take care of her, to protect her from the world, but he could see that that was not in the least what she wanted. Quite the reverse, in fact. In a burst of entirely characteristic frankness and not quite characteristic volubility, she had told him one brisk, cold day, as they strolled together in the park with Cassandra and Georgie a week or so before the Duchess's ball, that she had come to London to escape from her parents and a concern for her that she had begun to experience as stifling and oppressive, though she understood why they should feel so anxious about her always.

Their companions being ahead of them, arm in arm, clearly exchanging confidences, Countess to Duchess, Lady Ashby had spoken openly to him of her illness; he had not at the time understood why she had chosen to confide in him of all people, but had been glad of it, taking it as a sign that their relationship was deepening and heading in the direction that he so ardently desired it should. 'I was mad, for a while,' she said, looking up at him with those liquid brown eyes that made him melt into a puddle of wanting. He must have made some instinctive protest, for she said matter-of-factly, 'No, I really was. It seemed to me so... so wrong that Ash should be dead, and I just could not believe it for the longest time. He was so very alive, you see, and then such a short while later... The sight of him, so terribly wounded, in such dreadful pain, was always present to me, and... It was a nightmare time. But one does not speak of such things; forgive me, sir.'

He hastened to tell her that he understood, that there was nothing to forgive. And it was true, of course; he too had seen terrible things, things of which one did not speak, things which most young ladies could have no comprehension of, and why should they? Was that not one of the reasons men fought, to shelter women from such things? But she had not been so sheltered. And he knew she'd loved her husband, and he her – he'd seen them together, glowing with happiness. But of course he could not say so.

She was not done; she continued bravely on as the autumn leaves fell around them in a whirl of bright colour. 'Ash and I had so many plans for our life together, and it was very hard for me to understand at last that none of them would come to pass. My brother-in-law had not the least intention of marrying at that point in his life, you know, before he met your cousin. He was quite open about the fact with everybody. And so it was generally expected that Ash and I would have children and raise them at Northriding, and then in the course of time he, or our son, would eventually inherit the ducal title and the estate. So far more was lost than our future together; Northriding itself was suddenly in peril, with nobody to inherit after Gabriel. Their poor young cousin John, the next heir, died after Waterloo too, you see. And I felt such a failure, you know, because I had not been able to give Ash, give all of them, an heir when they were all depending on me. I knew they were counting on me for that, though of course they never spoke of their bitter disappointment. They scarcely needed to. And so somehow I persuaded myself that not all of him was gone and that I was indeed with child. I could easily have been so, you understand.' He did. Once more they were speaking of matters that were not generally discussed, but he could not think to stop her. And it was ridiculous and unseemly to be jealous of her intimacy with a dead man, and one furthermore who had fallen in battle, given his precious life and all his future for his country, even though he had been a duke's son and surely need not have put himself at risk.

'But I wasn't. I was deceiving myself. And that too was a great grief to me, when I was forced to realise it, and my illness came back, and I was truly not in my right mind for quite a while. I was under the care of a doctor in York, where they specialise in such matters. Everyone was very kind to me, and patient, my parents most of all. But now I am better, and although I am very grateful, and always will be, for the care they took of me, I can quite understand that it will take them a long while to accept that I am well now, and stop treating me as though I were made of china. Because I'm not.' She tilted up her chin adorably when she said this, and he wanted to kiss her then and there, but of course he couldn't. It would be most improper and she could not possibly welcome it.

'They are bound to be protective of you, I suppose,' he said instead.

'I know they are. But that's why I came away, to stay with my sister-in-law. I think it will be good for them as well as me, not to always be worrying that I am becoming unwell if I say the least little thing that makes them think I am cast down or low in spirits, as anybody must be every now and then. Because,' she said with a perfectly straight face, 'sometimes when they hover over me with anxious expressions on their dear faces, much as I love them, I want to scream and throw things.'

'Which would relieve your feelings for a short time, no doubt, but hardly reassure them as to your complete recovery.'

'Exactly,' she replied in tones of satisfaction. 'And that is why it is so much better to be staying with Blanche and her daughter Eleanor, because although they are very fond of me and were worried about me when I was ill, they were naturally never concerned about me in just the way that my parents were, nor did they see me at my very worst.'

'I do understand,' he said. 'I too have a mother, who worries.'

'I did not know. Well, obviously I did, for everyone has a mother, at least to begin with.' They laughed a little awkwardly, both visibly relieved to speak of less intense matters. 'Does Mrs Winterton not care for London society, then?'

By tacit mutual consent, their conversation turned to lighter topics, and presently they caught up with Cassandra and Georgiana, who appeared to be still so absorbed in their conversation that they had not even noticed their absence.

After this moment of closeness, Leo met Isabella frequently and danced with her on several occasions, but he had no opportunity to converse privately with her again until she engineered their moment together at Georgiana's ball. *That* was entirely unexpected. At first, he had feared she was unwell, and no thought of anything else had entered his mind, but when she pressed herself against him he realised – for he would have been very dull-witted indeed not to realise – that she had planned this. She soon admitted as much. She wanted him to kiss her, she said she did, and Christ knew he wanted that too. When he brushed her lips with his a little tentatively, her mouth opened to him in invitation, sweet and wet and tempting. It was all he had dreamed of, and when he nibbled on her full lower lip she gave a tiny gasp and her arms came up to clasp about his neck, and she pressed her lush body closer yet. God, it was so good.

Leo had himself under very strict control, and so it was a kiss, the kiss she had asked for, and nothing more. He held her tightly about the waist and she fitted into his embrace as though she belonged there, warm and soft and gloriously right, but he did not allow himself to explore her body. He wanted to run his hands down her back and caress every curve and hollow; he *wanted* to pull up her gown and petticoats and touch her bare skin; he *wanted* to lift her up so that she could wrap her legs around his waist while he pressed himself, hard and hot, against her belly. He *wanted* to plunder her mouth with his tongue and then kiss his way down her shoulders to her breasts. He wanted all sorts of things that would be wonderful, but wrong. He kissed her and she kissed him back, and if she were aware of the urgency of his desire – and he thought she must be, as a woman who had been married – she gave no sign of it.

When the kiss was finished, and it had to finish before he lost his self-control entirely, he spoke to her – he wasn't entirely sure what he said – but she seemed to gather her wits more quickly than he did. At first, he thought she might be proposing marriage to him, and although it was undoubtedly unconventional and sudden, he would have been perfectly happy to accept, to say, *Yes, Isabella, I will marry you, please let it be very soon, and in the meantime may I kiss you again?* But no. It didn't seem to be that at all. He couldn't imagine what it could be.

He was still holding her and had no wish to let her go; she didn't seem to want to be released, was still relaxed and warm in his embrace. Every inch of him was still thrumming with unfulfilled desire, and he would have wagered she was in the same state. His body had decided opinions about all this: about the desirability of continuing, and the madness of stopping. And it was almost impossible to think, to do anything at all but feel, while he held her, but he must. 'A proposition...' he said dazedly. 'You have a list...? I'm afraid I don't perfectly understand what you mean, ma'am.'

3

NUMBER ONE, AGAIN

'I don't suppose you do,' Isabella said. Again, she had to exert conscious effort to control her voice, to keep it level. She didn't want to talk at all, in fact – she wanted to pull his head down and resume the interrupted kiss. To deepen it. She could feel his heart thudding fast in his chest, just as hers was. He was still erect, his stand pressing urgently against her belly through her thin gown and petticoats, and she was all too aware of the pressure. It was an intimate sensation, no question of that, and she'd wondered how she'd feel when she came to experience such things again, but she found she liked it. She had an enormous desire to touch his body, to explore his muscled back and his chest and beyond, but that would have to wait. Everything would have to wait. 'And I think we should probably go back into the ballroom now before we are missed. Perhaps we could meet tomorrow afternoon, sir? Blanche has an engagement at four; I shall plead the headache and remain at home if you care to call on me then.'

Captain Winterton hesitated, and she believed she could divine his thoughts. 'I'm not a young lady who requires to be chaperoned at all times,' she reassured him. 'You need not worry about my reputation on this occasion. If you enquire whether Lady Blanche is at home and then in her absence ask for me, I don't suppose any of the servants will think it the least odd. There are some advantages to being a widow; you are a family connection, after all, and four o'clock is a perfectly respectable time to call. You can say you have some commission for us from your cousin Georgiana if you wish. She is Blanche's sister now, and mine, and might easily ask you to do some small thing or other for her if you had happened to call on her first.'

He made a visible effort to gather his composure, and a part of this, it seemed, meant releasing her from his embrace. She thought he did it reluctantly, and as for her, it was certainly true that she had been warm in his arms, and now was conscious of a chill. It was an October evening, after all, though for a short while it had felt like high summer in his embrace.

'I will call on you tomorrow, then, ma'am,' he said. He was a little distant now, but she would not regard it; he had agreed to come to see her, and that was the important thing. They moved towards the door, but before he opened it for her she said, 'Wait! Am I... dishevelled? I would not want anyone to suspect...'

He looked down at her, and even in the little light that came spilling out from the windows that overlooked the garden she saw his eyes kindle with renewed desire. Or perhaps it had been there all along.

She had put off her mourning recently, on her mother's urging and not without a pang of disloyalty that she had ruthlessly suppressed, and soon after her arrival in London, she had acquired a new wardrobe suitable to her social standing and her purpose, which was, as the Captain had divined, seduction. Her new gowns were fashionable but not excessively so, and perfectly respectable by the current standards of the ton, but many of them were cut quite low across her bosom and her shoulders, and it was clear that this one, her finest – which was a deep blue silk overlaid with gauzy fabric of the same colour embroidered with myriad silver stars – met with his approval. 'Your sleeve is a little disarranged,' he said, his voice very low and husky, and he reached out and pulled it up a little where it had unaccountably slipped from her shoulder. His gloved fingers brushed her skin, the lightest of contacts, and it was all she could do to suppress a whimper of pleasure at his touch.

'Thank you,' she said breathlessly. 'I fear your cravat is some-what disordered, but I do not think I can help you with it.'

'I will adjust it when I find a mirror,' he said.

'My hair has not come down?' Her maid had dressed it in a new style that was all the rage in London; the long braids were coiled in elaborate fashion high upon her head, with a few strands brought artfully down and curled to fall becomingly in front of her ears. She wore no widow's cap, of course, on such a formal occasion. It felt as though the confection was still all securely pinned in place, but it was as well to be sure, and men could be terribly unobservant where such things were concerned, she knew.

'It has not,' he reassured her, and then, as though he could not stop himself, as though he scarcely knew what he was saying, 'I wish it had, in all honesty. I would love to see you with your beau-tiful hair down about your... your shoulders.'

It was ridiculous to blush, considering what she meant to propose to him tomorrow, but Isabella was conscious of her cheeks becoming hot, and bit her lip in frustration. She meant to be a dashing, daring, unconventional sort of a person, at least for a short while before she returned home to Yorkshire and a quiet life of respectable widowhood, and to colour like a schoolgirl at the slightest suggestion of intimacy did not suit her resolution. It was provoking.

He was observant, after all, for a man; he said contritely, 'I'm sorry, have I offended you? I did not mean to. It was an improper wish, I suppose, and I should not have uttered it aloud. Forgive me.'

'Oh no,' she said. 'It wasn't improper – or, if it was, it is of no consequence. I must not be a hypocrite, and I expect you will think that what I mean to say to you tomorrow is far more improper; indeed, by conventional standards, it is.'

'Really? Shall I be shocked?' She thought he sounded quite cheerful at the prospect.

'I hope not.' She bit her lip again. 'Possibly.'

Before her rational self could take charge and stop her, she gave in to an overpowering impulse that shocked her with its strength. Standing on tiptoe and pulling his face down to hers, she fastened her hands on either side of his face, and then she kissed him once more, his mouth opening to welcome her, then she nipped gently at his lower lip with her teeth. He gasped, and though she knew she should stop there she simply could not. She sucked on the sensitive flesh, allowing herself just a taste, and felt his whole frame quiver at her touch. She too was quivering. With an enormous effort of will, she pulled her hands from his face and stepped away.

'Tomorrow at four,' she said. It was not a question, and she did not wait for an answer, but whisked away, back to the ballroom and the dancing. She did not look back to see if he was following, either. She knew he would be. It was working.

Later, alone in her bedroom, she would take out her list from where it was locked securely in her jewellery box, pick up her quill, dip it in ink and draw a firm line through the first item: kissing.

And then, with an unconscious little sigh, she drew a blank sheet of paper towards her and began writing.

Dear Mama

I hope you and Papa continue well. Blanche and all the rest of the Mauleverers require me to send their best regards to you both. I am in excellent health and spirits, so there is no need to be the least concerned about me. And though you were quite right to say in your last letter that the London air cannot be considered healthful and is liable to cause putrid sore throats, I promise that I have taken no ill effects from it. Tonight was Gabriel and Georgiana's ball at their house in Grosvenor Square, which was a great success, and I wish you could have been there to see it, even though I must admit that it was very crowded in the way such things always are, which you could not have liked. But otherwise, it was so very splendid in every respect and must have impressed you greatly. Georgiana looked lovely in white silk and diamonds, and I am sure no husband could be more attentive than Gabriel, which is most gratifying to see. I know that you think the waltz fast and not quite proper, but it is now danced everywhere – even at Almack's Assembly Rooms, I believe! – and I am sure if you had seen the great ball-room full of couples dancing it in the most unexceptional manner possible you might have changed your mind and approved it. I have no particular plans for tomorrow, so you will be happy to know that I am not burning the candle at both ends, as you feared I might...

4

Lady Blanche and her daughter Eleanor accepted Isabella's excuse of a headache without the slightest sign of suspicion; they were all a little out of sorts, they agreed, after the excitement and exertion of yesterday's ball, and she promised she would rest while they paid their dreary duty visit on an elderly FitzHenry cousin who was, in any case, no sort of relation of hers and could have no interest in meeting her. She did not care to deceive them, but it was necessary, and, if her plan worked, would continue to be necessary. *I must learn to be ruthless,* she told herself. *The new Isabella is a ruthless woman. I have so little time before I must go home.*

She dressed with care and sat waiting for Captain Winterton in a state of suppressed nervous agitation. Again she wore one of her new gowns; this one was olive green, with long sleeves that were slashed in fashionable Elizabethan style to reveal the fine, almost transparent habit-shirt she wore beneath it. She knew – she did not care to think just now of how she had gained that knowledge – that sometimes a few tantalising glimpses of naked skin, or the sugges-tion of naked skin, could have a more powerful effect on a man than large expanses of bare flesh. Although he hadn't seemed to object to her low-cut, short-sleeved gown last night. He had seemed to like it, rather. When his fingers had brushed the skin of her shoulder... But she couldn't dress like that in the daytime, for it would present a very odd appearance. She was aiming for subtlety, in her dress at least, though she would be obliged to say some truly outrageous things before she was done today.

She sat pretending to sew, waiting. How she hated sewing. Recovering from being ill had seemed to involve a lot of sitting around sewing with her mama – she had understood after a while that it was a sort of public sign that she wasn't mad any more, since presumably a woman who could set a straight stitch couldn't possibly be deranged – and she wouldn't care if she never picked up a needle again.

He arrived on the stroke of four; she was listening intently and heard Lady Blanche's butler climbing the stairs in a slow, stately fashion to enquire if she was at home to Captain Winterton, who had brought Lady Blanche a present from the Duchess of Northriding, he said. His normally impassive face showed disapproval, but not of her, she soon realised, nor even of her visitor himself. The ducal gift, he informed her, occupied a box, and appeared to be moving within it, and making noises. 'Goodness,' she said calmly. 'Whatever can it be? I think you had better show the Captain in, Hodge.'

When her visitor entered the room and the door closed behind the rigid back of an offended upper servant, she saw that the gentleman was indeed carrying a fairly substantial container: a bandbox, which had at a previous period of its existence apparently contained a hat, but obviously did so no longer. 'I think I'd better open it before I explain,' said the Captain after he had greeted her punctiliously, his firm mouth quirking into an infectious smile.

'Please do,' she replied, intrigued, and glad to delay for a

moment the extremely awkward conversation they would soon be
having. At her invitation he sat, setting the box down on the floor
and lifting off the lid; carefully he reached inside and to her
surprise extracted a small ball of black fluff, which was emitting
furious squeaking noises and appeared to take grave exception to
being held, however gently, in the Captain's large, capable hands.

'This,' he said gravely, 'may appear to be a decoration for a
lady's winter hat in some outlandish new mode, but in fact, is
nothing of the sort, but a mouser of an illustrious Yorkshire line. I
was to tell Lady Blanche, or you, that his name is Billy Biter, and
although this means nothing to me, I can vouch for the accuracy of
the sobriquet, for his teeth are like needles. May I set him down?
Please say I may, ma'am, before he draws blood.'

She was laughing at the comical expression on his face. 'Of
course! Billy Biter is a figure of Yorkshire legend who killed a
dragon. Does Blanche expect such a ferocious guest?'

'I believe so. I understand that any person of discernment
should know that mere London cats are vastly inferior to Mauleverer cats from Yorkshire and that Lady Blanche greatly desired one
for her household, and will be delighted to receive him. Whether
she will be equally delighted to see him climbing her sitting room
curtains, I cannot say.'

Isabella had been taking tea, and now had the happy inspiration of pouring out a dish of milk for the tiny creature. After a few
moments' coaxing, he paused in his perilous exploration,
descended from the pelmet, and condescended to lap from a saucer
set down for him, with a miniature pink tongue not much bigger
than Isabella's fingernail. His attitude suggested that he regarded
Lady Blanche's precious Sèvres china as nothing less than his due.
Once finished, he performed a thorough set of ablutions and fell
asleep on the satin sofa next to her, white paws tucked neatly in,
but not before glaring at Captain Winterton, whom he clearly

regarded as a vile abductor who would not soon be forgiven or forgotten.

A slightly charged silence fell. Then they both spoke at once, and entangled themselves in apologies as a result, but in the end, Captain Winterton prevailed and insisted that Isabella should speak first.

She found she unaccountably had an obstruction in her throat, but she cleared it and pressed on. 'As you know, sir, I am a widow, and my husband died very suddenly. You might say that I should have expected to lose him, since he was a soldier...'

'I would never say that,' he responded quietly. 'No one truly expects to lose a dear one in battle; it is simply impossible to accustom one's mind to such an idea, or to live in the constant expectation of bereavement. Anyone who says that they have reached such a state of resignation in advance is merely lying to themselves. But I'm sorry, I did not mean to interrupt.'

'Thank you,' she said. 'You're right, I think. Of course, I knew in theory that Ash could die, but I had not expected it. Not really. All the more because of the bizarre circumstances of our life in Brussels last summer. I had been dancing with him at the Duchess of Richmond's ball that very evening before the battle – he was all but wrenched from my arms, it was almost impossible to comprehend and still seems like a fever dream when I think of it. I know so many other women of all ranks and nations were bereaved in those dreadful days, and I know too that many of them were left in want and destitution as a result, whereas I am fortunate enough to be financially secure. I am aware that I am very lucky, in comparison with so many. But... for the longest time, I did not feel lucky.'

'You told me of your illness.' She could see that her words affected him, but she had no time to dwell on the significance of this; she went on before her courage deserted her.

'I did. But I did not tell you of the resolutions I took that helped me to feel better.' She was silent for a moment, choosing her words. 'I was married quite young, by my own most happy choice, and – as most women do – passed from the care of my parents to that of my husband and his family. I have never met with anything but kind concern from any of them, and again I know I have been excessively lucky in that too, but I have never known independence. As a man you probably cannot understand that. I was not aware of it myself, until I began to climb out of my illness, as out of a pit, and realised how little control I had over my life. For a long time, my mother did everything for me, obeying the orders of my doctor, and she decided when I rose each morning, or if I stayed in bed, what I wore, what I ate... She is the best mother in the world; do not think I am ungrateful for her care, and her motives were the most unselfish possible. But I resolved at last to take a little, just a little control for myself.'

'I believe I can understand you, ma'am. But I must ask, and forgive me if I seem unduly blunt, what this has to do with me.'

'I will explain. I am aware that it is not obvious. I have two courses open to me, that must be clear. I can accept my widowed state, or I can remarry.'

It seemed to Isabella that her companion was regarding her with the most intense attention now, though she was not sure why. Perhaps he was concerned that she intended to entrap him, or otherwise manipulate him into offering for her – that seemed quite likely, and she hurried to reassure him. 'Please understand that I have no desire to remarry; Ash was my love, and I cannot look to find another. I can never contemplate it, and I never will.' She too was watching him intently. Did he suddenly grow pale under his tan? It must be relief. 'I am resigned to living and dying as a widow, and when my stay with Blanche is done I will return to my parents' house near Harrogate and take up that quiet life again. I will. But...'

She hesitated for a moment, and he supplied, 'But...?'

'I want a little something for myself first. Perhaps it is selfish, and probably it is immoral, but... When Ash and I last kissed, last... held each other, I didn't know any of it was the last time. I didn't know it was the last time *ever*.' Her throat closed up with tears and she was obliged to pause for a moment before continuing.

'You are so young,' he said in a low voice that resonated with some powerful emotion; she hoped it was not pity. She had had enough of being pitied.

'I don't mind that, or not very much. But I would like to have some last times that I *know* are last times. I can see that many people feel terribly sorry for me – my own parents do – and this is perfectly understandable, but I don't like it. And to help me cope with it all I want to have something that I can hold to myself and think, *Ah, but you do not know. None of you knows.* I want to have some choice in what and when my last times are, and I want to have a secret or two. Something that is just mine, for the long, cold years ahead. Can you understand that, sir?'

He was not meeting her eyes now, and she could not read his face. 'I... I think I begin to perceive what you want from me, but I am not completely sure, and so although it is indelicate I believe I will have to press you to be a little clearer, ma'am. You said...' He swallowed, and his voice was a little hoarse when he continued, 'You said you had a list, if I heard you correctly.'

'I did.' It was almost a squeak, and the kitten stirred indignantly in his sleep before settling to slumber again.

'And what exactly is the nature of this list?'

It was her turn to drop her eyes. 'The first item was kissing.'

'And the second?'

She could not make her voice any louder than a whisper, but she continued bravely on. If she could not so much as utter it, how could she expect to do it? 'Kissing with... tongues.'

'I hardly dare ask what the third is.'

'It's probably best you don't. I'd rather not have to say. But do you grasp the idea?'

'I think I do. Good God. But... but, forgive me for asking this, why me?'

'I have another list, this time of possibles. Possible men. Obviously, they had to be unmarried, unattached, and not, not disagreeable in any way, and I had to find them reasonably attractive, and trustworthy, as far as I could tell. And it had to be men who seemed to find me attractive too. So it's not a very long list. And I thought you were the best.'

He let out a dazed sort of a laugh. 'Thank you, ma'am. I think. And how far, I'm sorry, but I have to ask this, how far does this list go? Do you just want—?'

'It goes as far as you can possibly imagine.'

Now their eyes did meet. They were both blushing furiously, and the room seemed very small, and very hot. 'You don't know anything at all about my imagination, and how far it might go,' he said huskily.

'Some of the items on the list are illegal,' she whispered resolutely, her cheeks burning. 'Some of them are things I couldn't possibly have believed, before I was married, that people would do to each other.'

'To each other...'

'Oh yes,' she said urgently as she apprehended his meaning. 'I don't mean to just... tell you to do things to me. I promise I don't. That would hardly be fair.'

He shifted a little uncomfortably in his seat. His cheeks were quite scarlet; he seemed deeply affected. 'Fair. Good God,' he said again. And then, 'And if I said no? What would you do?'

She had been prepared for this question and shrugged with a fair assumption of carelessness. 'I will be sorry, of course, but I will

approach the next man on my list, and put the same proposition to
him.'

5

He couldn't help himself. He had to ask. 'Who might that be?'

She told him; it was a name he knew, and he muffled a curse. 'That... that popinjay? No!' Every human feeling must revolt at the prospect. After a moment he realised that he had not said the last part of this thought aloud, and he was glad. She looked at him, her liquid brown eyes wide with surprise.

'But if you refuse me, sir, what can I do but continue? It would surely be no concern of yours.'

'A man whose figure owes everything to padding, and nothing to nature? A man whose calves are carved out of pieces of cork? A man who wears a *corset*?' He was suddenly and unreasonably angry, though not with her, and if the gentleman in question had entered the room, had minced across the threshold in all his artificial glory – admittedly an unlikely occurrence – he would have been sorely tempted to knock the jackstraw down, and see how he liked *that*.

'Well, I didn't know,' she said. 'How could I? I'm not quite sure how you do, for that matter.'

He looked at her, frowning. 'One can simply... tell. He creaks!

Audibly. Like a stable door in a gale.' He might have been exaggerating slightly, but his point still stood.

'Oh. I had not observed that. I'll have to listen next time I dance with him. But it doesn't sound very appealing, I must say.' There was, he thought, amusement dancing in those extraordinary brown eyes. 'I have been proceeding in the belief that all the gentlemen under consideration were exactly what they pretended to be. Perhaps that was naïve of me.' She did not run her eyes over his frame assessingly as she spoke, but he thought it cost her an effort not to do so. He was, he realised, highly attuned to her slightest movement and change of expression.

'I presume your list, as it progresses, is going to involve the removal of clothing, including, if necessary, corsets?' he blurted out and was instantly sorry for his cruelty and crudeness. But she did not blink. She had been embarrassed before, but she had regained her composure now. For him, it was otherwise.

'Yes,' she said. 'Inevitably.'

He looked at her as she sat there, demure in green silk and crisp white lawn, her hair securely braided and coiled upon her head and an absurd little scrap of lace perched upon it to serve as a widow's cap. The habit-shirt she wore under her gown was almost transparent, offering him tantalising glimpses of the warm skin beneath it, and it fastened at her neck with tiny mother-of-pearl buttons. Two of them. He would very much like to unfasten those buttons and press a hot kiss to the hollow of her throat. To taste her skin. He remembered now how she had nipped at his lower lip with her teeth yesterday and sucked on it. If he understood her correctly... He knew he did understand her correctly, incredible as it seemed. He had no option.

'Yes,' he said.

'Yes?'

'Yes, I will do as you ask. Yes, I will help you cross off the items

from your list.' He was, in a detached sort of a way, impressed at
how steady his voice was as it emerged. He sounded – he *hoped* he
sounded – entirely unconcerned, as if he did not care one way or
the other about the bargain he had just entered into. He might have
been ordering a new pair of boots, or recommending the latest
novel from the circulating library. Cool, gentlemanly, correct. He
thought his heart was breaking a little in his breast, at the prospect
of making love to her when she had explicitly said that she could
never love him, would never marry again. He felt suddenly cold
now, as though someone had stabbed him with an icicle. But he
was almost sure he did not show it. He must not show it, for the last
thing he wanted was for some other man, some unconscionable
villain, to sit in his place and hear this extraordinary proposal.
Proposition. Whatever it was.

'Good!' she said. And then after a moment, blushing a little,
'Thank you.'

It was close to unendurable that she would say such a thing to
him, to think to express gratitude in such extraordinary circumstances, and he found he could not, in fact, endure it. He had to
protect himself somehow, to claw back some shreds of self-respect.
She was an exceptional woman, but she was still naïve – had she
never paused to consider why any man, why any decent man at any
rate, would agree to her scheme? If the fellow she approached with
her outrageous plan was not a complete scoundrel, there could be
only one reason he would countenance it for a second, surely? But
obviously, it had not so much as crossed her mind that he or any
other man might already harbour tender feelings for her, and he
must think of another reason, for the sake of his own sanity.

'I am glad to agree, ma'am, because it suits my current state of
mind very well,' he said stiffly. She shot him a questioning glance,
and he explained, 'I too do not mean to marry. I am resolved not to.
I love, I adore, another, and she is unobtainable to me. She can

never return my regard; my great love for her must always be unrequited. And so I am able to oblige you, madam.' That had all sounded rather well, he thought, until the last part, which was somewhat unsatisfactory, possibly slightly ridiculous, but it was too late to do anything about that now.

'I'm sorry,' she said, and her ready sympathy almost unmanned him. It was preposterous. He could happily have laid his head in her lap and cried for his lost, unobtainable love – who was, in fact, her. Instead, he was, presumably quite soon, going to kiss her again. With tongues. And whatever came after that. Her confounded, mysterious, damnably enticing list.

'I am so sorry,' she said again, her face soft and open and entirely enchanting. Her eyes were deep forest pools and a man could drown in them. And then, devastatingly, 'Who is she? Do I know her – is she a married lady?'

It was so typical of her terrifying frankness to ask. Oh God. His mind was blank, and in his extreme agitation, it did not occur to him for a second that he could simply refuse to answer, to say that it was a private matter, a matter of honour even, and not to be discussed. They had gone beyond that, somehow. Far beyond that. He felt he had to say something. Anything. In a strangled voice quite unlike his own, he said, 'It's my cousin's wife. Lady Irlam. Cassandra.'

6

Isabella was sorry for his distress. In fact, she was sorrier than she could have imagined and sorrier than she should have been since the gentleman could mean nothing to her except that he was attractive enough, and had agreed to... what he had agreed to. There was no reason at all why the news of his love for another should feel just for a moment like a blow to the chest. No.

In fact, she should be pleased – she *was* pleased. Not that he was sad and suffering the pangs of unrequited love, obviously: poor man. But if he loved another, would always love her and nobody else, would go to his grave dreaming of her, et cetera, et cetera, he couldn't possibly become over-attached to Isabella herself, and that could only be a good thing. Clearly. She didn't have a very high opinion of her own charms and hadn't really considered previously that the man of her choice might fall in love with her, which would lead to all sorts of awkwardness, but it occurred to her now that it was at least possible. Ash had, almost at first sight, after all, despite being a duke's son and a major, and one of the handsomest and most dashing men in Yorkshire.

Banishing the thought of Ash and of their courtship firmly from her mind, she said, 'That must be very awkward.'

He seemed distracted. 'I'm sorry?'

'Being in love with your cousin's wife, I mean. You're staying with them, aren't you? It must be torture. Seeing her every day.'

'It is. Torture. Yes. I am undergoing a form of torment.'

He was terse. Clearly, he did not want to speak more of his deepest feelings, and she could not blame him. 'I promise you I will not refer to the matter again, just as we will not speak of my husband. We are both in the same case, are we not?'

'I suppose we are,' he said hollowly. And then, 'I have stayed too long, I think, for a mere visit of courtesy, and should leave you.'

'That's true,' she replied with an unconscious little sigh. 'I will pass on your gift and your message to Lady Blanche. Do you mean to attend the Singletons' party tomorrow night? We do, for Mrs Singleton is a bosom bow of Blanche's.'

'Yes,' he said. 'I believe we shall be going. I understand that Mrs Singleton's sister-in-law, Lady Silverwood, is Cassandra's... Lady Irlam's oldest friend from Yorkshire.'

'What a curious coincidence that is. The world is very small, is it not?' He agreed that it was. 'I shall see you there, then, sir.'

'You will.' He bowed over her hand. 'I presume you mean to... to advance your list on that occasion. I don't know how you will contrive...'

'Leave it to me,' she said. 'I know the house; we have paid morning calls there.'

He smiled faintly. 'You are very organised and determined.'

'I mean to be.'

He bowed over her hand and was gone; Isabella sat in silent reflection. The interview had passed off as well as she could have hoped, and, although she felt a little flustered in its aftermath, it was only the natural reaction to a tense encounter. He had been quite right to leave when he did.

Her feline companion awoke as the door closed, yawning hugely and regarding her with large eyes that were, she saw now, a striking shade of green. Lady Irlam's eyes were much the same colour, she remembered, not boring brown like her own.

He loved Lady Irlam, and it was perfectly understandable that he should. She was short in stature, like Isabella, but of a very different build, slight and delicate, with short red curls. Fairy-like. Ethereal. Nobody had ever likened Isabella to a fairy, that was certain, nor would they, not even a Yorkshire fairy. Was that what he liked? They were two women very different in appearance and… endowments. Would that be a problem, as the list progressed?

She chided herself for folly; if she knew anything at all, she knew that he had enjoyed kissing her last night. It was not possible for a man to feign such a reaction. She shivered as she remembered it: his arms tight about her, his mouth on hers, the pleasure-dazed darkness of his eyes, the hot hardness of his body against hers, his gasp when she had bitten his lip. No, he desired her, she was sure of it. A man could be attracted to more than one type of woman, just as a woman, such as she, for instance, could be attracted to more than one type of man. This was undeniable.

Tomorrow she would go apart with him and they would kiss, but more deeply. She replaced the empty Sèvres saucer carefully on the tray and picked up the kitten. He did not seem to take exception to her hold as he had to Captain Winterton's, and did not sink his teeth into her; she did not venture to put him back in the bandbox to which he had so greatly objected, but cradled him against her bosom. A bosom which, she could not help thinking, was considerably more substantial than that of Lady Irlam; again, she had not received the impression that this difference was in any way disagreeable to the Captain. When he had said he would like to see her with her hair about her shoulders, she had thought that he did not truly mean shoulders, but was afraid to say precisely what he did mean. But he would.

She suddenly felt more cheerful and thought she would rather enjoy seeing Hodge's face when he realised the precise nature of the gift the Duchess had bestowed upon the household. 'Come along, Billy Biter,' she said, tickling him gently under his miniature chin with her free hand as he lay comfortably curled against her warmth. He was purring. 'I have some introductions to make, lad.'

7

Isabella wore her new velvet gown for Mrs Singleton's rout party. It had long sleeves, which were now securely à la mode for evening wear – it had been an excessively cold and miserable summer followed by a cold autumn, and gooseflesh could never be fashion-able – but it was, like all her other new formal gowns, cut quite low across the bosom. It was a rich, dark brown – that sounded dull, but Blanche and Eleanor assured her that it was most certainly not; the colour complemented her skin and hair, they confirmed, and with it she wore a necklace of gold and smoky quartz which Ash had bought for her in York not long after their wedding because he said it matched her eyes. When she'd worn it for him, she'd paired it with gold silk, or white (or on one memorable occasion nothing at all), but she had not dressed in chocolate brown as a young married woman and was surprised how well it suited her. She felt older, sophisticated, experienced even. It seemed appropriate; it gave her strength.

It gave her strength, at least until she saw Captain Winterton entering the room with his family party, which included, of course, Cassandra, the woman he loved so hopelessly. The

Countess of Irlam had also chosen to wear a long-sleeved gown, but hers was a glorious, shimmering shade of sea-green silk, against which her short hair was a bright flame. She was wearing emeralds, her animated little face was alight with amusement, and she had a gentleman on each arm: her tall, dark husband – Isabella had heard him described as excessively handsome, but she had no eyes for him – and the Captain. Suddenly her own brown velvet felt irredeemably dowdy, and her necklace mere trumpery stones. A moment ago she had felt rather dashing; now she knew without a shadow of a doubt that she was plump, frumpish and ridiculous. Whatever had possessed her to wear brown?

She was engaged in an entirely frivolous conversation with a gentleman – with, in fact, her second candidate, whose person didn't seem to be creaking as far as she could hear – but she was making only mechanical replies to his remarks because she was watching over his shoulder, his allegedly padded shoulder, as Mrs Singleton greeted her guests and the Captain was presented to her. He bowed over her hand, and as he straightened to his full height she smiled up at him; their hostess for the evening was as short as Isabella herself, but not frumpish in the least. *She*, though an older lady, was elegant in pale green, with diamonds. Isabella didn't have any diamonds, or emeralds, and had not previously regretted their absence in the least.

Luckily, Isabella's companion in conversation didn't seem to require that a woman responded intelligently to his constant stream of chatter; it was enough that she agreed enthusiastically with him whenever he paused the flow for a second for that express purpose. She was with some small part of her brain rapidly reconsidering his status as first reserve; if he jabbered ceaselessly like this during intimate congress or any other kind of intimacy, he would give her the headache, which was scarcely part of her plan.

But the larger part of her brain was still occupied in observing the Captain and his companions.

Another couple stood with the Singletons to receive their guests: a fair, handsome man, whose classically regular features were rendered more individual by a nose that had obviously been broken at some time in the past and mended badly, and a tall, voluptuous, dark-haired woman who was plainly his wife. Isabella had heard somewhere that Kate Silverwood was of Italian descent, and could believe it to be true now that she saw her. Never in her life had she felt more pasty, uninteresting and sadly English by comparison. Lady Silverwood was wearing a beautiful ruby necklace and had a truly magnificent bosom upon which to display it. Matching earrings glowed and sparkled against her dark curls. And her gown was velvet too, but it was flaming red. (Isabella was beginning to hate with a deep passion the very thought of the colour brown, which she would never wear again as long as she lived.) Lady Irlam had embraced her friend, and they were moving aside now to engage in animated conversation, leaving their husbands to chat easily together.

This left Captain Winterton at a loose end as the Singletons greeted another party of guests, and with a little spark of pleasure which she refused to examine more closely, Isabella saw that he was moving through the throng towards her. He greeted her companion courteously but perhaps a little stiffly, and before she knew quite what was happening he had extricated her with ruthless naval efficiency and was drawing her apart to stand in a little alcove, partially sheltered from the rest of the company by a large Grecian urn.

'I thought the creaking might be wearing on your nerves,' he said with a perfectly straight face.

'I wasn't aware of any creaking, I must admit. But that could be because he never stopped talking for long enough to let me hear it.'

'He is a terrible rattlepate, it's perfectly true, along with all his other faults. I really do think you should consider removing him from consideration. Even if you can overlook all the padding he'd have to remove, which I am sure would take a tedious amount of time, imagine him afterwards droning away while you were...' He trailed off provocatively, and Isabella could not repress a little snort of amusement, since she had been thinking exactly the same thing not a moment since. 'Quite,' he said. 'You can't cross things off your list if you've fallen asleep mid—'

'Thank you,' she said repressively. 'I believe you've made your point.' Curiously, now that they were more or less alone together, her earlier pangs of insecurity had dissipated. She knew that he was irrevocably devoted to Lady Irlam, and she could perfectly understand why, for she was lovely, but as he looked down at her, Isabella, with that teasing light in his eyes, she could be confident that he didn't find her dowdy. There was no need to burn the brown gown just yet.

As if he echoed her thoughts, he said abruptly, 'You are in high bloom tonight.'

'I was just wishing I had not worn brown – such a dull shade when all the other ladies look so glorious and colourful. I feel like a sad little sparrow among tropical birds.'

'Nonsense,' he said. 'Sheer nonsense. You are nobody's sparrow. You look... edible. Touchable. Your lovely fair skin against the dark velvet is having a most extraordinary effect on me.'

There could be no doubting his sincerity. She blushed, and as she felt the heat race across the pale skin he had so fervently described, she saw that he was watching its progress intently; there was a tinge of red across his own cheeks now. A little silence grew between them, electric with possibilities.

She said briskly, 'There is to be music soon; apparently Mrs Singleton is famous throughout the ton for her musical parties.

And I am told that Lady Silverwood, her sister-in-law – that's the tall lady in red with the magnificent... rubies – is renowned for her performance of operatic arias in Italian.'

'Oh good,' he said, sounding anything but enthusiastic. 'Opera.'

She sighed at his slow-wittedness, but then, he was still looking at her as though he wanted to eat her up, so perhaps that accounted for his failure to catch on to her meaning. 'There is a music room with seats set out for the audience, I understand, but there is to be a great crush and some guests will have to stand at the back.'

Amusement lit his face again as he understood her. 'And we are to be among these less fortunate guests?'

'We are. So we can then slip out...'

'I look forward to it,' he said. 'Eagerly. I am sure you have reconnoitred the terrain well in advance, and chosen the perfect spot.'

'I have.' She had. 'Let us part now, sir, and I will come and stand near you when the music begins. When I leave the room, you can follow me in a discreet fashion.'

He bowed, and she left him, hoping that her flush had subsided so that nobody would notice anything amiss. Edible, indeed. They were, she realised, flirting, and though it could lead to nothing lasting, it was undeniable that she found pleasure in it. There was nothing wrong with that. She knew she must savour every moment, and store up memories against her lonely future.

8

NUMBER TWO AND NUMBER THREE

Everything was exactly as Lady Ashby had predicted. Mrs Singleton – who didn't strike Leo as the sort of woman anybody would care to argue with, or, at any rate, not more than once – mustered her guests and shepherded them firmly into her music room. Cassandra took a seat quite near the front, in order to support Lady Silverwood, no doubt, and waved at him in a friendly fashion to indicate that she had saved him a place, but he feigned not to see and suppressed a smile as he saw the resigned expression on Hal's face. He didn't believe that his cousin was any fonder of opera than he was himself. He thought that Irlam would make a fuss about passing an evening in a deadly dull manner, while all along not truly minding because he was doing it for and with Cassandra. He was a lucky fellow, but tonight he, Leo, was also to have his share of good fortune. It might never lead to anything, it might end in heartbreak as he had feared the other night, but at least he would be able to hold her in his arms, to kiss her – yes, with tongues – and to know as he did so that further delights, as yet unspecified, lay in store. It might be a painful situation in which to find himself, hurting him now with the anticipation of greater hurt to follow, but it was also damnably exciting.

She stood close by him but did not look at him, and as the chattering crowd began to settle she slipped away; he was willing to swear that nobody saw her go. She had a talent for intrigue; if her plan was to go smoothly, she would need it. She could be a spy, he thought, and a good one. Were women spies? Probably. He felt slightly feverish.

A few moments later he followed her. She was waiting outside the door and took him by the arm, drawing him swiftly across the hall into what appeared to be Mr Singleton's library. A shrewd choice, as he doubted any of the other guests would be seized by the overwhelming urge to read a book in the next half-hour or so. Singleton, though appearances could be deceptive, he knew, looked like a man who hadn't so much as opened a volume in twenty years.

There was a key in the lock, and she turned it. She was in charge, and there was something undeniably arousing about the fact, something he had never experienced before, or not for many years, but found he liked. She wanted him; she had chosen him above all others. She'd said she could never love again, she'd said there was no future in it, but to be chosen by a woman like this was a hell of a thing.

She was in his arms. He was prepared for it this time and didn't hesitate for a second. His hands were about her waist and his lips fused with hers. It was different, it was much better, because before they had both been a little unsure, for their own separate reasons, but now they both gave rein to the hunger they shared and devoured each other shamelessly. It was his turn to bite her gloriously full, sensual lower lip, and to hear her let out an adorable little moan when he did so. He felt the whisper of it against his tender skin. And then her tongue came out and sought his; she teased him with the tip first, then withdrew, and it was his time to moan, but then she relented and gave him the length of it, and he did the same. It was hot and wet and erotic, messy, urgent, wonderful. Her hands came up and tangled in his hair and held him close and tight, a hold he would have struggled to escape from if he'd had the least desire to do so, while he felt the softness of the velvet and of her under his palms.

His left hand was fixed about her waist; his right was inexorably drawn upwards to cup her breast. His fingers spanned and held it, their tips found the edge of her velvet bodice, and brushed velvety skin. He felt a jolt run through her, and she pulled away a fraction to gasp against his lips, 'That was supposed to be next!'

She was a little incoherent, but he understood her. His hand stilled, though he did not quite have the strength to remove it, and the pads of his fingers still lay warm on her bare, pliant flesh. 'Do you object?' he said unsteadily.

'No!' she said. 'Don't stop!'

'I won't. I need...' He raised his head, and saw a convenient wall of books close by; he pushed her up against it and pinned her there with his body, and thus freed his other hand to cup her other breast. He had the fleeting thought that all of it – their seeking hands, hers as well as his, her ripe breasts, the sensual softness of velvet, the very existence of walls – was designed for this very purpose and no other. Their tongues still tangled together, he ran the tips of his fingers across the perfect lush curve of her upper breasts and felt her shiver at the contact and press fiercely back to fill his palms, to urge him wordlessly to give her firmer caresses. He held her and squeezed her; she pressed her body into his, and he pressed himself against her as she clung tightly to him. His fingers slipped under the velvet neckline of her gown and encountered flimsier fabric, which he pushed down ruthlessly.

His lips explored the rich curves of her mouth, then feathered across her cheekbone, and when he reached one deliciously plump pink earlobe he bit it gently. She jolted again, and he took this as encouragement to draw the little bud of flesh into his mouth and suck on it. This was both enjoyable in itself and a tiny foretaste of further, more intimate delights. It seemed that it was pleasing to her too, for she threw back her head in response and bared her throat to him. He licked the tender spot behind her ear, which made her gasp again, and commenced kissing his way down her throat. He had no idea if this was or was not a separate entry on the list; just now he didn't care, and it seemed she didn't either.

But it wasn't all plain sailing. He desperately wanted to push her sleeves down from her shoulders and release her breasts from her bodice so that he could see as well as touch them. He wanted his mouth, his lips, his tongue on them more than anything. But her sleeves were long and quite tight, and he found he couldn't do it. His right hand had slid fully inside her bodice and cupped her warm naked flesh, his thumb and forefinger had found her nipple and encircled it, it was erect under his touch and she made a wonderful low sound in her throat as he played with it. But he couldn't see it or taste it, and the bodice was tight-fitting too and restricted his movement considerably. He wanted to kiss it, to lick it, to fucking eat it, and he couldn't. Life was manifestly unfair.

He raised his head a little and said, 'I want to worship your lovely breasts with my mouth. This gown is very becoming, but it won't let me. And I don't want to tear it.' He did want to tear it, in truth, he wanted to rip it off her with his teeth, but he still retained some shreds of sense and would not do so. Not here.

'Number four, I think that was number four,' she moaned. And then, soft, aroused, infinitely alluring, 'No, don't tear it. We should stop soon, and go back, but not quite yet. What is to be done?'

His eyes darted around the room, examining the furniture and rejecting most of it as useless for his purpose. But there was a low, odd little chair a few feet away, plainly meant for a gentleman to lie back at ease with legs stretched out, reading or drowsing; it looked comfortable, and fortunately, it did not have a high back. 'Sit down,' he said hoarsely. 'Sit in that chair.'

She sank into it, and he came to kneel behind her on a footstool. 'Oh!' she said as she understood. 'Oh goodness, yes!'

He reached over the low chair-back and slid his hands down under the edge of her bodice once more so that he could cup both of her breasts fully; in this position, he could also kiss the back of her neck. And lick it. And bite it. There were a few wispy strands of honey-blonde hair that had been too short to be caught up in the elaborate plaits that crowned her head; for some reason, they affected him deeply, and he tugged at them with his teeth. All the while he held her warm, heavy breasts in his hands and played with them in a way that seemed to give her a great deal of pleasure, judging by the noises that she was making and the way she was moving in her seat. Almost all of him was focused entirely in the moment, in the wonderful sensations that came from touching her with his fingers and his mouth, but his erection was hard and urgent, almost painful, and some insistent part of his physical being was screaming in a language older than mere words that making love to this woman, when he finally did make love to her fully, would be like nothing he had ever experienced in his life.

After a little while he realised that he must stop, or risk discovery; slowly, reluctantly, he withdrew his hands, and after one last lingering kiss where her neck met her shoulder, he stood. She still lay sprawled in the chair, her hands clutching its arms, her bosom heaving, straining at the fabric of her gown. He thought that he had never in all his life seen such an enticing sight. In a voice he hardly recognised as his own, he said, 'You should go back. I will wait here a moment.'

She rose a little unsteadily and shook out the velvet folds. She was flushed, and visibly struggling to regain her composure, plainly unwilling to face the eyes of others. 'Should you not go first?' she said in little more than a whisper.

'Look at me,' he ground out. 'I cannot go into company in this condition. I don't mean my cravat, my hair – that's nothing, I can mend that in the mirror. Please do look at me. I want you to know exactly the effect you have on me.'

Her wide brown eyes ran down his body and halted where he had meant them to halt, where his erect member stood visibly proud, stretching the fine black silk of his evening breeches. She bit her full lower lip at the sight, a characteristic gesture, and a number of all too readable thoughts flitted across her face. Not a single one of those thoughts helped his sad predicament to lessen in the slightest. She looked as though she was about to lick her lips, he would swear he could see the tip of her pink tongue creeping out, and if she did so he wouldn't be answerable for his response. She must be a terrible card player; but then, it wasn't faro he wanted to play with her, but a far more dangerous game, with much more than money at stake.

'Number six,' she said a little breathlessly. And she was gone.

He groaned and closed his eyes for a moment before he went to find a looking-glass to show him what a wreck she had made of him. Number six. If his calculations were correct, and they easily might not be, that left four and five still undone. Four he'd been told, and God knew he could picture how wonderful it would be to have his mouth on her where his hands had just been, but five remained a mystery. He could speculate, but it would perhaps be better if he did not just now. He needed to be alone and in his bed before he could indulge in a healthy bout of speculation. In a moment, he would have to go back among people and see if he had escaped the threat of opera entirely, or still had a few arias to endure.

Number four, number five, number six...

For the first time, it occurred to him to wonder just how many items her list contained. Ten? Surely not. Twelve? Fifteen? More? How many more? It was an interesting thought, even an absorbing one, but he couldn't really say it helped in the attempt to recover his composure.

Jesus, but he was in a woeful state.

9

Isabella's maid had helped her undress with silent efficiency, and she sat in her chamber crossing an item – crossing *items*, two of them – off her list before she climbed into bed. Her elaborate coiffure had been unfastened, though it still lay in heavy plaits down her back. She should unfasten it and brush it before plaiting it again for sleep, but she wasn't inclined to make the effort. She had an awful lot of hair, which took an awful lot of brushing. These thoughts must lead her to what Captain Winterton had said the other day, of his desire to see her hair unbound. She remembered how, only an hour or so since, he had kissed the back of her neck, and tugged on the short strands of hair there with his teeth. She had lain back in the chair with her eyes closed and he had... handled her with intense focus. Her nipples peaked and her breasts tingled at the mere thought of it. She was conscious of the soft fabric of her nightgown against the sensitive, aroused flesh. What had he said? He wanted to worship them with his mouth.

That, of course, was number four.

There was no denying that everything was proceeding

extremely well, and Isabella had to admit that the experience of taking control of her life was even more exhilarating than she had imagined it would be. Her mood in the last few days had been light, even giddy; Blanche had remarked upon it only today, with approval. If this was what it took to finally drag her fully out of the darkness that had enfolded her when Ash had died, then it was well worth the doing.

She put away her list, locked the box, and hid the key among the trinkets on her dressing table, taking up her pen again to add a few lines to her letter to her mother, which she could then send off tomorrow to allay any maternal heart-burnings over her wellbeing.

Mama, tonight we attended a musical evening at Mrs Singleton's house in Clarges Street. I was not previously acquainted with that lady, but she is a friend of Blanche's. Several ladies and gentlemen of great musical ability performed songs for us, including some from the Italian opera, though I am afraid I cannot precisely recall any of the titles of the arias now, and it was all very entertaining and agreeable. I wore my new brown velvet, which you have not yet seen...

She added a few more harmless platitudes of a similar nature, signed off with her love, and set her letter aside. Climbing up into bed – it was a Mauleverer bed and so it was excessively high, and a little dab of a woman such as she was required a set of steps to reach it – she blew out her candle and stretched out under the soft covers, wriggling her bare toes. She had not put on her nightcap – a small act of rebellion, and one she would not have been able to undertake at home in Harrogate, for her mother had developed the habit of coming in to see her and to kiss her every night before she slept, just as she had when she was small, and would no doubt have told her that she would catch her death of cold if she even contemplated sleeping without a cap. In October, too! Reckless madness! It was comforting, to be so fussed over, so deeply loved, and it was also irritating beyond belief. No wonder her letters home were so ruthlessly edited to remove anything that might be the least worrying or shocking, or even excessively interesting, since her mother had once warned her that the interesting could so easily shade into the scandalous before one was aware of it.

Isabella sighed, and let her hands drift down over her body. No – that wasn't what was happening. In her new spirit of taking control and admitting what she wanted, at least to herself, she would own what she was doing. She wasn't finding her hand between her legs by accident. Oh dear. No, she was going to touch herself, to pleasure herself, and she was going to think about Leo Winterton while she did it. She'd done it after he kissed her the other night, and she was going to do it again now. On purpose. She was going to think about – she *was* thinking about – his hands on her breasts, tweaking at her engorged nipples, and his breath hot on her neck behind her. The feel of his lips and his tongue as they trailed across her skin. She was going to think about, *was* thinking about, the sight of him, big and hard for her, stretching the black silk of his breeches. She had shocked herself by how very much she had wanted to put her hand on him and stroke him and see how he reacted; well, soon she would. As she touched herself, she thought of things they had done, and things they had not done yet, but would do very soon. Number four, number five, number six...

She had thought that she would float off to sleep afterwards, with the release of tension, but she was surprisingly wakeful. It would not do to delude herself, and there were undoubtedly problems ahead. Not problems – she would not be negative – but challenges. Obstacles to be overcome. It was all very well to kiss in a corner, to slip aside to an unoccupied room and caress each other.

Number five, certainly, could be carried out without a great deal of fuss, and probably quite quickly, given the effect he had on her. The thought of his hand sliding under her petticoats, the roughened pads of his fingertips finding the top of her stockings, exploring further... She was halfway there in a matter of seconds. Again.

But number six, number seven, good God, number eight – *they* would need time, and privacy, and a certain amount of preparation. She hadn't thought that far ahead, and she didn't suppose the Captain had either, but now she must, because it was really happening and she didn't want it to stop.

She couldn't bring him here. Lady Blanche was an easy-going hostess, had told her to treat this elegant house as her own home, and appeared to mean it, but even she would presumably draw the line at her guest sneaking men into her bedchamber. A man. Besides, it gave the whole business an air of sordid intrigue that displeased her. She had an odd sort of feeling that Blanche, who was a widow too and appeared to have no intention of remarrying, might have some sympathy for her situation, but even if she did, she surely wouldn't condone... that. She had her young daughter's morals and reputation to think of. She wondered if Blanche was lonely; if she ever regretted her empty bed, even if remarriage with all its many risks did not appeal to her. It wasn't the kind of thing she could ask.

The thought of going to the grand mansion in St James's where Leo was staying with his cousin – and the woman they both loved, of course – was plainly ridiculous, and she wasted no time on it. That left a rented room, she supposed; there must be rooms that people hired for short periods of time for just such purposes. That was sordid, too, and probably left one at risk of robbery and black-mail. Not to mention fleas. It was most provoking.

If only she knew somebody of great experience who could

advise her. She did, of course – her brother-in-law; she thought the Duke was equal to anything, and wouldn't turn a hair at the oddest request, and he had had the most terrible reputation as a rake before he married. He would surely know all a person could about such matters. But although she didn't lay claim to much sensibility these days – she had suffered from an excess of sensibility after she was widowed, and look where that had got her – she didn't find herself capable of asking for an interview with Northriding and explaining that she, his brother's widow and recent patient of a doctor who specialised in the care of lunatics, would very much like his advice on how best to arrange to meet a man in secret for the purposes of engaging in sexual congress. Gabriel could, if he wished, have her incarcerated for such a suggestion. He was her trustee and head of the family into which she had married. The weight of public opinion would surely be on his side in dealing thus with an inconvenient and unruly woman. He wouldn't do it – she knew he wasn't at all that sort of a man – but many another brother-in-law, husband or father would. It wasn't that she feared at all: no, it was hurting him. He had loved his little brother Ash deeply; he too had been devastated by his loss. She had no desire to distress him further. The thought of such a conversation made her feel hot all over, and not in a pleasant way.

She found herself defeated for a moment and then smiled in the darkness as an idea occurred to her. An excellent idea.

* * *

Blanche thought it was an excellent idea too, when she raised it over breakfast the next day. 'I think you should,' she said. 'You know they leave soon to go back to Yorkshire, and you're quite right, you're barely acquainted with Georgiana, and heaven knows when you will set eyes on each other again. It's not to be expected that they'll be coming to Harrogate once the winter sets in. I dare say they will pull up the castle drawbridge and not emerge till spring, for we know how they are together. Go alone, a little early so that no one else will be there, and you may have a comfortable coze with her and get to know each other better, as you should, being sisters. Please do thank her for Billy for me, too, though of course I will call on them before they leave.'

Billy, it seemed, was not destined to be a kitchen cat, or not exclusively so. Perhaps his taste of milk from a Sèvres china saucer had turned his tiny furry head, or perhaps he was of a naturally haughty nature, having started life as a ducal beast, but in any case, he had taken to spending most of his time above-stairs, and Blanche and Eleanor indulged him shamelessly. He was present at breakfast every day and had his own special plate now. He was already visibly larger than he had been upon his arrival not long since.

Isabella set out for Mauleverer House a little in advance of the correct hour for paying morning calls; she had despatched a note to the Duchess via a footman that morning and received a cordial response.

One of the advantages – and there were not many – of having been mad at an earlier period of one's life was that it gave a person, once recovered, an insight into the real natures of one's acquaintance. There had been the former bosom friends at home who had crossed the street when they saw her approaching, as though losing one's husband at the age of twenty and going crazy with grief over it were contagious. That had stung, but perhaps not so much as the behaviour of the gentleman, for want of a more accurate term, who had decided that her previous indisposition gave him licence to manhandle her at a recent public assembly. There must be a process of thought behind his actions, though she could not fathom it, and did not truly wish to for fear of what it might reveal.

Widow, not a year married, loved her husband – went mad – better
now – must want me to grope her bottom painfully hard after the
cotillion. It remained a masculine mystery, and she had no wish to
delve into it further.

Of those people who had not known her before and had been
informed of her illness, in Isabella's mind the two people who had
acquitted themselves with the greatest credit were Leo Winterton
and his cousin Georgiana, Duchess of Northriding. She must
presume then that they were a tolerant sort of a family, not prone to
judging others. Georgiana, too, had not merely heard of her tribu-
lations but had seen her in a state of great distress on the day of the
Duchess's own wedding in York. They had by malign chance
encountered each other in the street as the happy pair returned
from the ceremony in the Minster, and Isabella had been momen-
tarily overcome by the sight of Gabriel, with his bride on his arm in
all her wedding finery, and the extent of his resemblance to Ash. It
had been horrible, painful, but only a momentary setback, and the
shock had helped her in a perverse sort of a way, for when she
became aware that Gabriel had married, and realised from his
demeanour and his bride's that they were deeply in love, she had
felt a burden lifting from her shoulders. It was a liberation, and not
a small one. She need no longer think that she had let everybody
down irrevocably by her failure to produce an heir, nor need she
believe that the Duke had been obliged to upend his whole
comfortable, dissolute life and enter into a marriage of convenience, much against his inclination, because of that failure. No
one who saw the pair together for more than a moment could
imagine *that*.

Georgiana had never referred to that embarrassing time, nor
had she shown the least sign of resenting the temporary pall that
Isabella's reaction had thrown over her happy day. If she felt pity
for her new sister-in-law, she did not show it, and Isabella was

always on the lookout for pity. The new Duchess treated her just as she might treat anyone else in the family she had just joined, with open friendliness. There was not a hairsbreadth of difference between her manner to Isabella and the way she behaved towards Blanche and Eleanor.

There were, of course, many self-absorbed people in this world who showed no pity to anybody because they thought of nothing but their own fascinating affairs, but Isabella did not think that the Duchess was one of them. She had seen little of Georgiana, but what she had seen she liked. It was perhaps rash to pick her out as a confidante, but she had very little choice, and the risk involved was not enormous; if she were disapproving of or horrified by what she heard today, all that Isabella would ask of her would be not to tell her husband.

But 'disapproving' was the last word that anybody would think to apply to Gabriel's bride, surely? The gossip in the haut ton said that she had been engaged to be married to an eligible gentleman last year upon her come-out, and had jilted her betrothed on some sort of whim, and further gossip, the sort that was whispered avidly behind hands and fans, would have it that she had been so instantly enamoured of Gabriel upon meeting him that they had been caught in a highly compromising position a mere day or two after they had been introduced. The way their eyes had remained locked together as they danced at their ball, the unavoidable impression of utter physical harmony that their every movement gave besides, made Isabella think that this tale, or some version of it, might easily be true. And if it was, who better to ask for help and advice? Furthermore, the Duchess was known to be close friends with Lady Carston, the poetess, who had been Georgiana's aunt's companion for many years until her recent and entirely unexpected marriage; *she* was the subject of some most peculiar rumours. Taken together, all this hardly screamed 'censorious and a stickler for proper behaviour'. It was encouraging.

She was shown into the Duchess's own charming, newly decorated blue sitting room, rather than one of the more formal salons, and Georgiana greeted her with a friendly kiss and a welcoming smile, and poured her tea. 'I am glad to see you, Lady Ashby,' she said as she did so. 'We have had so little chance to become acquainted, and I am happy to rectify the omission today, at least a little. You know that we return to Northriding Castle in a few days? Gabriel has had his fill of being stared at by the ton.'

'I had heard as much,' she said, taking the cup with a word of thanks. 'Well, not the part about being stared at, though I am sure it is no wonder he should dislike it so, but the fact that you mean to leave. And please, do call me Isabella. Blanche asked me to bear the message that she will be sure to come and see you before you go, and furthermore to thank you in person for the kind gift the other day.'

'I will, of course, and please call me Georgiana. The kitten? I hope he is not too much trouble. She did say she wanted one, and we have several.'

'I understand he is supposed to grow to be a famous mouser, though I don't suppose he'll ever rouse himself to show us his skills if we all keep feeding him tidbits from our plates. I swear he sleeps on Eleanor's pillow, though she denies it.'

'All the Mauleverers have a soft spot for animals, I have noticed, as you must have done.'

'It's true. Ash was the same,' she agreed with a small smile. She appreciated Georgiana's tact; an opportunity to speak of her dead husband, if she cared to, but something that could easily be turned aside without the least awkwardness if she did not. 'Thank you,' she said quietly.

'For what?'

'People don't usually raise topics that invite me to speak of Ash if I should wish to do so – well, Gabriel and Blanche do, but nobody else. My own father will go to enormous lengths to avoid speaking his name or alluding to the fact that he so much as existed. I know he means well, I know people in general do, but it's not as though I'm likely to just forget about him if he isn't discussed for a sennight or two. You know: "Was I married, and he died horribly? Oh, you did not mention him, so I had quite forgot!"'

'I don't suppose you are in the least likely to forget him. And why should you? But is it easier for you, being in London? I know Blanche hoped it would be.'

'Yes,' Isabella said. 'It is just what I needed, being here. And not just because it is a change of scene. I have a plan, you see.'

'That sounds intriguing.'

'I'd like to tell you about it. But I fear it will shock you.'

The Duchess burst out laughing in a most unladylike fashion. 'I think you can hardly have heard the rumours about me! Did you not know that all the polite world is a buzz with the scandalous fact that Gabriel seduced me within a day of meeting me, and we were caught in flagrante delicto in his garden by the Archbishop of York?'

'It sounds a little unlikely. I hardly think it can be true,' Isabella said calmly.

'Oh, it isn't. The Archbishop didn't come into it at all,' said Georgiana wickedly, her bright blue eyes still sparkling with mirth and mischief. 'In fact, the truth is much, much worse.'

'Oh *good*!' Isabella replied with feeling. 'Then I *can* tell you!'

'Tell me instantly!'

They put their heads close together, the blonde and the black, and in a low tone, Isabella poured out all of it, or almost all: her complicated feelings after Ash's death, and her plan. It was an exquisite, unexpected relief to share everything with another woman. When she had done, her sister-in-law looked at her thoughtfully, betraying not the least appearance of disapproval, and said, 'I do understand, I believe. You want something for yourself, to give you comfort. If you were a man, of course, and widowed and heart-broken, you could play the rake with half the women in England and very few people would have anything but sympathy for you. Perfectly respectable ladies of the ton would sigh sentimentally over your tragic story, and think it terribly romantic. You'd be besieged by women desperate to console you in any manner you chose. But because you *are* a woman, you must sit quietly at home and cry into your stitchery.'

'Exactly so. But not too much,' said Isabella with a trace of bitterness. 'Just the approved amount. Excessive grief is also unwelcome. It makes people uncomfortable.'

'It's ridiculous. Who among us has not lost loved ones whom we will always mourn? Isabella, I hope I have time before we go to introduce you to my friend Jane Carston – she was at the ball, but I don't think you are acquainted. She has strong views on a woman's place in the world, and she's very good at slipping below the notice of society in order to live the life she wants. I'm sure she would approve of your plan.' Georgiana saw the expression on her guest's face and interpreted it correctly. 'I know – she knows too – that there has been a certain amount of gossip about her sudden marriage. But then there is always gossip when someone, when a woman in particular, does anything the least bit out of the ordinary. I think she will carry it off. I can't tell you what she's doing now, it's not my story to share. But I promise you she would be sympathetic. And you to her, I think.'

'I'd like to meet her.'

'I hope you will. I'm glad you told me, you know,' said Georgiana. 'Another time I'll tell you *my* story. I think you of all people might understand. I too have struggled with how I wanted to behave and how people thought I should behave not being at all the same. I've done dangerous and foolish things, and been very lucky not to suffer the worst consequences of them. So don't take me up wrongly when I say that I hope you're being careful – I don't mean that as a criticism at all. I understand what you're trying to do, but I hope you're protecting yourself in any way you can. Men can be... predatory. Untrustworthy. Even men we think we can trust. I had personal experience of this, last year, with someone I thought loved me but most definitely did not.'

'I've chosen well, I think. No, I know I have.'

'Do you want to tell me who it is? You don't have to, of course. But perhaps it's a good idea to tell somebody, for your own safety, in case something should go wrong. You could use my knowledge to threaten him, say, if you felt yourself suddenly to be in peril.'

'I don't see why I shouldn't tell you. I won't insult you by asking you to keep all this secret, because I'm sure it's obvious.' Isabella was silent for a moment, then said, watching her hostess carefully all the while, 'It's your cousin. Captain Winterton.'

Georgiana's face was a picture of astonishment. 'Leo? Good God!'

'You don't approve?'

The Duchess spluttered for a moment, then laughed aloud again. 'It's... it's not that! It's just that one never imagines one's own cousin... Or at least, I don't. No, of course I don't disapprove. He's a good person, he's like a brother to us. And he's attractive, I suppose. I'm not saying he isn't. I've just never thought of him in that way. I'll stop talking now. Oh Lord, though, Leo!'

'It is a little awkward, I can quite see that. But you don't think I've chosen badly?'

'No, I'm sure you haven't. I'm sure he'd never hurt you or take advantage of you.'

'Well, I don't know him very well...' The Duchess was grinning, a rather wicked twinkle in her blue eyes again, and Isabella could not help but smile in response, her cheeks colouring a little. 'I don't! I've just danced with him a few times, and conversed a little, and... and so on. So far.'

Georgiana snorted. 'So far! But the more I think about it, the more I can see that you've chosen rather cleverly. You want to be in control, don't you? That's a large part of the point of what you're doing. And I'm sure that Leo would never... deny you that. Force the pace. If you see what I mean. Goodness, he would have me to answer to if he did, as well as my brother Hal! But he wouldn't. It's very hard to be sure of such a thing about a man. But I trust Leo as I trust Hal, and I don't think I'd say that about many men.'

'Gabriel, of course,' said Isabella with a sad little smile. Gabriel, and Ash, before she had lost him.

'Oh yes,' replied Georgiana with complete confidence. 'From the first time I met him, when I didn't even know his name... But that's for another day. It occurs to me, as it must have occurred to you – how are you going to manage? It's all very well to kiss in a garden or a private room during a ball, goodness knows I've done it myself, as I'd be the first to admit, but when you get a little farther down your list, isn't it going to be excessively awkward? There's a limit – believe me, I know – to what you can get away with while being secure of not being interrupted, and if you were interrupted...'

'It doesn't bear thinking about,' said Isabella with feeling.

'You wouldn't enjoy the sensation it would cause, in the first place, and the result of it would be that you'd be forced to marry him, which I collect is just exactly what you don't want.'

'I don't. And neither does he, for that matter. Which is one of the reasons I'm so glad I chose him, though I couldn't have known it when I did.'

'Why doesn't he?' asked Georgiana with sudden curiosity. 'I can see why you don't, of course, after all you have lost, but I'd have thought he might be ready to settle down, now he has left the navy. And he's obviously attracted to you. From what you've said.'

It was unsurprising that Georgiana had no idea of her cousin's secret; Isabella had no intention of sharing it. 'He is in love with someone else. Someone unobtainable.'

'Goodness,' said the Duchess. 'Poor Leo, I had no idea. Did he tell you...? No, I should not ask. Forget I said that, please. And it's a distraction, anyway, and not relevant. How will you manage, that's the question? Finding a place to go to, I mean. I'd say come here, but I don't really think...'

'Oh no!' replied Isabella swiftly. 'I wouldn't want that. It would hardly be fair to Gabriel. And I'd rather he didn't know! I'm sorry to ask you to keep a secret from him, it's very bad of me, but I hope you can see why. It might distress him, and I wouldn't want that after he's been so good to me always.'

'Of course!' Georgiana hastened to reassure her. 'I promise I won't tell him if you don't want me to, though I don't think he'd disapprove. He's not a hypocrite or one of those tedious people who think men should be allowed to do everything they want and women nothing at all. He was a rake, and I suppose rakes must rather count on women having desires too, or however would they manage? But I can quite see why you feel uneasy... Your late husband's brother.'

'Exactly. I had thought that there must be places one can hire, couples can, I mean, for a short time...'

Georgiana shuddered slightly. 'I expect there are. Can you imagine what they must be like?'

'I keep thinking about fleas,' said Isabella hollowly.

'Fleas would be the least of it, I should think. You need... I know what you need!'

'You do?'

'Yes! You need a place that's safe, definitely without fleas, where you can go and be private and nobody will take the least notice of you, or think to blackmail you or threaten you.'

'That sounds impossible.'

'But it isn't! I know just the place, and I can tell you exactly how to go on there!'

10

The very next evening, Lady Ashby sat in the Duchess of Northriding's elegant black and silver carriage, feeling ridiculously nervous. She was wearing an anonymous sort of a dark cloak, and a loo mask, which she had concealed in her reticule until she was alone in the vehicle and then put on with hands that shook slightly. She was *supposed* to be going to Mauleverer House to spend the evening in quiet conversation with Georgiana; Blanche had been touchingly pleased that her two sisters-in-law were growing so close and had not blinked when Isabella had said that she might be back in the early hours of the morning. She'd be late herself, she said, since she and Eleanor were going to the theatre and on to a supper party afterwards. Enjoy yourself, she had said, and Isabella, feeling hideously guilty, had murmured the same. She hoped they all would. Enjoy themselves.

She wasn't going to Mauleverer House. She was going to what had been described to her as a respectable-seeming townhouse in a fashionable street quite close by, where Captain Winterton would be waiting for her outside, according to instructions she had whispered urgently to him when walking in the park that morning. In her reticule, she had a *carte de visite* that Georgiana had passed to her, but it was a card with a difference. It was printed on heavy, creamy rag paper, and it bore no name or title, just an address, and a printed picture of a black mask very much like the one she was wearing. It, and a handful of guineas passed discreetly to the servant on the door, would be enough to gain admission, the Duchess had assured her. She had described the place and what went on there, and after her initial shock Isabella had admitted that it sounded perfect. Terrifying, but perfect. There were private rooms that could be locked, she had been told, and nobody would disturb them. Nobody would know who they were, no names would be asked for or given, and if they should happen to recognise any of the masked fellow guests – which was unlikely since they did not mean to linger in the public salons, which were not for the faint-hearted, she had been warned – why, they had as much to lose as she did. More, possibly. And Georgie had assured her repeatedly that there wouldn't be any fleas.

The carriage drew to a halt, and Isabella gulped and jumped nervously when the footman – the very discreet Mauleverer footman in black and silver – opened the door and let down the steps for her, his face quite expressionless. She had been hesitant at first in accepting Georgiana's offer of her carriage for the evening. 'What if it is seen and identified as yours?' she had said worriedly.

The Duchess had smiled in a feline manner and replied, 'How do you think I know about the place?' This had silenced Isabella quite effectively, and she understood then the full nature of the favour that her sister-in-law was doing her; if the carriage was seen, everybody would assume that the occupants were the scandalous Duke and his bride, who was known to be entirely in his thrall in a thrillingly wicked sort of a way. Georgiana had said that it was just the place, and just the occasion, and on reflection, Isabella could see that she might well be right.

As long as the Captain was there waiting for her. She didn't know what she'd do if he wasn't.

She got down, and scanned the street anxiously, her heart pounding. But he *was* there, already masked, standing a few paces away, and he stepped forward to greet her. Isabella hurriedly fumbled in her reticule to take out the card and give it to him. She supposed the footman climbed up into his place on the box beside the coachman and they drove away; she wasn't paying attention. Leo looked down at her and she saw the gleam of his eyes, if not their colour, by the light of one of the new gas-lamps. 'Are you sure you want to do this?' he said in a low voice. 'It is not too late to change your mind, if you should have qualms.'

'Yes,' she answered firmly. 'Yes, I am sure. Let us go in.'

The Captain managed things well, though she was reasonably sure he was not an habitué of such places. His hand went out and slipped something into the palm of the tall, imposing man who stood on the doorstep with an air of discreet watchfulness. It was all so neatly done that she would hardly have noticed it if she had not been looking. And then they were inside.

Isabella did not know what she had been expecting, despite Georgiana's description – somewhere that, inside, looked obviously depraved, she supposed, though she wasn't entirely sure exactly what form this depravity would take. Depraved... furniture? Paintings? Statues? Worse somehow than the ordinary paintings and statues of semi-naked or entirely naked deities and mythological personages that decorated most of the mansions of the ton? Anatomically correct statues of the male form, perhaps, because she had noticed that they generally weren't... Her mind was flitting from one thought to another in a nervous fashion. Her mouth was dry.

She knew, because of Georgiana's warning, that in the public salons other guests, if that was the correct word, would be doing things that most people would not countenance even if they were done in private. Sinful things. But she and the Captain weren't intending to go into the public salons, and out here in the hall, at least, it appeared to be a perfectly normal London house belonging to someone of rank and fortune. There were walls, with elegant wallpaper. There was a floor. Obviously. There were candles in sconces of classical design. It was, in fact, not at all unlike Lady Blanche's home. Perhaps slightly bigger and more sumptuously decorated. Isabella was, if she was honest, rather disappointed at how very ordinary it all was. The Captain must be feeling the same sense of anti-climax, for she heard him murmur by her ear, 'I'll swear my Aunt Mary had that exact same striped wallpaper. It doesn't seem right, somehow.'

There was a small private room leading off the hall; Georgiana had described its location with exactitude. They opened its door and found it empty, providentially, but then it was still quite early. Georgiana, who really was extraordinarily well-informed, had advised her what time was best to arrive. They entered the room, and she locked the door, but left the key in the lock. And then she turned to look at him, her heart pounding.

11

NUMBER FOUR AND NUMBER FIVE

Leo had never been so full of nervous anticipation in his life. He wasn't, if he were honest, a man of any great sexual experience. He'd done quite a lot of kissing and mutual exploring with a slightly older neighbour when he was young, just before he'd gone to sea, experiences which he remembered with enormous fondness. His companion in pleasurable discovery – in some respects his teacher, for she had been from the outset far surer than he of what she wanted – was now a married woman of thirty with a parcel of children of her own, and he hoped she was happy.

There were many and varied opportunities offered to a sailor in every port, of course, not to mention on board ship, if one were so inclined, which he wasn't. But then again, a large proportion of those opportunities were of a frankly terrifying nature, for anyone who valued his health and his self-respect. He had heard of a perilous game rich, bored gentlemen played, a series of wildly irresponsible dares involving loaded pistols, though he didn't know if it was anything more than a rumour, and dallying with pox-ridden dockside whores struck him as even more dangerous. At least a bullet was quick. Naturally, he had indulged his sexual impulses sometimes, in places that seemed safer – he was only human, and he'd spent his whole adult life and half his boyhood in the navy – but he had done so prudently, always. That was something he should tell her, probably, Isabella; that he had always been careful to be safe, and he would, if things progressed in that direction, which it seemed they would, continue to do so. He would protect her. He didn't suppose she would be any more eager to risk pregnancy than he was, even if no other kind of risk had ever crossed her mind.

He didn't believe that the danger of parenthood, at least, was something he need worry about tonight. He imagined that there were a few items at least on her list before they came to that point. He thought too that he had a shrewd idea of what number six was, and she'd alluded to four, though he had no idea about five. It made him nervous, therefore, but it was also still damnably exciting. He'd probably be considerably less anxious if he didn't care about her so much. Of course he would. But he pushed that thought away since it led nowhere but to painful places. Dwell on the excitement. Dwell on making it – whatever *it* was – as wonderful for her as possible. He wanted to do that.

She locked the door of the dark, intimate little room and turned to look up at him, unfastening her cloak and throwing it aside without any apparent regard for where it landed. She licked her lips, involuntarily, it seemed to him, rather than in any deliberate attempt to tantalise him. Though it did. So, she was anxious too. It made him feel better somehow, made him all the more aware of the arousal that hummed in his blood, in every inch of his body, and set his head spinning. He said, and he had to clear his throat to say it, 'What do you...? May I kiss you? First?' Was that wrong? Were they perhaps not going to do that again, now she'd crossed it off? That would be a shame, for him at least.

But she said, 'Yes!' and then she was in his arms, as eager as he was, apparently. They'd done this before and they knew they liked it. They were on solid ground. His tongue brushed hers and hers came to meet it; they held each other tightly, fitting together like pieces of a puzzle, and gave licence to their mutual hunger. In the quiet room, there were little inarticulate murmurs of pleasure, and soft gasps that could have come from either of them. All thoughts, all worries about the future left him, submerged in the rush of pure sensation as their mouths devoured each other.

When he came back to himself, his hands were on her buttocks – that was new – squeezing her soft, abundant flesh, lifting her off her feet, pulling her as close as she could be. This was one of the many, many things he'd dreamed about doing, and it was even better than he'd imagined.

Her hands were inside his waistcoat – she must have unbuttoned it. With an adorable little cry of triumph, she pulled his shirt free of his breeches and slipped her hands under it to touch his bare skin at last. He loved to feel her hands upon him. It was another thing he'd thought about; it seemed he had a list too. He should probably write it down. Maybe later. Not now. Definitely not now.

She was exploring his back, her small, determined hands warm on his skin, but after a little while she pulled away slightly and said breathlessly, 'Number four...'

'What's number four?' he managed to say, though she'd mentioned it and he thought he knew.

She could write it on her list, she could think it and want it, but apparently, she couldn't say it. It seemed that she was going to show him; he was more than willing to be shown. She had worn, he saw now, since he hadn't been attending before, a silvery gown with a bodice that fastened with tiny pearl buttons. Sometimes, he knew – he wasn't *that* inexperienced, though he didn't claim to know much about women's clothing – these buttons on ladies' gowns were mere decoration. These ones weren't, though; these ones were functional because she was unfastening them. All of them.

Once undone, they revealed the straps of her stays and a scandalously flimsy chemise that covered, just barely, her breasts. Did that have buttons too? No, it had ties, she'd probably chosen it tonight because it did, and she unfastened them. She was determined, clearly, to do all this herself, and it was powerfully erotic to him, and also new. Everything was new. She was blushing, but she faced him bravely and bared herself to him. Good Christ in heaven. Her beautiful, beautiful, big breasts, which he had touched but never seen, and her erect pink nipples, erect just for him. He made some sound in his throat and it seemed to give her courage to speak at last. He couldn't have said a word in that moment, and any shred of rational thought he might have clung to deserted him entirely when she said, 'Would you like to... kiss me? I don't know if I told you that that's number four.'

He made a strangled sort of a noise that she could take as, 'Would I *like*...?' if she so wished, and then they were tumbling onto the sofa, fortunately there was a sofa, but of course there would be, and he was pushing her back into the soft cushions, or she was lying back herself in delicious invitation, perhaps both, and his hands, his mouth were on her.

Leo lost himself again. He wanted to lick her, so he did. Around and around her nipples, and she moaned and arched her back against him. He drew one aroused little bead into his mouth and sucked on it, and tongued it as he sucked. His hands were on her, too, exploring, enjoying the weight of her exposed breasts. Her skin was flushed and she made little noises once again that showed how much she liked it all. Her fingers were in his hair, holding him against her, urging him on, not that he needed any urging. She smelled wonderful, she smelled of herself. She tasted wonderful. When it was all too much for him for a moment, just too damn good, he buried his face in her glorious flesh and she held him there and stroked his head. He could hear and feel her heart pounding under him. He pressed his lips to her skin again and put out his tongue to taste more of her. Salty, sweet, unmistakably her.

He wasn't aware of it, but his right hand had crept down across her gown, across her lush curves, and was searching blindly for the hem of it. He only realised when she said, when she moaned, 'What you're doing with your hand—'

'I'm sorry!' he gasped instantly.

She chuckled, a low, rich sound he hadn't heard from her before and wanted to hear again. It was his new favourite sound. She said, 'That's number five. Don't you dare stop, sir.'

He was nothing if not obedient. He found the hem and raised it, and his fingers were on her knee, on her thigh; she wriggled under him, pleased with the direction he was taking, clearly. So was he. The silk was glorious to touch, but her skin, when he came to it, was better. So much better. He traced the top of her stocking where it met her velvety thigh and thought to say, 'My hands are rough; I wish they weren't. I'm sorry, I don't want to hurt you...'

'Don't be. I like it,' she almost growled. 'It doesn't hurt me, I mean, but I like the feel. I like it very much.'

So did he. The calloused pads of his fingers were rougher than a gentleman's hands should be, but she'd said she liked it so that was good, was better than good. He stroked her lush thigh and then continued upwards, to tangle in her curls. To find her secret places. He loved the noises she made when he touched her, and when he came to the little bud of flesh he was seeking, it seemed to swell under his caressing fingers. He loved, when he explored further, the undeniable fact that she was wet for him.

'I don't know what you like,' he whispered, his hand cupping her, stroking her. 'I want to please you. So much.' He wanted to make her cry out with pleasure. He hoped he could. God knows it wasn't about anything at all to do with conquest, or even skill – he didn't think he had any great skill to speak of – but he wanted to give her something, he wanted with passionate intensity to know that they were in harmony with each other, that she was enjoying this as much as he was. Her pleasure seemed much more important to him than his own just now, and that too was something he'd never experienced before.

'Oh...' she said breathlessly, moving under his hand, pressing herself against him. 'Shall I tell you?' It seemed she had lost all the shyness that had overwhelmed her when they'd first arrived, now that he was touching her at her direction.

'Please!'

'If you touch me... there... that's good.' His fingers were on her peak again, circling it, coaxing a response from her willing flesh. They were both breathing raggedly.

'Like that?'

'Yes, a little harder, even.' He was glad to take instruction, if she would consent to give it, and moved harder and faster on her, using her wetness to ease the motion of his fingers, anxious lest his rough skin should irritate her most tender and delicate places after a while, even if it did please her too. His mouth was still on her breast, kissing, sucking, his other hand was there as well, and she had her hands fixed tight in his hair, holding him to her. He wanted to give her everything.

'And this? Shall I do this?' His fingers slid to her entrance, and he slipped the tip of his index finger into her just a little, into the glorious, silken, liquid core of her.

She moaned, 'Yes!' and he dared to venture further, not wanting to be too tentative, but not wanting to push too far or too fast, not wanting above all to hurt her. She seemed to sense his uncertainty and gasped, 'If you touch me a little more on my... my seat of Venus, then presently you can put your fingers in me fully.'

'One finger, then two?' he asked, obeying her instructions and pressing more firmly on and around her peak, stroking it with his thumb, as she writhed beneath him and arched her back. His voice was muffled in her flesh, low, intimate, urgent. All he cared about was making her happy.

'Yes, so good, please,' she gasped, the power of articulate speech apparently on the point of deserting her. Which made him very happy. He pressed his finger into her and then slid out, and soon established a rhythm that had her pushing her pelvis up against him and clinging to him even more tightly. Two fingers after a while, stroking in and out, and she liked that, she was moaning low and breathing hard. He was more confident now and surer that he would not hurt her, and he slid between her bud and her entrance, really fucking her with his fingers as she had asked him to. He was enormously responsive to every tiny movement of her body, to the depth of her arousal, and he felt her hot flesh tensing and tightening as her climax approached. He could hear it in the increasingly guttural sounds she made and feel it in the slick wetness of her. She was close.

'Oh God!' she gasped, and he felt the beautiful moment of her release, when she started to peak and little convulsive movements spread out through her whole body. He knew not to stop, he didn't know how he knew, and his fingers still slid over and into her as she jerked under him and her limbs relaxed and melted into the sofa. She was no longer holding him to her. He buried his face between her breasts and closed his eyes for a moment.

His rhythmic movements slowed and at last stopped, but he didn't take his hand from her. He didn't want to. He'd lost all sense of time, but every now and then a renewed little spasm of pleasure shook her body and she pressed herself up against him again. He didn't want to deprive her even of one convulsion of sensation. Each was infinitely precious to him. He was still kissing her breasts and murmuring incoherent endearments but – probably fortunately – she seemed too lost in her orgasm to hear him. He opened his eyes and lifted his head so that he could see her face. It was soft, flushed, vulnerable, and her mouth was open. He felt enormously protective of her and knew in that moment, if he had not known before, just how much he loved her. At least he had been able to give her this, even if she didn't want anything else from him. This wasn't nothing. He felt tears building behind his eyes and in his throat and indulged himself for a moment in letting them free. A hot salt droplet trickled down his face and lost itself in his neck, and then another. She wouldn't see, and even if she did see she wouldn't know what it meant. He was safe for a little while, he thought. He slid his fingers from her at last but couldn't bring himself to release her completely. His hand lay loosely on her sex. If he took it away, he'd want to taste it, taste her on him, and she might think that was odd. Was it odd? He was a long way past being able to tell.

She sighed and opened her eyes. They were enormous velvet pools that, not for the first time, he knew he could lose himself in forever. Perhaps he was already lost. He had another hand, he realised – he wasn't quite himself still – than the one that was still cradling her secret places, and he could not help reaching out with it and touching her face very gently. She smiled at him. *Please don't say thank you*, he begged her silently. I'll *break down and sob if you say thank you. I'll wager* that's *not on your list. It certainly isn't on mine.*

She didn't. She said, 'That was…' She didn't seem to know what to say, and he had no objections to that. He had no idea what to say either. He should probably move his hand. His head. His whole body. He had – for what seemed like years he had had – an intense, almost painful erection. He might or might not have been grinding it against her thigh as he pleasured her. But he wasn't planning on mentioning it if she didn't. It would presumably go away eventually. Next year, perhaps.

But she shook her head as if trying to clear it. He could see now that there were tears on her cheek, but he wasn't presumptuous enough to assume that they had anything to do with him. They couldn't be. He had no idea what was going through her mind and wasn't sure he wanted to know. It was quite likely, after all, that she was thinking about her husband, her lost love, and that would be only natural even if the idea was a painful stab in the chest for him.

Isabella said, 'I was wondering... about you. About number six.'

12

NUMBER SIX

He'd had an idea what number six was, he recalled. His body recalled it, too. He croaked, 'You don't have to do anything. I didn't do this, any of it, in the expectation of some sort of—'

'I know you didn't,' she said swiftly. 'But I want to.' A glimmer of a smile. 'It is next on the list, after all.'

'Oh well,' he said, trying to match her humour, 'if it's next on the list...'

He moved away from her – he hoped he hadn't been crushing her with his weight, but if he had she hadn't seemed to mind – and she slid to her knees at his feet and looked up at him. Her gown was still undone and he was glad she didn't think to cover herself. She looked so beautiful, so infinitely desirable and so much more than that in his eyes. She put her hands on his knees and pushed them gently apart, then settled herself more comfortably between his thighs. He leaned back against the sofa cushions as she reached for him, stroking his visibly aroused member through the silk of his pantaloons. He shifted in his seat and throbbed under her caress. She'd feel that; the thought made him twitch again. She left her hand on him, she stroked him confidently with her thumb,

Jesus, and as she did so she looked up, saying, 'Now it is my turn to ask you what you like.'

'I like this. In fact, I can't imagine you doing anything I wouldn't like,' he said honestly.

'Very well.' Her fingers worked deftly to unbutton him, and as she pulled away the fabric he sprang free. He had no time to be embarrassed, for she wrapped one small fist confidently around his width and ran her thumb, her amazing, clever thumb, very gently along the slit. He leapt under her touch again and made an inarticulate noise in the back of his throat. If she felt any awkwardness in seeing him, in touching him like this for the first time, she did not show it. Kneeling at his feet, her breasts exposed, her hand holding him, she was smiling. He didn't care to imagine what manner of foolish expression he had on his face. And then he simply didn't care about anything at all, because she bent her head and put out her tongue, and with the very tip of it, she licked him where her thumb had caressed. A bolt of electricity shot through him and his whole body jerked in a convulsive movement. She laughed in what sounded like triumph and took him in her mouth; he sagged back against the cushions and gave himself up to her and whatever she chose to do with him.

She sucked on him for a little while, just on the head of him where he was most sensitive, and her fist still gripped him and pumped him. It was wonderful, it was the best thing he'd ever experienced in his life, but it wasn't going to last long at this rate. He couldn't stop her – he wouldn't dream of it, he'd have to be insane, but... She took her mouth off him, but not her hand, and looked up at him. She was still smiling. 'I was going to ask you if you liked that, but I see you do.' He whimpered assent, and somehow he must have managed to convey more than he knew, for she said. 'Too much, too fast?'

'I don't want to... too quickly.'

Her fist relaxed, and now she held him in a much looser grip, her fingers spread wide. She bent her head to tongue him delicately as she had before, again he gasped at the jolt of pleasure she caused, and then she released him so that she could lick down his length, and up, and back down. He closed his eyes.

After a few moments he opened them – it pulled him back from experiencing the pure sensations, but he didn't want to miss the sight of her, in case this never happened again and he had to survive on the memory of it. This was about so much more than simple physical pleasure. Although... She was licking him, having established a rhythm that appeared to please them both, and her left hand lay on his thigh; somehow his pantaloons had been pulled down to bare the upper part of his legs. Leo was a hairy man, much of his body covered in a thick golden down. He'd been teased over it frequently by friends, which had made him self-conscious about it in the past, and he would have been tonight if he had thought to anticipate her seeing him thus, but he never would be again, not with her, because it was clear that she liked it. She was stroking his leg as she pleasured him, and her right hand – good God – was on her breast, playing with her engorged nipple. He remembered that all this was happening because it was what *she* wanted. Happening at her direction. It was all her. He could almost feel doors in his mind – that was how he pictured it, a thought strong enough to be a physical sensation – opening. It was a wonder, he realised later, that he didn't spend himself then in sweetest release. He was entirely in her power, and it was glorious. It was exactly what he had always wanted, always needed, and he had never known it till now.

She must have become aware that he was watching her – perhaps he'd moaned or cried out, he couldn't say – because she raised her head to say, 'I'd like to suck on you now, if you are ready for that.'

'Yes,' he whispered. 'Yes, please do. But I don't... I don't want to spill in your mouth.'

'Are you sure you don't?' Her wicked little tongue came out and slid along his slit again, and of course he gasped and jolted.

'I do, but...'

'You don't think I'd like it?' Again she tongued him. 'You think it's too soon?' Again. 'You'd like to do this again?' He whimpered. 'Oh! You want to come somewhere else?'

'All of those things,' he ground out.

Her hand was still on his thigh and she was still touching herself. He reached down with a shaking hand and caressed her lovely breast, the neglected one. Would she understand him? 'If that's on the list...?' he said.

13

NUMBER SIX AND NUMBER FOURTEEN

She understood him perfectly. 'Not if it isn't?' But Isabella could see that he was in no state for dealing with double negatives, lying here aroused and helpless as he was, so she added, 'You don't want to do that if it isn't on the list?'

'I do want to. But... Just tell me, please, is it on the list?'

'It is, as a matter of fact. Much later. I wasn't sure anyone, you, would want to...' He groaned at the confirmation, and she laughed low in her throat, and rewarded him with another lick, more lingering this time. She was playing with him and they both knew it. The sense of power he gave her was intoxicating, there was no denying. He would obey her without question, she realised; if she asserted, *That comes later*, or *That is not something that I choose, do this instead*, he would accept it. This was new, this was not how it had been for her before, but she did not have time now to think about how and why it should be so, or what it meant.

'Very well,' she said, her breath caressing his most tender flesh and making him twitch. 'I will suck on you for a while, for that was my intention and I think you will like it too, and then, when I feel that you are close, I will pull back and let you spend yourself... where you desire to. This will mean, of course, that number six will have to be revisited, another time. Another time, I will taste you fully.'

'Please...' She could see that he was almost frantic with desire.

She relented, and put her mouth on him, closing her eyes and holding him lightly as she sucked and tongued him and he gasped. She knew he could have little control now and it was tempting to continue, but she had promised, and so she did not. When his breath was coming fast and ragged and she could taste the close-ness of his orgasm, strange and yet familiar too, salty, she slid her mouth slowly, reluctantly from him and sat back on her heels, looking up at him, panting; he staggered to his feet almost by instinct, eyes closed still, and she rose up on her knees and pressed herself to him, surrounding him, her hands tight on her breasts, as he moved urgently against her, between her. His hands came down to clasp her head and she buried her face in his abdomen, inhaling the masculine scent of him and revelling in his warmth as he thrust into her flesh and soon cried out in powerful release. It was animal-istic, perverse, fierce, wonderful. It was a powerful new memory.

A short while later he loosened his hold on her and sank back into his seat. She was still kneeling at his feet, exposed, and he drew her up to join him on the sofa. She was pink, flushed and sticky, and he whispered, 'I should help you... Clean you...'

'Yes,' she said. 'Yes, you should.'

An hour or two later, Isabella sat in her chamber, crossing items from her list. Four, five, fourteen. Six she left alone; it could be fully scored out another time. On reflection, she crossed through five again. It was only right to be accurate. He had commenced wiping his seed from her with his handkerchief, but it had been insufficient, he had worried that it would abrade her tender skin, and so after a while, he had lowered his mouth to her again and with infinite care licked away all traces of what had occurred; after that, she had been so aroused that he had been obliged to put his hands on her again and bring her to a second orgasm. He had been less tentative this time, more confident in his ability to give her pleasure, but still – always – acting only at her direction.

They had stayed in the room for hours, all told, and lost themselves so deep in erotic reverie that it had been hard indeed to compose themselves at last and leave. They had both felt that their occupation must be perfectly obvious to any persons who saw them as they emerged – but then, everyone else in the house must be presumed to be in a similar case, and it was true that they drew no attention as far as they could tell. Once home, Isabella had gained her room without meeting Blanche or Eleanor and had no idea if they had returned before her or not. Her maid had helped her undress, and if she had noticed anything amiss in her mistress's demeanour or appearance she had not betrayed any sign of it. She wasn't an old family retainer, but a Londoner of foreign birth, hired recently; she was a well-spoken and enormously self-contained young woman, so much so that it was evident she had her own mysterious life and cared little for Isabella's as long as she was properly paid for the work she did, and this seemed to suit them both.

Isabella locked her list away and climbed into bed, considering and then immediately discarding the idea of commencing a new letter to her mother. Somehow she couldn't... She'd do it tomorrow, perhaps. Her mama worried if more than a day or two passed between letters, and she had promised to be a faithful correspondent. But as her complicated reality and the anodyne world of her missives home drew further and further apart, she could see that it would become harder and harder to write and calm her mother's fears, even though she must.

She felt no desire to lay hands on herself tonight; she was, for the first time since Ash's death, entirely sated. Her limbs felt heavy, relaxed, languorous, and her breasts, her nipples and her secret parts were still tingling at his touch. Leo's touch. Ash, Ash, Ash... She realised she was weeping softly. She supposed it was no wonder. She had achieved so much of her aim: when she thought of a man's hands on her, wreaking precious oblivion, she would no longer think always of that last urgent coupling in their lodging, uniform undone, ballgown pushed aside, before he left her with a swift, desperate kiss and rode off to his waiting death. The memory of that day and its awful aftermath was a little weaker, she thought, and would be weaker still once her list was completed. It was a loss, but it was what she had wanted, what she wanted now, and if it cost her a tear or two it was worth it.

But if she were honest, that was not the sole source of her distress. She had thought herself armoured against all possibilities, in embarking on her mission to take charge of her life: she had resolved to stop at any point if the gentleman's attentions did not please her; she had been reconciled to the fact that Ash had been a considerate and skilful lover and it was unreasonable to expect as much of another, chosen almost at random as he had been. So she had accepted that the intimacy might be clumsy, awkward, perhaps unfulfilling. She hadn't expected it to be better.

Not better, she instantly corrected herself. Not better. Never that. But different. She had been a virgin, of course, when she had married. Ash had not been similarly untouched – he had been a man of seven and twenty, and experienced. He had taken the lead, inevitably, for she had been ignorant and unsure, and had always tempered his desire with gentleness and care for her. They had found themselves well-matched in passion, and explored what gave them pleasure over the months of their marriage, until they met as equals, or nearly so. Everything that passed between them had always been a matter of mutual consent, leading to mutual ecstasy. But having first taken the lead he had always done so afterwards, and Isabella had never thought to question the rightness of it. Perhaps they might have lived a whole happy life together without her ever questioning it: forty years of marriage, a deep mutual satisfaction that endured. Who could tell, since it was not to be?

But now Isabella had her list, and her wish for control – control in her own life, and control in intimate matters. She had not known, when she embarked on this course, that it would set something free inside her, something entirely unsuspected till tonight. Because when Leo had submitted himself so humbly to her wishes, she had realised that his willingness to do so – no, God, much more than that, his intense pleasure in doing so – was more powerfully arousing than anything she had ever experienced with Ash. He had given himself to her without reserve in a way that Ash never had, in a way that she had never dreamed a man could. And she loved it. It was idle to deny that she loved it. She could not help seeing it as a betrayal of her lost husband and all they had shared. And so she wept. She was conscious of the folly of it – if letting another man touch and caress her was not a betrayal of Ash, and she had firmly decided it wasn't, why should this be? It was just a quirk of her nature that had been revealed to her by circumstance. It wasn't as though she was in love with Leo. That was obviously quite out of the question. And that *would* be treachery.

She turned restlessly in her bed, and with a decisive thump reversed the pillow for a moment's blessed coolness. This was not what she had thought she wanted. How could she ever have envisaged this? But she had tasted it and now she needed it. Her body and her mind and her spirit craved it, all the more because she knew this opportunity was a brief one, never to be repeated. She refused to pick over the whys and wherefores of it and make herself miserable; she'd been miserable for so many months and it had driven her mad. No more.

14

Certain circumstances of a private nature meant that Lady Ashby was able to make no progress with her list for several days. Their next casual meeting naturally took place in front of others, and Leo grew anxious when she smiled on him but made no effort to arrange a further rendezvous. He began to wonder if something was amiss until she contrived to whisper that she was suffering from a feminine indisposition. He was conscious that his face cleared in comprehension and relief – she had not tired of him, she was not regretting all that had passed between them so far, she meant to continue – and he pressed her hand with what he hoped was a very speaking look of sympathy.

He was both sorry and not sorry that their intimacy proceeded no further for a while. Sorry because he was speculating on what might come next; he thought that there were a couple of things that were obvious – but he might be wrong – and he was tormenting his nights with dreaming of them. Dreaming of her. He was in an almost constant state of sexual arousal and was, he knew, responding almost at random to remarks addressed to him. She was a drug to him, and he craved her like any addict.

But he wasn't at all sure that sexual release would cure him. It hadn't yet. He'd spilt himself between her lovely breasts and he was still obsessed; he didn't imagine that coming inside her, greatly though he desired it, was any likelier to set him free. God knows he didn't want it to. He was a prisoner who dreaded the day of his release and hoped it would be long delayed. He knew with painful clarity that all this must end one day, and he was more than content to wait and postpone the dreadful hour a little. His body might not be so patient, but his heart was. He didn't want her to cross the last item from her list, whether that was fifteen or fifty or five hundred, and send him on his way. So a pause was welcome. He was, in this as in everything else, her servant.

He was also, he was brought to realise a day or so later, painfully obvious in his affections. Leo did not know if Cassandra had noticed and told Hal, or if Hal – newly attuned to the tender emotions as he was – had observed his sad state, but in any case, one afternoon when they were alone together in Lord Irlam's library his cousin said abruptly, 'Not been quite yourself these past weeks, Leo, wouldn't you say?'

He looked up from his wine glass, startled, and saw that Hal was regarding him with affection, and a little concern. He thought for a moment of denying everything, saying he had no idea what Hal was babbling on about, but it would be futile – Irlam wasn't stupid – and unfair to one who was the closest to a brother he had, or would ever have. 'No,' he said, and took an incautiously deep swig of Madeira that made his eyes water. 'No, I don't suppose I have.'

'Care to tell me about it? There's no need to reveal to me with a fanfare of trumpets the object of your attentions, old boy – I'm not a complete imbecile.'

'I never thought you were. Yes. I do love her, Hal.'

'Of course you do. No reason you shouldn't. I don't think she's indifferent to you, either. You seem to get along famously, the two of you. So why do you hesitate to declare yourself, and why are you so down in the mouth?'

'She doesn't want to marry again. Is determined not to.'

Hal made a rude noise and said, 'Nonsense. The way she looks at you... I'm sure she's been hurt, had a terrible time of it, poor girl, to be widowed so young. But I'm sure all you need is a little time and patience. Has she explicitly refused you?'

'I haven't asked her. I don't intend to – it's the last thing she wants from me, and it would ruin everything. It's far more complicated than you can know, Hal.'

'It always is,' said Lord Irlam with weary resignation, as if he spent half his life hearing that something or other was more complicated than he could possibly suspect. 'Always. It's this family – touched in the upper works, the whole lot of us, I'm beginning to think. Wouldn't have said you were one of those with his attics to let, of course, before this, but very little surprises me now. I'm used to dealing with Georgie's affairs, remember. Nothing you've embroiled yourself in could possibly be more tangled than the unholy mess she and Northriding made for themselves a couple of months back, and yet look at them now, smelling of April and May, enough to make a fellow queasy.'

Leo laughed hollowly. 'You're wrong, you know. I don't know the ins and outs of Georgie's troubles, and Lord knows I don't want to, but I don't see how this can be solved. It's quite hopeless.'

'I don't know about that, but I can see it's causing you pain. I'd like to help, if I can. I can listen, anyway. It might relieve your feelings, you never know.'

Captain Winterton looked at his cousin's open face and knew that if he were to tell anybody at all of his predicament it must be Hal. This was a man who'd shouldered more than his fair share of life's responsibilities, though he was not yet thirty, and he was utterly trustworthy and unlikely to judge. Setting aside Georgie's doings over the last year or so, Hal's brother Bastian and his aunt Louisa, though they were necessarily discreet about it, both lived what most people would consider highly irregular, even sinful lives, with companions of their own sex, and he thought no less of them for it, and loved them both as much as he had ever done. It was probably true that nothing could shock or surprise him. He was sorely tempted, and almost sure he could trust Hal to be discreet – but it was not his secret alone, and so he couldn't take the risk.

He said, 'I appreciate the offer, Hal, don't think I'm not sensible of your kindness. But I can't go into detail – forgive me. It's enough to know that I love her, and there's no future in it. She may, as you say, not be entirely indifferent to me. But it's of no consequence since her mind is quite made up that she will never marry again. Can we speak of something else?'

Hal, his face troubled, had no option but to agree, and the painful subject was abandoned.

15

Lady Ashby was surprised, and a little disconcerted, to receive a morning visit from the Countess of Irlam. She was not greatly acquainted with that lady, despite their connection by marriage, and at first thought that she must be calling on Lady Blanche, who happened to be absent with her daughter at the modiste's that day. But no; once the Countess had been admitted to the drawing room – Isabella had had a wild idea of telling the butler that she was not at home, but a second's reflection told her that this was impossible – she smiled and said, 'I'm glad to find you alone, Lady Ashby, for I confess it's you I most particularly hoped to see.' Cassandra was a little occupied in stripping off her gloves and removing her fashionable bonnet and braided blue velvet pelisse, and so presumably did not see the fleeting expression of sheer panic that passed across Isabella's face. She murmured some polite response, she could not have said what, and waited. What could this woman she barely knew possibly want with her? She was alone, without even little Billy to keep her company and give her courage.

Tea was brought, and once it had been poured the two ladies regarded each other. Isabella was glad that she was wearing one of her new gowns: the green one, in fact, with the slashed sleeves and habit shirt, which most unaccountably she always associated with her interview with Captain Winterton, in this very room. She couldn't hope to compete with her ethereal guest in terms of style and elegance and beauty – that had already been established at Mrs Singleton's party – but at least she was fashionably dressed today, and well groomed, and not wearing brown. She refused to dwell on precisely *why* the idea of competing with Lady Irlam – over what, pray? – should so much as have entered her head.

Cassandra went on, 'I thought we should become better acquainted, as two ladies from Yorkshire among so many southerners. You're from Harrogate originally, I understand? I have been there often, but I grew up in Skipton – do you know it?'

Isabella did, and they conversed easily for a little while, discovering that they had some acquaintances in common, and might easily have met on several occasions, had they but known it. She began to relax. Clearly, her wilder imaginings – in which Lady Irlam betrayed an unexpected possessive streak over Captain Winterton, her cicisbeo, and upbraided Isabella in deeply mortifying terms for stealing him away – were ridiculous. They must be entirely preposterous, surely – this was a friendly, happily married lady, who had no sinister intentions whatsoever, and furthermore could know nothing, nothing at all, about her husband's cousin's illicit relations with Isabella. Nor could she have the least suspicion of the Captain's unrequited passion; of course he would have been discreet in such excessively awkward circumstances. These were reassuring thoughts and enabled Isabella to converse with her unexpected guest with perfect composure.

It would be good, she thought, to have a friend of her own age to talk to – and to write reassuringly to her mother about – at least for the short while she remained in London, and one with whom she had something in common in the way of background, even though their current circumstances were very different. It must pain her somewhat to think that if Ash had lived she and her guest might very well have become bosom bows, through their tenuous family connection, and seen a great deal of each other as the years went by. All this could never come to pass now, of course; she'd be back in Harrogate soon enough, under her parents' roof. But she pushed that thought aside; she had a great deal of practice at banishing unwelcome thoughts, and barely flinched now when one threatened to assail her.

'I was wondering...' said Lady Irlam – she had been invited to call her Cassandra; said Cassandra. 'We plan to leave London soon and return to our home in Hampshire, so I thought we might make up a house party there. Nothing grand, just a few friends who will spend some weeks with us there in a very relaxed, informal sort of a way. Town is emptying out, it seems to me, and I believe Lady Blanche plans to return to Ireland while the weather remains relatively clement. You will be at a loose end, then, so would you care to accompany us and make one of our party?'

It was perfectly true; Lady Blanche had discussed her intention of leaving England in a few weeks' time, and Isabella had been closing her mind to all that this implied. She had even formed some vague idea of taking lodgings in London, although it would be hard to do so without some respectable lady to accompany her, which naturally was the last thing she wanted, and even with such an inconvenient companion, her parents would hold the idea in great disfavour when they heard of it. It seemed likely that her father would be despatched to fetch her home, and though he couldn't and wouldn't drag her back to Yorkshire against her will, the pressure he and most of all her mother could bring to bear would be considerable. Women of her age, even widows, simply did not set up house in London with no close male relative to lend them countenance. Whatever would their friends and neighbours say when they heard of such peculiar and not quite respectable behaviour? But here was another alternative...

Cassandra saw her momentary hesitation and said, 'Of course, you might very easily dislike the notion of committing yourself to a party where you are not well acquainted with any of the other guests, and I quite see that it is unfair that I should ask it of you, so I shall describe them to you, to allow you to make a more informed choice. I had hoped that my great friend Lady Silverwood might come, with her husband Sir Benedict and daughter Lucy and little son Teddy – he is the sweetest baby – but she is increasing again and prefers to stay at home. My husband's aunt, Lady Louisa Pendlebury, will be with us, and her friend Lady Carston. I don't know if you have met either of them in more than a casual way?'

'I haven't,' said Isabella, 'but I was talking with Georgiana, with the Duchess, a few days ago before she left London – of course, how foolish of me to forget that you must already know her far better than I do yet – and she said that she had hoped to introduce me to Lady Carston, as she was sure we would deal extremely well together. But in the end, she had no chance to do so, as Gabriel was so eager to leave.'

'Did she say that? That's interesting,' said Cassandra rather enigmatically. 'Well, I'm sure she was right, and you may take her word for it that you and Jane Carston will be firm friends. And Lady Louisa is excellent company, you know – not like an aunt at all, if you have aunts and are picturing someone terribly stuffy and dull and disapproving. She was very kind to me when I first met her, even though I was a mere nobody; she's not at all high in the instep. Let's see, who else...? My husband's friend Mr Wainfleet, who is not in the petticoat line, as he'd say himself. Oh, I should not use horrid slang, forgive me! I spend altogether too much time with my husband and his brothers! If you do not know, to be or not to be in such a line signifies a gentleman who does or does not

frequent the company of women, with all that that implies. Poor
Mr Wainfleet very much does not, and I think is a little scared of
young, attractive ladies, if truth be told, so he won't trouble you at
all.'

Isabella was quite touched that Cassandra thought of her as a
young, attractive lady, though of course it was not true and could
not signify in the least, and was smiling a little at this as her
guest went on, 'There may be a few other people present, I'm not
sure yet, but nobody intimidating, I assure you, and besides that,
we will be a family party, more or less. My brother-in-law Bastian
will be there, and my childhood friend Matthew Welby – you'll
have a great deal to say to him, he's from Yorkshire too, he's like a
brother to me and has become very close to Bastian; they share a
set of rooms in London now. And my husband's Aunt Sophia,
Mrs Winterton, of course, and her son Leo, Captain Winterton. I
know you are acquainted with him, so that will be a friendly face
– did he not accompany us on a turn around the park a few
weeks ago? And I am sure I have seen you dancing with him
once or twice.'

Isabella gulped and gazed at Lady Irlam in wild surmise, but
her face was completely open and innocent, and it was ridiculous
to think she meant anything particular by her last remark. 'Yes,'
said Isabella slowly. 'Yes, of course I am acquainted with the
Captain, though I have never met his mother.' Good God, his
mother!

'He is a most agreeable man, is he not? I do not know him very
well – he was at sea, I believe, when Hal and I married, and then we
went abroad for several months, so I have only properly met him
this year while he has been staying with us. But I like him very
much.'

'Just so,' Isabella replied in hollow tones. There were many
other things she could have said, things that she'd wager would

have made her companion's fiery locks stand on end, but perhaps fortunately she refrained from giving utterance to any of them.

'Well,' said Cassandra with a mischievous smile that Isabella could not help distrusting, 'I suppose I should not ask a young lady's opinion of an eligible gentleman; indiscreet of me to enquire, and it would be indiscreet of you to answer, so you are very wise not to do so.'

'I do not consider myself a young lady – or not in the sense I believe you mean,' Isabella responded with a tolerable assumption of calm. 'I am not on the hunt for eligible gentlemen, not in the slightest, I do assure you, even though you must be right to say that the Captain is indeed extremely so.'

'Oh goodness,' said Lady Irlam, flushing, 'I am so sorry – of course you are not. Forgive me for my clumsiness, I beg you. I have indeed spent too much time with my husband's family, and they do tease each other so terribly that I dare say I have fallen into the habit of it myself. How provoking! Now I have offended you, and given you a disgust of the Pendleburys and their rag manners besides, and the result of it all is that you will not come, and it will all be my fault when I am sitting alone in the Castle with no other young lady to bear me company.'

She did appear to be genuinely distressed, and Isabella was obliged to rush to reassure her that she was not in the least upset, and the upshot of it all was that she found herself agreeing to accept the invitation, and with a speed that took her breath away all was arranged; she would travel down to Hampshire with Lady Irlam in her carriage the very next week.

When her guest had taken her leave, Isabella reflected that, although the entirely unexpected invitation had been initially alarming – and the thought of keeping company with Captain Winterton's mother remained so, for how would she contrive to look her in the face? – it would at least enable her, enable them, to continue to make the necessary progress on her list. This would have been difficult enough upon Blanche's departure, and impossible if the Captain was engaged to go down to Hampshire with his family, which appeared to be the case, though he had never told her of it. Perhaps he had not known how to broach the subject. She would ask him, next time she saw him, and they could make a plan for how to proceed once they were at the Castle. It suddenly occurred to her that, if they were discreet – and they would have to be – they would for the first time have all night, or most of it, and the comfort of a bed at their disposal. That was food for thought.

Isabella remained touchingly confident that Lady Irlam – indeed, that everybody not directly concerned, apart from Georgiana, in whom she had confided and who was now safely in Yorkshire – remained in ignorance of her plan and its execution. She would not have been so sanguine if she had been privileged to read the letter that Cassandra dashed off to the Duchess of Northriding as soon as she arrived home, and she would have been quite appalled if it had been possible to overhear the conversation the Countess had with her lord when next they encountered each other.

* * *

Cassandra had almost finished dressing when Hal lounged into her chamber; she dismissed her maid Kitty with a smile. Or attempted to. Kitty could not be described as the regular sort of lady's maid, but was a tall, imposing, buxom and outspoken countrywoman who had known Lord Irlam from the cradle, and although she took her leave, she did so shaking her head and muttering that she could tell they were hatching some mischief between them, and not to come running to her when it blew up in their faces. 'We won't,' said Hal, bussing his old nurse soundly upon both cheeks and practically pushing her out of the room.

He turned to survey his wife, who was looking particularly becoming in an evening gown of deepest indigo velvet, which flattered her pale skin and flaming curls. He was obliged to tell her so, and kiss her shoulders and her graceful neck, and it was a little while before he gathered his wits enough to ask her what he had come on purpose to enquire: 'Is she coming?'

'Yes, she has agreed to stay with us, and did not think it the least odd that I should ask her, as far as I can tell.'

'Good. And can you divine what she thinks of him – are her affections in the least engaged? The poor fellow is at the end of his tether, you know, and we must do anything we can to help him.'

'I don't know,' said Cassandra, lovingly smoothing back the rakish black lock that fell across her husband's forehead and would not be tamed. 'She was initially very nervous when I arrived, and I'm not quite sure why.'

'Perhaps she has some inkling that he cherishes warm feelings towards her, and is wary of him and of his family as a result?'

'I couldn't tell. Possibly. At any rate, I was very clever and put her in a position where she had no choice but to accept my invitation; I can't say if she thought I was matchmaking or not, but in any case, I'm tolerably sure she has not the least suspicion of me or my intentions. I hope she does care for him – I do like her, Hal, and I'm sure you will too. There's something straightforward about her that is very engaging.'

'Leo's head over heels in love with her and that's good enough for me. I only hope the whole affair isn't as desperate as the poor fellow seems convinced it is. But I dare say we shall know soon enough!'

16

NUMBER SEVEN AND NUMBER SIX

Lady Ashby was able to contrive another meeting with Captain Winterton a night or two later; she was becoming quite disturbingly skilled in deception, she reflected, as she put her gloved hand on his arm and accompanied him into the house of assignation, loo mask firmly in place. They needed to talk with some urgency; perhaps all they would do this evening was talk.

Or perhaps not.

Alone with him in the small candle-lit room with its red and gold furnishings, she stripped off her evening cloak, mask and gloves, and turned to look at him. 'I presume you have heard that your cousin's wife has invited me to stay with them in Hampshire, and I have accepted?' she said, frowning unconsciously.

The Captain had removed his outer clothing too, and undid his mask now with elaborate care; she thought he was purposely not meeting her eyes. She could not wonder at it. It must be difficult for him, this conversation. 'Yes,' he said. 'Cassandra, Lady Irlam, did mention it. Of course, I did not reveal that it was of any particular interest to me.'

Isabella was conscious of an inevitable awkwardness – they were discussing the woman he loved, as they had at the outset agreed never to do – but it must be overcome. God knows she had no desire to hurt his most tender feelings, but she must know if she would be walking into some hideous situation that would end badly for all of them. 'Why has she asked me?' she demanded. 'I hardly know her. Is she trying to make up a match between us, do you think? In which case it must be horribly painful for you, and perhaps I should invent some excuse to withdraw my acceptance.'

'No!' he said with surprising heat. Perhaps he needed her there as some sort of shield against his feelings for Cassandra, Isabella thought. A distraction, a protection. Not very flattering, but understandable, she supposed. His motives for acquiescing to her plan were, after all, none of her business. And then he went on more calmly, 'No. I'm sure there's no need for that. She might be – matchmaking, I mean, in a mild sort of way. But even if that's true, I'm sure she'd never do anything more than put us in proximity, the natural proximity that must arise in a house party of this kind. Perhaps she has hopes of bringing us together, but it can't be of any great moment to her, and if we both show we have no such inclination, I am sure she will have good breeding enough to do nothing more.' His face seemed troubled, and no wonder, but his voice was firm and even as he continued, 'She said she liked you – why should she not? – and hoped you would bear her company. I dare say she misses Georgie now she's married and gone to live in Yorkshire, for they are very close, you know.'

This gave Isabella a momentary pang – what if the two women corresponded and discussed her? What if the Duchess revealed her secret to her bosom bow and sister-in-law? But that was folly, she reassured herself. Georgiana had appeared fully to understand the reasons for keeping the matter secret, had agreed not even to tell her own husband. And Cassandra herself could know nothing, had appeared to know nothing whatsoever. It must be as he said, and certainly if he could overcome the awkwardness, which he had said he could, it would be most convenient, apart from the presence of his parent.

'Will you feel uncomfortable... continuing when your mother is staying in the house?' she asked him, her eyes fixed intently on him.

He held her gaze steadily, his expression one she could not hope to interpret. 'No,' he said shortly. 'Perhaps I should, but I won't. We shall be discreet, of course, and nobody will suspect anything. As far as anyone knows, we are barely acquainted. Will *you* feel uncomfortable?'

'Maybe a little, but I will overcome it, I dare say. My own parents would be different, naturally, and I imagine they might easily notice, or my mother might, which would be excessively awkward. Disastrous, really. But you are a grown man, after all, and have been independent for years.'

'Yes,' he said, 'I am.' His voice was very low, and she was suddenly aware that, despite his troubled mind, he was aroused, simply being here with her in this intimate little room where so much had already passed between them. She knew he wanted her, and she knew that he was waiting, patiently or impatiently, for her to tell him what number seven was, because he didn't know. And at some deep level, she thought, he didn't care what it was – whether it was something that would lead to his fulfilment or hers, or both. He would perform whatever task she set him with equal willingness. It was intoxicating, the power she had over him.

She said a little breathlessly, 'Well, there is no denying it will be excessively convenient, to be sleeping in the same house together.'

'Will I be doing much sleeping?' he said. He was smiling now, all disturbance apparently banished, and his blue eyes were glittering.

'Perhaps not.' How her heart was racing! 'But now I must discuss a delicate matter with you, sir, that affects us both. The fact is, I have every reason to believe myself unable to conceive a child; no, more than that, I know...' Why was she telling him this? It was private, a source of deepest pain, and no affair of his. But in a sense it was his business, she had made it so, and she must reassure him. 'When I did not conceive after many months, I consulted doctors, the most renowned practitioners in London. And they told me I was barren. There would be no child, and the fault was mine. They spoke of hysteria, and wandering wombs.' Her voice faltered, recalling the utter humiliation of it, then somehow she found the courage to continue. 'I didn't understand how they could be so sure, and God knows I didn't want to believe them – as I think I've told you, I later persuaded myself I was with child when I was not and could not have been. But that does not signify now. It is all past and gone. I only mention it because you need have no fear that I, that we...'

He said, his voice unsteady, 'I hate to see you so distressed, Isabella. I'm sorry you were obliged to tell me, but of course I understand why you did. Thank you for confiding in me. I will not insult your trust by asking you if you are sure; I see that you are.'

'The most eminent doctors, and such certainty...!' she responded in what was almost a cry of pain, and then, 'Please, may we alter the subject?'

'Of course. Forgive me, my dear. Perhaps tonight is not the time to do more than talk, after all – would you like me to escort you home?'

He was so considerate; how well she had chosen! 'I would not,' she said firmly. There were tears on her cheeks, but she would not regard them. No, she would push these darkest memories away, down in the darkness where they belonged, and she knew exactly how to go about it. Release, and the momentary oblivion that it brought, was what she needed. She felt herself drawn inexorably to him; he was only a few steps away, and she closed the distance in a rush. She reached up to caress his cheek, and he turned his mouth and pressed a hot kiss into her palm. 'Number seven...' she said, her hand still on him, 'is long overdue, it seems to me.'

'Before we proceed to number seven...' His voice was hoarse. 'Before we do that, I must repay your confidence in me and tell you, as I should have told you before we commenced on number six, that you stand in no peril from me. I have not indulged a great deal, before I met you, in... pleasures of the flesh, and when I did I was always extremely careful to be protected. To protect others.'

'I would expect no less of you,' she said composedly. Ash had told her the same; had said that any decent man must do as much, or never think to take a woman as his wife or lover. He had been safe, and therefore so was she. But she could hardly tell Leo that; it would be in poor taste. It seemed he had harboured no such concerns about her. How complicated it all was. She shook her head and returned to the moment. 'Number seven, then...'

'What is number seven?' he asked huskily. 'Dare I guess...?'

Isabella drew him over to the red velvet couch and seated herself, pulling him, unresisting, down beside her. She lay back, smiling, and said, 'I think you must know that now it is your turn to kneel before me.'

'Oh God, yes,' he said fervently and slid instantly to the floor at her feet.

She looked at him expectantly and he gazed up at her, flushed, his pupils dilated so that his eyes were dark as sin. 'I want to please you,' he whispered, 'as you pleased me. I don't have a great deal of experience of this particular delight – but I want to learn. There's nothing in the world I want more than to give you pleasure.'

'I know,' she said. 'I know you do. And you will.' She was suddenly, ridiculously, on the verge of tears again. Why should it mean so much? It was merely the execution of her plan. Another memory to keep. But she refused to stop and think and let doubts creep in. She wanted his mouth on her. She would have it. 'Uncover me. I don't care if it's fast or slow. Let that be as you please. Uncover me, kiss me, lick me, eat me.'

'It will be as slow as I can make it,' he said raggedly, 'which may not be very slow, after all, for I am eager to taste you at last.'

'You will find that I am wet for you,' she replied with equal unsteadiness. She almost shocked herself, saying such a thing to him, but she was full of raw emotion after her painful disclosure, and perhaps that was why the extraordinarily frank admission had slipped out. She'd been able to speak so to Ash; she'd never looked to utter such words again. But she could trust Leo with so many of her secrets.

He couldn't know what she was thinking, but her honesty was plainly too much for him; he groaned, and pulled up her skirts with clumsy, determined fingers that shook. He shoved the rich fabric layers roughly aside and lowered his head, and she opened her thighs to him and lay back against the cushions, desperate to lose herself in sensation.

He paused for a moment with his hands on her, and she had to restrain herself from squirming with impatience for his touch – it would be unfair, for she had said fast or slow, had she not? But then he was kissing her inner thighs, his lips hot and hungry, pushing her wider apart with his shoulders so he could reach her fully, and his hands slid up and clasped her bottom, lifting her to a better angle. Then with a groan he buried his face between her legs and commenced devouring her. He'd said he hadn't much experience of this, but he wanted to give her pleasure so badly, and was so highly responsive to her every gasp and sigh and subtle movement, that he could not help but please her, move her deeply. She felt worshipped, and her hands crept down and held his fair head to her, as he lapped and sucked and tongued her with intense concentration. She wouldn't compare it with anything she had experienced before with Ash. She needn't, because she was in control and Leo was her willing captive, and as with all their previous encounters the power she knew she had over him added enormously to her arousal.

She felt herself on the verge of coming, the waves were building inside her, and she gasped, stilling his head with her hands, 'Slower, slower, Leo, please!' and he heard, smothered though he was in her flesh, or else he felt her and knew instinctively what she needed, and so he drew back a little, glancing up at her and smiling wickedly.

'Is what I'm doing to your liking?' he murmured against her wet flesh, and she was so aroused that the whisper of his breath on her most tender places made her gasp anew. He was teasing her; he must be very well aware that it was precisely to her liking.

'Good God, you know it is.' It was a wonder she still had the power of articulate speech. 'Are you fishing for compliments, sir?'

He laughed and said, 'I must have a natural aptitude. Who would ever have guessed?' And then he bowed his head again and began to lick along her seam with long, deliberate strokes that set her body arching and made her press herself up against him, her breath ragged. He had slowed the pace a little, as she had demanded – begged? She was past telling – but the imperative of her body would not be denied, and in a moment she was crying out and clutching the sofa cushions as an intensely powerful orgasm claimed her and carried her away.

When she came back to herself, he was still buried in her, languorously licking, kissing, nibbling gently with his teeth. Little aftershocks still jolted her, and only slowly ebbed away. At length, he sat back on his heels and raised his eyes to hers. Their gazes locked, and Isabella felt suddenly as though she stood outside herself, above herself, looking down on the body of a woman sprawled lewdly on a couch, skirts about her waist, in a room that must have seen a dozen, a hundred of such meetings. A woman, with a man between her legs, a man she barely knew. She felt dizzy for a moment, disorientated, and then he said, 'I think that was the most wonderful thing that's ever happened in my life. I can't ask if it was anything like the same, but I do hope it was good for you.' His face was wet, dazed, and she could not doubt the truth of what he said. It wasn't a question and she couldn't answer him in words: dared not, perhaps.

'Come and kiss me,' was all she could reply. He rose and joined her on the sofa and she seized his face between her hands so that she could taste herself on him. They were the most urgent kisses they had yet shared, and in a little while Isabella had to pull away to catch her breath. He was beneath her now and she had rolled to straddle him. Her skirts were still rucked up in wild disorder and his hands were on her bare bottom, clasping it tightly. She could feel his hardness against her naked skin, through the thin fabric of his evening breeches. 'We never completed number six!' she gasped.

'You don't have to,' he ground out against her throat. 'I don't expect—'

'But I want to,' she said. She slid off him and took his place on the floor; she all but tore at his breeches buttons to free him, and there was no finesse in her touch this time, no teasing and slow exploration. He was fully aroused, big and hot, the silky skin straining and begging for release, and she would give it to him, devouring him as he had devoured her. She closed her eyes and took him eagerly into her mouth, glorying in the way his whole body tensed as she claimed him and set to work, glorying in his moans, and in the escalating rhythm of his breathing that told her, if she had needed to be told, that he was about to spend himself in her in helpless surrender.

A while later, Lady Ashby, alone in her chamber, firmly crossed numbers six and seven from her list and then took up her pen again for a very different purpose.

Dear Mama, once again my fond love to Papa and to you. I received your last letter safely, and continue well, as I hope you both do, apart from his troublesome rheumatic pains. I hope the flannel is helping. But I have some news! I have, as I am sure I must have told you, become acquainted with Lady Irlam, Cassandra, who is married to Georgiana's brother and so in some sense a family connection of mine too. Her maiden name was Hazeldon and she is from Skipton, imagine that, and later I will tell you all the Yorkshire people we can count as shared acquaintances, for I know it will interest you greatly. She is making up a house party, chiefly the Pendlebury family, at her home in Hampshire, Castle Irlam, and has asked me to join them for a few weeks. I have accepted; indeed, it would have been discourteous not to do so when she has been so kind and welcoming. I know that you expected me home before long, and are anxious for me to return, and I promise I will come well before Christmas, but I thought you could not possibly object to my accepting such an unexceptionable invitation...

It wasn't the easiest of letters to write, as Isabella could well imagine her mother's reaction when she read that her daughter was leaving Blanche's home to spend time with a group of fashionable people quite unknown to Mrs Richmond, and of whose characters and motives, she could not doubt, knowing her mother as she did, she would be suspicious. She was at pains to reassure her anxious mama of their utter respectability, and she hoped their connections to Yorkshire would render them acceptable, which was why she stressed it. She wasn't writing to ask for permission, which was just as well because she'd never have received it, and by the time her mother replied with all the reasons why she shouldn't go, it would be too late and she'd be there. She wasn't looking forward in the slightest to receiving that letter.

Writing left her unsettled, then, and on top of that it had been an extraordinary evening, full of extremes of emotion. She had told Leo one of her darkest secrets, something she hadn't even confessed to her mother during the long months of her illness. It had been an entirely private thing till now. That encounter with the doctors had been one of the worst humiliations she'd ever suffered, and speaking of it ought to have drained her – instead, she'd felt liberated, and now she felt almost giddy in reaction.

She could not help but reflect that soon they would be at Castle Irlam, for good or ill, and soon, Leo would be inside her at last performing that basic, primal act which seemed to hold such significance. If anyone had known that they were lovers – for that was what people would say they were, and she supposed it was true despite the highly peculiar circumstances she had devised – they would assume that they'd been doing *that* all along.

'I have a lover,' she said aloud. Odd that she'd never thought to say it or even to think it before. She, Isabella Richmond Mauleverer, a barren, sad, previously mad widow from Harrogate whom everybody pitied, if they were kind, and shunned, if they weren't, had a lover. They, she and her lover, had committed sodomy – because, she'd looked it up, what he'd done to her and what she'd done to him tonight, both of those things were defined as sodomy by whoever it was who spent their precious time defining such matters, and were illegal. Even when she'd done them with Ash, her lawfully wedded husband, they'd been illegal, and presumably, if things could be *more* illegal – could they? – they were even more illegal when done, when committed, thrillingly, with a naval captain you hardly knew in a dubious house of assignation in Mayfair. 'Excellent!' said Isabella aloud in the silent room, and when she fell asleep she was smiling.

17

Leo wasn't easy in his mind. His body – that was a different matter. His body was happier than it had ever been in its, in his life. It was Christmas and birthday and carnival all rolled into one, as far as his body was concerned. But his mind, and for that matter his poor heart, they were an entirely different kettle of fish. He hadn't in the least enjoyed the conversation with Isabella that had preceded the best hour or so of his existence so far. He was deceiving her, and he hated it. He hadn't lied to her on that occasion, not in so many words, because it was perfectly true that he remained in ignorance of what Cassandra knew or didn't know about what he'd confessed to Hal. He could say that if he wanted, but he had a pretty shrewd idea that Hal had told his wife everything he knew. Of course he had, because Leo would have wagered a large sum that he always did, and furthermore, why otherwise would Cassandra have suddenly taken it into her head to invite Lady Ashby to be her guest in Hampshire?

She hadn't set up the party for Isabella's benefit – that had been happening anyway, and Leo had been just about to tell Hal and Cassandra that he wasn't joining them as he'd previously agreed to but was staying in London and taking lodgings, for excellent reasons of his own. He just hadn't thought of the reasons yet, and now he didn't need to. And yes, all he'd said to Isabella about Cassandra and her possible matchmaking was true, in a way. Lady Irlam might very well be doing that, inspired by some sweet but misguided desire to help him, but if he and Isabella showed they weren't receptive to being subtly pushed together he was sure, as he'd said, that she'd stop. He could get Hal to tell her to stop, he supposed, if it became necessary, though that was a conversation he'd rather not have.

What really made him uncomfortable, even in the aftermath of an incredible orgasm wrought by the mouth of the woman he adored, and with the prospect of so much more to come, was the knowledge that she believed him to be helplessly in love with Cassandra. Because he'd lied and told her he was. He had been able to tell from her expression – he chose to believe that other people couldn't read her face as easily as he could – that she'd seen how agitated the whole conversation made him, but had ascribed all of it to the fact that he was in love with Cassandra and didn't want to discuss her. Jesus. It was a kind of protection for him – in that sense, it was working better than he could ever have anticipated when he'd blurted out Cassandra's name *in extremis* that day – but it was a lie, and he could dimly envisage all kinds of hideous scenarios, all kind of monstrous complications, that might arise from it now that they were all going to be living cheek by jowl for several weeks. With, as if all that wasn't bad enough, his dear mother.

And that was another thing. He'd told Isabella, in another of his patented not-quite-a-lie-but-not-quite-a-truth-either statements, that he didn't mind in the least creeping around Castle Irlam in order to make passionate love to her while his mother stayed under the same roof. Well, roofs – it was a castle, after all. It wasn't as though he feared bumping into his mama in the early morning as he crept back to his bed. He had his own room there, which he had occupied since he and Hal had graduated from the nursery to more adult quarters, and his mother had a suite of her own since she had spent so much time there when the boys and Georgie were growing up. They weren't in close proximity. He knew that that wasn't what Isabella had meant, though – she had meant, did he have a problem with deceiving his mother while engaging in a sordid sort of an intrigue? And he had said that perhaps he should, but he didn't. He wasn't sure what she had made of that – they'd been rather delightfully diverted and perhaps she hadn't had time to dwell on it – but he thought now that there would be an inevitable awkwardness to it, and of course he didn't want his mother to know what he was doing, because she wouldn't understand. But the reason he didn't mind the whole situation as Isabella had thought he might was that, for him at least, this wasn't some sordid intrigue. This was the woman he loved. And the pain would come, must come, not from the deception he was engaged in, but if he saw his mother beginning to like her, beginning to see her as exactly the sort of young woman her only son should marry. She might easily see that, he thought, because she was his mother, and knew and loved him. She might even speak to him of it, ask him if he had not thought to seek Lady Ashby's hand in marriage, and then what would he say? That would hurt. Lying to his mother about his deepest feelings, if it came to a point where he was obliged to do that, would hurt.

What would hurt the most, of course, would be the end of it all. He didn't know, and wouldn't ask, how many more items there were on the list. He couldn't know the extent of her experience with her husband. Perhaps they could explore new things together; he thought she might easily agree. It would still be her list, if she chose to make it so, he could say to her. He wanted to marry her and live with her, and make a life together, but if he couldn't have that he was quite prepared to grow old in her service, to take the list into the hundreds and the thousands. Yet he knew she wouldn't. He knew that once her purpose was achieved, once she had regained the sense of self that she had lost, she would call a halt, and he would bow his head and agree, raise not a word of protest though his heart would be shattering into a thousand pieces in his chest. She would leave, hugging her secret to her.

It might be that this would happen quite soon; when the house party ended, in three weeks, or four. Before winter set in, certainly. Before the first snows fell, she'd want to get back to Yorkshire.

It was with a deeply divided mind and heart, then, that Captain Winterton swung himself into the saddle as Hal did the same at his side, and set off, accompanying the coach that carried his love and his torment, his mistress in every possible sense of the word, along with Cassandra, whom he'd said he loved but didn't, to Hampshire and his fate.

18

Isabella faced the idea of many, many hours alone in a closed carriage with Lady Irlam with a certain amount of trepidation. She had been informed that the Earl kept teams of fine horses stabled on the road to his principal seat, and would face no delay at any of the changes, being well known at each and every superior inn, but it was still a long journey. Their maids were travelling separately with the luggage, and the gentlemen were riding. Thank heaven for that, at least. But what would they talk about, she and Cassandra? She could think of several topics of conversation that really would be best avoided, for everybody's sake.

It had been decided that they would make better time if they left together early in the morning, rather than stopping to pick Lady Ashby up on the way, so Isabella bade farewell to Blanche and Eleanor, and Billy too, late one afternoon, before going to spend the night at Lord Irlam's mansion in St James's Square. She found herself surprisingly emotional at the parting, and Blanche shed tears when she tried to express her thanks for what had been so much more than a casual, brief visit. 'I'm so glad you came to us,' said her hostess, embracing her. She had sent her daughter from the room on an errand to fetch something that had been forgotten, which all three women were quite aware was the merest pretext. The kitten was present, but he showed no interest in the conversation, being quite absorbed in his meticulous ablutions. 'I'm not imagining how much being here has helped you, am I? I don't mean to say that you weren't well when you arrived – you were – but you seem so much better now. Back to your old self, almost.'

If only you knew, thought Isabella. But she must be grateful to her sister-in-law for her kindness, and said so again. Blanche brushed aside her thanks. 'You will always be my sister,' she said. 'I hope you know that. You will for ever be a member of this family, no matter what happens. Gabriel is of the same mind, I know. And I shall miss you.'

'No doubt we will see each other next year,' Isabella murmured, touched. 'You will pass through Harrogate on the way to North-riding Castle, surely, or I will be with you in York as we were this year, for the assemblies and the races. I will miss you too, both of you, but it is not so long until the spring, after all.'

'Hmm,' said Blanche, mopping her eyes. 'Do not take me up wrongly, my dear, if I say that I hope not to see you in either of those places, unless of course you are accompanied by a new husband. Then I shall greet you – both – with a great deal of pleasure.'

Isabella was astonished, and could only gaze at her hostess in incredulity. 'I don't...' she spluttered at last. Tears were starting in her eyes too.

'It's absolutely none of my business, which is why I have not spoken till now, but now that you are going, I find I must say some-thing or be out of reason cross with myself. My dear...' Blanche took Isabella's hands in hers and leaned forward urgently. 'My dear sister, Ash would have hated the idea of you living as a widow for the rest of your life. Hated it with a passion. You must know that I am right.'

Ash's widow was crying in earnest now, strong ugly sobs racking her despite all her attempts to control them. 'I can't betray him!' she managed.

'It wouldn't be a betrayal. It would not! I didn't mean to distress you, and I am sorry for it. We all loved Ash; his death hit us all hard. I was as worried about Gabriel as I was about you, for a long time – you let your feelings out, which perhaps was healthier, rather than bottling it all up inside as he did and pretending to be unaffected. But he is healing now, with Georgiana, and making a new life for himself, and you deserve no less.'

'I don't want to forget him!' she almost wailed. 'I don't want to, I won't!'

'No one is asking you to. We will all remember him, and love him, as long as we live. I hope Gabriel will name a son for him one day soon. But you might easily have another fifty or sixty years to live, and you are owed some happiness after so much misery. I'm sure your parents would agree, and I am entirely confident Ash would have said so himself if he had been able.'

'*You* haven't remarried,' said Isabella, sniffing, aware that it was a foolish thing to say as soon as the words left her lips. She knew that Blanche had been widowed a few months before her own wedding; she did not know, because Blanche rarely spoke of her husband, whether her marriage had been a happy one, but she had sometimes suspected it had been not always been easy.

'Oh, me!' replied Blanche with a slightly twisted smile. 'Who would I marry? Some old gentleman who wants a nurse in his declining years, or thinks to live on my son's estate at my son's expense? I thank you, no. I am too set in my ways by now to want to see another nightcap on my pillow and accustom myself to another man's snoring. But it's different for you.' Isabella made no reply but shook her head in stubborn, mute refusal. 'Very well! I have said my piece. You will do as you think best, and so you should, but I want you to know one thing. If some gentleman should aspire to your hand – don't worry, I shall not be indiscreet enough to name him! – then when you are assembling frivolous reasons for refusing him, assuming of course he should be a worthy candidate for your affections, do not think to use the disapproval of the Mauleverer family as one of them. I simply won't have it. I would very happily dance at your wedding, and so would Gabriel. I should tell you that I speak for him in this.'

'I... I don't know what to say.' Eleanor was taking an unconscionable time about finding her mother's missing hartshorn, or whatever it was. Isabella wished she would come back and put an end to this.

'Say nowt. Just think on what I've said,' Blanche responded, sounding very Yorkshire suddenly. They found themselves laughing after their tears, and soon they parted, Isabella kissing her hostess, Eleanor, and the entirely indifferent cat goodbye and wishing them all a safe journey to Ireland.

It was ridiculous, of course, thought Isabella as she lay sleepless under Lord and Lady Irlam's roof later that night. It could not affect her intentions in the least, and she would pay no attention to Blanche's words, kindly meant though they were. Blanche had no desire to marry again; well, neither did she. Ash had been her one love, and that would never change. And Leo, if Blanche had divined something, some spark between them, and had been speaking of him, did not, in point of fact, aspire to her hand in any case, because he was in love with Cassandra and always would be. Which was absolutely fine, and suited her perfectly. She was employing him – that was a horrid way of putting it, but it was true – to heal herself, and it was working. It was definitely working. He didn't do so badly out of the bargain, after all, and she had no need to feel guilty. She didn't feel guilty. He had told her that he wasn't enormously sexually experienced; well, by the time she'd finished with him, he would be, and what he then chose to do with all that skill was entirely up to him. He would marry, no doubt, despite his unrequited love, perhaps when he was older and had forgotten his beloved at least a little, and some unknown girl would be very lucky indeed, and perhaps rather surprised. Isabella fell asleep at last, dreaming of number eight, which for the Captain's benefit she had subdivided into parts (a) and (b), and his face when she told him so.

The household rose very early the next morning, and the two ladies were bundled into the travelling carriage and swaddled in luxurious rugs and wrappings, their feet set upon hot bricks, while they were both still half-asleep. It was seductively easy to slip into slumber again in the comfortably sprung modern vehicle, and it was not until the first change of horses that Cassandra and Isabella woke fully, yawning and stretching and eagerly drinking the hot coffee that was so solicitously brought to them.

Somehow, the fact that they had both been relaxed enough to sleep while together eroded much of the constraint that Isabella, at least, might have felt. It made no sense, but she was less worried about unwelcome topics of conversation. She felt warmly grateful to her hostess for the lovely carriage, and she was besides now a dashing, daring, unconventional sort of a woman, who had a lover, a lover with whom she had done outrageous, illegal, wonderful things, and she could quite easily deal with any slight awkwardness in discourse. What was mere conversation? She was a woman of the world, a woman who took charge, and equal to anything. Maybe there had been brandy in the coffee, also. She would make sure always to take it that way in future.

They ate delicious little morsels that Lady Irlam's pastry chef had prepared for them, and talked in a desultory fashion, and dozed a little more between changes, and in a surprisingly short amount of time, or so it seemed, they dismounted from the carriage to take nuncheon with their gallant horseback protectors. They had not encountered any highwaymen from whom they had needed to be rescued, the journey had been entirely without incident, and they were more than halfway there.

And so the day passed, as a half-seen late autumn landscape of bare fields and almost leafless trees unrolled outside the carriage windows, and in the chilly dusk they found themselves sweeping up the carriage drive to alight at last, a little stiffly, at Castle Irlam, to lights and a welcome from many liveried servants. Lord Irlam and Captain Winterton had ridden ahead at the end of the journey and so were waiting to help them tenderly down. The other guests had not yet arrived, Isabella was told; only family was present, and they had already dined. She was not obliged to meet them in her tired, dishevelled state – with exquisite care, she was whisked away to her warm, comfortable panelled chamber, and a bath was offered her, and, afterwards, her dinner on a tray, a glass of rich red wine, and sleep, in a deep feather bed. Tomorrow she would write home, with the reassurance that she had arrived safely, having met with no accident upon the way.

19

Isabella slept soundly and woke refreshed. She would have been perfectly capable of getting up for breakfast, not being an invalid, but this was brought to her in her chamber on a tray, and as she ate she reflected that it might be best not to meet Captain Winterton's mother and all of the rest of his relatives over the breakfast table. People were apt to be lax over introductions before they'd taken in the first cup or two of tea or coffee, according to taste, and she would prefer to be perfectly clear which lady, currently unknown to her, was Mrs Winterton, her lover's mother, and which was Lady Louisa Pendlebury, most unusual of aunts, and which the authoress Lady Carston. This third lady was quite newly married (though apparently minus her husband on this occasion) but not, as far as Isabella understood, a very young lady, and so she might possibly be confused with one of the others. She would prefer to avoid any such confusion. All these introductions, and the party she was going into alone, might sound rather daunting, but obviously, to a woman of the world such as herself, they weren't in the least.

Her maid had laid out her riding habit along with a day gown;

Lady Irlam was intending to go on a ride about the estate and would welcome her company if she cared for it, the woman informed her, but if not, the other ladies were in the morning room and would be glad to spend the forenoon with her. Without hesitation, Isabella chose the ride. It was quite likely, she considered, that Lord Irlam and his cousin the Captain would accompany them, and her new riding habit was extremely becoming, a fact of which Leo was currently and tragically unaware since she hadn't had a horse in London upon which to show it off.

A maid conducted her down a grand staircase to the morning room first, which was unavoidable, she supposed – it would be a dereliction of duty on Lady Irlam's part as hostess not to introduce her to the rest of the party now. At least the ordeal would be brief, which was, she was aware, not a very woman-of-the-worldly thought. She entered, and three very tall women whom she did not know rose to their feet, towering over her. No; that wasn't quite correct. Lady Carston, who was blonde and lean and athletic-looking, though not particularly fashionable or otherwise intimidating in appearance, was very tall indeed; the other two ladies were merely much taller than Isabella, which was after all not a difficult thing to be. Cassandra was there too, of course, and after making the introductions laughed as she said, 'I perceive upon your face, dear Lady Ashby, the identical expression mine must have borne when first I made the acquaintance of this family. You see now why I invited you – I am so tired of having a crick in my neck when holding every conversation.'

'I don't see why you should be, Cassandra,' said Lady Louisa. 'You know I never stand when I can sit, and never sit when I can lie. I am very pleased to meet you, Lady Ashby.' She suited her action to her words and reclined back on the sofa she had recently quit. She was dark, like her niece Georgiana, with the same bright blue eyes all the Pendleburys seemed to share, and extremely handsome, with a lush, voluptuous figure clad in a very modish deep pink gown. She wore no cap and nobody would have thought to describe her as a spinster, though she was over forty and unmarried. It was perfectly true that she bore no resemblance to any other aunt that Isabella had ever encountered in her life.

Isabella murmured the appropriate response and turned to greet Mrs Winterton. She beheld a lady of a comfortable figure with a great mass of beautiful silver hair arranged rather haphazardly. She had a kind smile and a kind face; she somewhat resembled, in fact, Isabella's own mother, though Isabella would much have preferred it if she hadn't. She looked... motherly, with all that that implied. How much easier if she'd been sour and horrid. Not that Leo was likely to have a mother who was sour and horrid.

There was no time for awkwardness; Cassandra said they must not keep the horses standing, and drew her away, out through the great hall and down the imposing stone steps they had ascended last night, where the Earl and Leo and another couple of young men stood waiting on the carriage sweep, with grooms and horses. Mr Pendlebury, Lord Irlam's brother and unmistakeably so, was presented to her, as was his friend, and Cassandra's, Mr Welby. He was an excessively handsome young man, not tall, angelically fair with features of classical regularity, and Isabella couldn't have said why observing him mount up didn't raise her pulse-rate even a little, and why she was so glad that the Captain, not he, stood ready to throw her up into the saddle. Leo stood, inevitably, close to her as he helped her, his hands firm and strong about her waist, and as he lifted her he murmured, 'That habit is extremely becoming. Excessively so. I am glad to see you in it and will be even happier to see you out of it. I hope you will say that it may be tonight. My blood is on fire as I look at you.'

She was aware of blushing furiously and hoped that if anyone observed it they would ascribe it to the cold and to the exertion of seating herself securely on an unfamiliar horse, a very prettily behaved grey which she assumed belonged to Lady Irlam, and which she was assured would not give her the least trouble.

Her new habit was very dark crimson, a striking colour expressive of her new attitude to life, and it did not follow the prevailing mode for high-waisted gowns, which Isabella sometimes feared made her look sadly dumpy. Instead, it was tailored very exactly to her frame, rather like a gentleman's scarlet hunting coat, but made up in velvet, and flattered, she hoped, her small waist and hourglass figure. The expression on Captain Winterton's face, and his whispered words, the very tone of his low voice, suggested that her hopes had not been in vain.

Isabella had spent half her childhood in the saddle, and it was exhilarating to be there once more, regardless of the company she found herself in. They rode out across the frosty landscape, and fell naturally into groups of two, since six persons plainly could not ride abreast without presenting a perfectly ridiculous appearance. The grounds of the Castle were immaculately maintained, and clearly had been conceived by Capability Brown or another of his ilk, and designed for an earl – Lord Irlam's grandfather or great-grandfather – who could never have lived to see the gloriously mature result of his investment. The land was gently rolling, picturesquely wooded with specimen trees, each notable eminence crowned with a temple or a folly or an obelisk. The building they were riding away from was large, rambling and obviously ancient in parts and more modern in others, but surrounding it was a very different landscape than the clifftop setting of Northriding Castle, where she had spent most of her married life with Ash after their honeymoon. That had been wild and starkly beautiful; this was tamed, controlled and gentler in its appeal.

'Did you grow up here?' she asked her companion. He seemed

entirely at ease in such grand surroundings, she could not help but observe.

'In large part,' Leo said. 'My father's estate – mine, now – is much, much more modest and only a few miles away. He died when I was quite small, and my mother and I have always spent a great deal of time here with my cousins. Hal and I grew up as brothers, in effect. After my uncle's and then my aunt's deaths, of course, which came in quick succession, my mother removed here more or less permanently in order to help look after the younger children; the twins were only five, poor scraps. But I was already in the navy by then.'

'You have all suffered grievous losses,' she said. 'I am sorry.'

'It is the way of the world, is it not? Only a lucky few can escape it. I barely remember my father, if truth be told. The late Earl was like a kind and loving father to me.' He hesitated, then pressed on. 'I know you had some qualms about coming here; have you overcome them?'

Such a question didn't really sit well with her new image of herself as wildly unconventional and thus indifferent to social difficulties, and perhaps therefore she should be irritated by his asking it, but she wasn't; she was a little touched by his evident concern. He was not so absorbed in his love for their hostess that he could not spare a thought for her. 'I think so. Lady Irlam has been very kind to me and said nothing at all to make me uncomfortable, and I have met the rest of the ladies, including your mother, who seems most amiable.'

He smiled. 'She is. And she has a rare and valuable quality among mothers: she doesn't pry.'

'How fortunate.'

Their eyes met, and they coloured, and laughed, and then, conscious that they were falling behind the others, urged their willing horses on across the frosty grass to catch up before anyone thought to remark upon their dawdling.

Lord Irlam's friend Mr Wainfleet arrived later that day, and so the party was complete. It was quite true, as Cassandra had said, that he didn't appear to be in the petticoat line. It was possible that he admired Isabella – certainly he blushed fierily whenever he was obliged to speak to her or look at her – but it would have been a determined hostess indeed who attempted to matchmake, given his almost total inarticulacy and the expression of poorly concealed terror that seized his otherwise pleasant features when he was forced to converse with any female.

When the ladies withdrew after dinner, Cassandra apologised to Isabella on his behalf; the rest of the party appeared to be tolerably well acquainted with him and accustomed to his ways. 'Hal says he's very amusing and often quotes his funny sayings, but I confess I can only take his word for it. He's very shy, poor man, in feminine company. It has occasionally occurred to us that he might have cherished a tendre for Georgiana, whom he's known for many years, in which case her marriage must have been a blow to him, but even Hal admits that he can't be sure. Of course – being men! – they have never spoken of the matter.'

Isabella was not comfortable with this talk of tendres, for all sorts of reasons, and so turned the topic, and the evening passed in pleasant conversation and light-hearted card games. Nobody pressed Isabella to sing and play the pianoforte, nor expressed an urgent desire to do so themselves, perhaps because there were no young unmarried ladies present who felt a compulsion to display their accomplishments to the four eligible gentlemen. It was in this sense an unusual party, and the more relaxing for it. The evening flew by, and soon it was time for bed; the ladies climbed the grand stairs together and parted to go to their various chambers along the many confusing corridors and galleries.

Or not. Isabella, perhaps because her new experiences had somehow removed the blinkers of ignorance from her eyes, believed that she had begun to sense undercurrents in the party which she didn't quite understand. Lady Carston, she knew, had been Lady Louisa's companion for many years, until her marriage a month or two since. Lord Carston was apparently a gentleman in his late forties who had been widowed years ago, and had several grown children, including an heir. Maybe it had been a case of love in later life, for him at least – he must be nearly twenty years older than his bride – but if so it was rather odd that he was not here. He was a family friend, and godfather to Lord Irlam, she had learned, so he would surely have been welcome. She thought... But perhaps she was imagining things. Perhaps the fact that she was currently engaged in illicit relations made her believe that everyone else was too. Perhaps she was obsessed and should be concerned about the tendency of her mind.

She would ask Leo. He would come to her tonight; they had communicated wordlessly downstairs, and she was waiting for him. It might take him a little while to extricate himself from his cousins and the other gentlemen, if they should happen to be playing billiards, or sitting up drinking, or anything of that nature. He would not want to provoke any comment or look at all suspicious.

She lay in bed in her new nightgown – a nightgown her mother would greatly have disapproved of, and all the better for it. It was the sort of thing she had worn, albeit briefly in both senses of the word, when she had been married to Ash. Those garments had mysteriously disappeared after his death, and she presumed her mother had removed them; they had never discussed the subject, and now never would. She experienced, as she often did when she thought of her mother, a disagreeable pang of guilt. She could not help but appreciate the thoughtfulness that had caused her mama to hide the flimsy, deliberately seductive night-rails; she could imagine herself coming across them in the weeks and months after Waterloo and collapsing in floods of tears at the tender, now painful recollections they called up. It would have been one of many such collapses, and she must be grateful to have been spared that one at least. Her mother had been endlessly patient, kind and thoughtful during the months of her illness, and she was not sure she had ever really thanked her for it. When she had begun to feel herself recovered, she had become impatient, touchy, quick to take offence. And then she had to all intents and purposes run away, to take refuge with Blanche. That must have stung. Poor Mama.

But she would not feel guilty that she was better, and no longer in a state of childlike dependency. She knew that it had been her mother's dearest wish that she should be restored to full health, and if the steps that she was taking to set the seal on her recovery were not quite what her mother would have liked – and they most certainly were not – well, she would never know it. She would be home at Harrogate soon and set about making amends as best she could. It was not as though there would be any shortage of time for them to regain their former closeness. It wasn't a particularly cheerful thought, but it was a necessary one.

Meanwhile... The door opened silently and with infinite slowness, and Leo, barefoot and clad in a silk dressing gown, slipped into the room and closed the door behind him with equal care. He had no candle; he must know the Castle well enough not to need one. She felt ridiculously shy suddenly and wished that she had not thought to lie in bed, like a bride waiting for her husband on her wedding night. Not that her wedding night had played out that way, they had both been so eager... But she would not think of that. Not tonight of all nights.

20

NUMBER EIGHT (A) AND NUMBER NINE

The whole situation at the Castle wasn't as awkward as Leo had feared. It might be difficult later, of course, but he couldn't think of that right now. No man could be expected to think of potentially embarrassing scenes with his mother, or any other relative for that matter, when faced with the prospect of number eight, or what he assumed must be number eight.

Isabella was so beautiful. She always was, but never more so than now, in the thinnest of muslin nightgowns through which her skin showed warm. It was held up by thin straps, and they were slipping from her shoulders. Her hair was down but not yet unbraided, and lay in heavy honey-gold plaits across her breasts. Her face showed a consciousness of the significance of what they were about to do, but her brown eyes were determined. She was so brave. She took his breath away. She said, 'I remembered what you told me once, about how you'd like to unfasten my hair, so I left it like this for you. In case you'd like to.'

'You added it to the list?'

'I did. It's eight (a), in fact.'

He couldn't speak. But his limbs and his fingers still worked, apparently. He sat down beside her on the soft bed and began to undo her hair, as he had dreamed of doing the first time he met her, and so often since. She'd removed whatever ribbons usually tied off the ends of each plait – she thought of everything – so all he had to do was unfasten each one and comb his fingers through it with care, and spread it across her bare shoulders. When he was done, she looked quite different. More distinctly herself, somehow, her private self, and therefore even more alluring. He gathered up a great hank of her hair and buried his face in its silky, fragrant mass, feeling her hand come out and stroke his head very gently. They stayed like that in silence for a long moment, and then he raised his head to whisper, 'I'd very much like to see you naked. You know I never have. May I?'

'Undress me,' she responded without hesitation. 'You said, I think, that you wanted to see me with my hair loose about my shoulders, but I thought at the time that you weren't being quite honest. Was I right?'

'Yes,' he said, his fingers already busy with the convenient ties that fastened the wispy garment. 'Of course you were. I could hardly say I wanted to see your breasts. People don't say things like that. Or I don't.'

'You just said you wanted to see me naked,' she pointed out, her voice not quite steady as he stripped her.

He checked for a second. 'So I did. Perhaps I'm changing, growing bolder. I suppose I must be. Well then – I want to see your glorious breasts, concealed by your beautiful hair. I want to uncover them and kiss them. Find them beneath their lovely covering, and feast on them. I've always wanted that, even before… anything.'

'Really?' Her night-rail was gone, pushed down, forgotten, and she shook out her hair to cover herself; it was almost waist-length, just as he had imagined.

'Yes,' he said, and hoped she would not ask any more. He didn't want to have to discuss his feelings for her; not how he'd felt before he knew her at all, and certainly not how he felt now. 'I want to see you naked and magnificent in this bed. It's been an exquisite torture to me, seeing tantalising glimpses of you partially undressed. I want everything.'

She smiled at him. 'So do I. I want to see you naked too. You've seen a great deal of me, one way and the other, you know, and I've seen very little of you.'

'You're serious?' He knew she was always honest, but he had to ask.

'Of course I am. Strip, sir.'

'I'm very hairy, you know.'

'I realise that. I like it. Strip.'

His dressing gown was gone in a second. He wasn't wearing anything under it. She was lying back against the pillows, cloaked in her glorious, dishevelled tresses, and he was kneeling beside her. He wanted to drink in the sight of her, small waist, lush thighs, rounded belly, but she was distracting him with her demands on him. Wonderfully distracting him. And after all, why should it just be about him looking at her? She wasn't a painting in a frame, a naked goddess put there for his titillation. She was real. She reached out and placed one hand on his bare thigh, stroking the downy golden hair. He didn't care to imagine what picture he presented to her gaze: naked, hirsute, powerfully erect already, displaying himself at her command. If women chose the paintings, would that be the sort of thing they'd choose to look at? He could hardly believe it could be so, but... Her fingertips trailed slowly, appreciatively, he thought, down towards his knee, and then up again, and a jolt of pure arousal shot through him. 'They called me Bear, at school,' he volunteered. They had, and worse things.

'I want to bury my face in it,' she said dreamily. 'Can I call you Bear too – would you mind? Tell me if you'd mind.'

'I'd like that. No one uses it now. A private name... No one must ever know, though, for it reveals so much.'

'Bear,' she said, naming him, running her hand up his abdomen to his chest, and then down again. And then he was on top of her – once again he couldn't have said whether he'd tumbled her back or she'd pulled him forward – and his face was buried in her hair, blindly seeking her breast through the silken locks. His mouth found her engorged nipple and seized on it, his hands were... everywhere. Hers too. Exploring his back, moving down and caressing his buttocks, pulling him to her, owning him. It was even more wonderful than he'd imagined it being, and he lost himself in it for a long time.

A glorious while later he found himself kissing his way up her neck to her mouth – it seemed like years since he'd kissed her – but when he reached her he suddenly became aware that he was crushing her into the soft mattress, and probably his damnably excessive hair was...

'Am I hurting you?' he gasped against her cheek. 'My weight, my hair rubbing you – are you uncomfortable? Please tell me.'

'No,' she said breathlessly. 'No, I like it, all of it. Your weight on me, your strength – and as for your hair, my God, push your thigh between mine and I will clasp it to me tightly and rub myself against it and you shall see how much I will like it.' No one had ever said such things to him before, and he had not even dreamed anyone might; she continued to astonish him.

She took his leg between her soft thighs, as they kissed fiercely and explored each other with eager hands, and he didn't think he'd ever known anything as raw and animalistic and perfect as her pleasuring herself shamelessly against him. It was not long before she growled in his ear, 'Now, please, now!'

'How?' he asked her. He could never forget that she was in control; he needed her to be. 'How shall it be, my queen?'

'I find I need your weight on me again. Come back and take me that way; I'll wrap my legs around your waist.'

He was inside her in a moment. It was utterly glorious to slip into her wetness at last, and she locked her legs around him, her heels in his buttocks urging him on as he thrust into her and they moved together in an escalating rhythm. They couldn't kiss as they coupled this way, the height difference was too great, but it didn't seem to matter. She had her face buried in his neck and was kissing him there and nipping him with her teeth. Their bodies were sweat-slicked and in utter harmony, he could have cried at the sheer rightness of it, when she began to clench on him, and her release triggered his, so that they came together in a moment of mutual ecstasy that was the most intense and perfect sensation he'd ever experienced in his life. He could not know how it was for her.

They rolled over together, panting, and he slipped out of her. She laid her head on his chest and he put his arms about her and held her as their breathing slowed and their hearts settled to a normal rhythm. She rubbed her face in the mat of hair that covered the muscles of his chest, and said, a little muffled, 'I am a loose woman. I probably was before, but I definitely am now.'

'Are you?' He almost added 'my love' – he had to bite his tongue to prevent himself from saying it. *My love, my love, my dearest love...*

'Yes,' she said. 'I am. I'm shameless.'

'I was thinking that, so far as I was thinking anything, while you rubbed yourself against me.'

'I told you, shameless,' she repeated happily. 'A hussy. A jezebel. A fallen woman. You're my lover; I'm your mistress.'

He took her hand and kissed it, turned it over and pressed

kisses into her palm. How he adored her. 'You are. In every possible sense, Christ knows.'

She sat up and looked at him. Her hair was wildly disordered, her lips swollen from kissing, and her face and neck and breasts and thighs were flushed with arousal and the friction of his rough body hair upon her delicate skin. She looked like a woman who had been thoroughly fucked in exactly the way she liked; she looked like all the things she'd said she was, he supposed. His mistress, if that was all he could have of her. Oddly, he thought, his friend, too. And then she said, devastatingly, 'That's what you like, isn't it? That's why we're really doing this, or why you are, at least. Because you like me to be in charge.'

He shouldn't be ashamed. Wouldn't. Didn't it suit both of them? 'Yes,' he said steadily. 'That's why I said, "you are my mistress in every possible sense". You are always in control. And I must admit I love it.'

21

NUMBER SIXTEEN, BRIEFLY, AND NUMBER SEVEN

'I thought so,' she said. 'I mean, I wasn't sure, I've not...'

'Nor me.'

'Really? You didn't know?'

'How could I? I could have gone my whole life without knowing, if I hadn't met you, Isabella. Men generally take charge. I always have. It's expected.'

'Exactly, Bear,' she said eagerly, shaking back her hair, which did absolutely nothing for his fragile composure. 'You know... We said we wouldn't talk about before, I know we did, but I think I have to. I was a virgin when I married, obviously, and Ash, my husband, he was not, and so naturally he took charge, as you said. He was wonderful – don't worry, I won't say any more, it wouldn't be right, but he was, it was. We were very happy. I won't have you thinking we weren't. But he was in control always. I mean, I could initiate things, in bed. I did, often. I could speak entirely frankly with him, and he with me. But I don't think I ever commanded him, "Do this, do that, pleasure me!" I'm sure I didn't, actually. I was young, and it would never have occurred to me that a woman might do such a thing.'

'But now it has. And...?' It was a struggle to speak. He didn't enjoy hearing about her husband, her lost love. But he would swallow it, in order to have this extraordinary conversation with her and to know her thoughts on this above all topics.

'I love it. I really do. I love being your mistress. I love commanding you. I love knowing that you will do exactly what I tell you to do. I thought you liked it excessively too; I knew somehow that you did.'

'I remember when I realised,' he said slowly as he absorbed the impact of her words. 'I was obeying you, making love to you as you ordered, and suddenly I knew that half the pleasure was in the obeying – that's not quite right, but you understand me, I hope. I might have come in that moment, just from the knowing. It was... freeing. Like nothing I've ever experienced.'

'Freeing,' she mused. 'Yes, that's precisely what it is. For both of us. So,' she said, a mischievous light in her brown eyes, 'we've established that you like the rules. My rules. Which means that you wouldn't want to see the list, which is in that little inlaid box over there, by the way, even if I offered to show it to you?'

'I'd have to read it, if you ordered me to,' he replied humbly. He was going to embrace this fully, it seemed. Whatever this curious thing was that they had found they shared. Even though it was like being offered the knowledge of how long you were going to live, of precisely when you were going to die. Imagine if he discovered that there were only twelve items on the list. Only ten. His heart was racing.

'I suppose you would,' she mused. She'd pulled back her hair completely to fall down her back now, leaving her lush, naked body entirely exposed to him once more, and he couldn't take his eyes off her. 'But I don't think I should do that. I think the anticipation, the not being sure what's next but knowing that I know, is part of your pleasure too.'

'It is.' His pleasure, and his torture. They were the same.

'Oh Bear, my Bear,' she said. 'I won't be cruel to you and make you read it. I think, though, that I should tell you that I've added some items to the list recently. I wasn't sure of them, but now that we've spoken about this so frankly, I am.'

'I was contemplating... asking you to do that.' It was a reprieve of a kind. At least he knew there would be more precious nights together.

'I think I've shown that I'm prepared to be flexible,' she said seriously. 'I added eight (a) for you. I could add other things. If you're good.'

'I do plan to be,' he said fervently.

'And I should tell you,' she went on, 'that you probably think that that was eight (b), but it wasn't. I changed my mind. It was nine.'

'What's eight (b), mistress?'

'Me on top, riding you.'

Of course it was. 'That would have been wonderful too.' He'd pictured it. He thought he'd probably pictured everything, but, of course, he couldn't know.

'It will be wonderful. Quite soon, I should think. Exactly how soon, of course, is up to you.' She commenced touching herself quite casually as she looked at him, her fingers teasing her nipple. She'd done that before, he remembered. It had affected him deeply then, and it did so again now, all the more since she was magnificently naked. And he was.

He swallowed. 'I had hoped I need not leave you quite yet. These autumn nights are so long.'

'You made certain assumptions, wicked Bear.'

'I wouldn't call it that. I was in the navy; I like to be prepared for every eventuality.'

'"England expects that every man will do his duty,"' she quoted idly. And then, 'Oh! Is that in poor taste? If so, I'm sorry.'

He was laughing. 'I think if we know anything at all about Admiral Lord Nelson – I did meet him once briefly when I was just a lad, though of course I never had the opportunity to speak to him – it's that he would very thoroughly have approved of a beautiful woman sitting naked in a bed, touching herself in a highly provocative manner and ordering a sailor to do his duty. His only comment, I imagine,' he said, putting his hand high up on her thigh and caressing it, 'would have been that an officer and a gentleman shouldn't need to be told. I expect he'd consider *that* a gross dereliction of duty.'

'Well,' she said, her own hand slipping down her body, to the damp curls between her thighs. 'I don't suppose you will need to be told twice. And in that spirit, before we come to eight (b), you remember number seven, for which you had a natural aptitude?'

'Of course I do. I don't think it's the sort of thing I could ever forget.' He was lying down so that he could kiss her inner thighs now, more slowly than he had last time, and her fingers were still buried between her legs. In a moment, he would nudge them gently aside with his nose. In a moment. Or perhaps he'd kiss them, while she continued. Lick them. That sounded messy but interesting.

'Is this on the list, you touching yourself?' he said against her skin, and then his tongue crept out to explore her fingers as she slid them back and forward across her nub. His eyes were closed, and so as he licked greedily he didn't know from second to second whether he would encounter her wickedly determined fingers, or her tender responsive flesh, or, wonderfully, both.

'Naturally!' she gasped. 'Number sixteen, I think. Would you like to watch that to its conclusion? Oh Lord, I think you would. But this doesn't count. I'm going to stop doing this in a moment, and let you take over. Since you're so good at it, Bear.'

He was, more than ever before, hers to command.

22

Captain Winterton crept away from Isabella's chamber in the early hours of the morning, long before the chilly autumn dawn broke. She staggered out of bed and relieved herself in her chamber pot when he had gone, but she simply didn't have the energy to take out her list and cross off the items, eight (a) and (b), nine, and seven again. Sixteen, briefly, but she'd already said that didn't count. She was far too tired to write to her mother, and not at all in the right frame of mind besides.

She ought to sleep, she needed to; her body, languorous and deliciously sore and sated, asked nothing better than to slip into deepest slumber. But her brain was buzzing like a bee trapped in a glass. Her thoughts were jumbled, fragmented, and she tried, incorrigible list-maker that she was, to bring some order to them. Whirling, disordered, uncontrolled thoughts frightened her. She wouldn't have it, the new assertive Isabella wouldn't.

She was thinking, inevitably, about Ash. About the last time she had wrapped her legs around a man's waist and taken him into her, and moved against him in urgent union as he spent himself inside her welcoming body. It was different, of course, in all sorts of ways.

And that was good, that was the point. She didn't want ever to obliterate the image, the feel of her husband, of the rough, familiar, comforting texture of his military jacket against her cheek, of his murmured endearments as he held her and loved her for that last time that neither of them had known would be the last. Tears sprang to her eyes now as she remembered it, and perhaps they always would if she lived to be ninety, but perhaps – perhaps – the pain was a little less sharp. She liked to think it was. It was no longer *her* last time, anyway, and that must count for something. She would make sure it did.

She had so many new memories now to sit beside the old ones. Physical sensations, extraordinary ones, but more than that. She'd mounted Leo, ridden him, taken her imperious pleasure from his more than willing body as she straddled him. It was hardly the first time she'd done such a thing; it was one of the more obvious positions for sexual congress between a short woman and a much taller man. Especially for a short woman with large, sensitive breasts and a tall man who warmly appreciated them. But the physical release she found now was inextricably linked with this new thing: with her command and Leo's submission.

It was, she realised now, a great responsibility that she had so lightly taken on. It wasn't about his feelings for her – he didn't and couldn't love her, they both knew that, and thank goodness for it – but it was no small thing, having someone who'd obey your every lightest whim. She needed to make sure that he really wanted to do everything she ordered him to do. He had so far, she was sure of that, but... She could dimly see, exhausted as she was, even as sleep tugged at the edges of her thoughts and blurred them, that two people with such a bond could let it lead them to some dark, dark places. He wanted to be commanded; he didn't want to be hurt. Or did he? Did he want her to be cruel, physically, emotionally, and if he did, would she fulfil those wishes? Would she enjoy fulfilling them? And if she did, what would that say about either or both of them? It occurred to her – and it was an unsettling realisation to hit her on the edge of oblivion – that it wasn't quite as obvious as it first appeared, who was truly in charge.

She slept at last, but her dreams were unsettling – arousing, too, which unsettled her more, though she only recalled scraps of them when she woke. Isabella was glad to take her breakfast in her chamber that morning, and glad to dawdle over dressing and coming downstairs. She wrote her duty letter to her mama, too, describing the uneventful journey, what she had seen of the Castle and its grounds, and most – but perhaps not quite all – of its current inhabitants. She did not rush over it. If by the time she had finished the gentlemen had gone riding again and she was too late to join them, on this occasion that would suit her very well.

They had. Most of the party had joined them, too, including, rather surprisingly, Mrs Winterton – but she was a countrywoman, after all, Isabella supposed, and there was no reason why she shouldn't take exercise on horseback. She found Lady Carston alone in the morning room, looking rather pale and leafing through an *Edinburgh Review* in a desultory fashion. Isabella imagined for a moment that Lady Louisa had gone out too, but when she mentioned it, her companion laughed and said, 'Louisa, riding! I wish I might see it. I am sure she would have you understand that she *could* – not in the theoretical fashion of Lady Catherine de Bourgh if you are acquainted with that lady, but really. Her nephew tells me that she is a most accomplished rider, as indeed they all are in the family. She merely chooses not to display her skills. Louisa's idea of healthy exercise is leaning over and reaching for the third volume of a novel. She is in bed still, reading.'

This comment naturally led to an animated discussion of the works of the lady author of *Pride and Prejudice*, as perhaps its utterer had intended. Isabella had been fortunate enough to read and enjoy that work, and *Sense and Sensibility* too, but had not known that there had been not one but two new volumes from her pen since. Her ignorance was not, perhaps, surprising, given all she had experienced in the last eighteen months. She was resolved to be open about her situation and told Lady Carston why exactly the omission had occurred.

That lady regarded her thoughtfully. 'Of course,' she said. 'I knew I had set eyes on you before. I saw you briefly in the street in York, the day the Duke and Duchess of Northriding were married, but we were not introduced, and I had forgotten it till now.'

Isabella grimaced. 'I did not see you. I am afraid I was in no fit state for introductions that day. I had not realised Gabriel was betrothed, even, and it came as a great shock to me to see him with his bride. Do not think I blame him – he wrote to my parents to tell them and asked them to tell me, but the letter did not reach us in time.'

'That's most unfortunate. No wonder you were taken aback,' said her companion comfortably. 'I understand that he had previously cherished a fixed intention never to wed.'

'That's true, but it does not excuse my behaviour. I can only say that I was ill at the time, and was overset. But the shock was a salutary one because it helped with my recovery.'

'How so?'

'I realised, even in the brief moments I saw them together, that Gabriel was in love with his bride, and she with him. Once I had overcome the pain that seeing him married must inevitably cause me, because of his great resemblance to my late husband, I was so glad to know that I had not been responsible for turning his life upside-down. A weight was lifted from my shoulders that day.'

'I collect that you mean,' said Lady Carston, 'and forgive me if my frankness causes you discomfort, that you feared he would be obliged to marry, greatly against his own wishes, because he had no heir after your husband passed away?'

'You put it very delicately, and I promise you it causes me no discomfort. I mean that after Ash died, and his young cousin John too, Gabriel had no heir because of my failure to provide one.'

'That is a heavy burden for any woman to bear. Or any man, for that matter.' She hesitated, then said, 'I believe I should tell you – it is no great secret, but perhaps it is a matter that people do not generally speak openly of in company, and so I collect you have not yet heard – that Georgiana is with child. I'm sure she wouldn't mind me letting you of all people know, since you too are a Mauleverer. She knew, I think, before she left London, but she has only written to share the news with her family in the last day or so. The letters were here when we arrived.'

Isabella found that tears stood in her eyes. But they did not sting. 'I am so glad,' she said simply. If she had ever held any foolish dreams that a son of hers would succeed to Northriding one day, they were long gone. 'I am very happy for her, and for Gabriel. I like her very much, and I can see that they are perfectly suited to each other.' She was thinking as she spoke of a certain house in Mayfair, which Georgiana had introduced her to; there could be no doubt, in the light of such private knowledge, that she and Gabriel were very well-suited indeed.

'Indeed they are,' said her companion with what she could only interpret as a naughty glint in her brown eyes. It was an expression she had observed on the faces of others when speaking of Gabriel and his bride, and Isabella could only imagine that it was connected somehow to the most irregular circumstances of their marriage, the full truth of which she did not yet know but hoped to learn one day. 'In fact,' she went on, 'Georgiana has written to me of you.'

'Really?' she said with profound unease. This was what she had feared when coming here; this was most unwelcome news.

'She betrayed no confidences,' said Lady Carston, hurrying to reassure her. 'I will tell you exactly what she said: it is simple enough. She said that she liked you, and wished she had had a chance to spend more time with you. She said that she thought you stood in need of a friend, and for Mauleverer family reasons that she did not propose to explain, Cassandra might not be best placed to be that friend. And finally and most intriguingly she said that you and I might find we had a great deal in common if we should come to exchanging confidences. We were both, she said, and she underlined the significant word, of a somewhat unconventional nature.'

'Oh,' said Isabella.

'Oh indeed,' her companion replied. 'Now, Georgie knows all my secrets and I know hers – or most of them, at any rate, for there are some things that even very good friends do not speak of – and I must presume she knows yours too.'

'She knows how matters stood a few weeks ago,' said Isabella mysteriously, conscious of being annoying.

'I can't endure it,' said Her Ladyship with a comical grimace. 'I will tell you. It will be fairly obvious that this must go no further, though indeed the first part of it is no more than the gossip of the ton, or will be soon enough. I too am with child.'

'Congratulations!' said Isabella politely, rather puzzled. There was nothing so terribly shocking in this news, coming from a woman not long entered into matrimony.

'Thank you. Congratulations are indeed in order since I married expressly for the purpose of conceiving.'

'Oh...?' said Isabella again.

'I have lived with Louisa for ten years or more. Not as her companion, but as her lover.'

'I thought so!' cried Isabella, unable to stop herself. 'I thought you were. I meant to ask Leo, but I forgot...' She halted, horribly conscious that she had betrayed herself.

Lady Carston smiled in a knowing sort of a way, but did not pick her up on all she had so carelessly revealed with one word out of place. 'I didn't leave Louisa,' she went on. 'Lord Carston, who is my very good friend, knew of my deep desire to have a child and offered to marry me. We agreed that once I had conceived, assuming I did, I would return to my life, and my love. And here we are.'

Isabella was silent for a moment, digesting all she had just heard. She had liked to think herself unconventional; why, she was a mere amateur compared with this woman.

'You have made your life exactly as you wanted it...' she said slowly.

'Not quite. Women can't; there's always a cost. I am now, according to the law, a femme couverte. I am legally Carston's property, and my child will be too, essentially. He is not the man to exert such power, or I would never have married him. But the stark fact of the law remains, and I loathe it.'

'There is always a cost,' Isabella repeated. There was nothing she could say to that. 'Why did he agree? I understand why you were prepared to enter into this arrangement, but what of him? What does he gain from it?'

'Apart from the obvious thing?' Jane said, smiling.

'He doesn't need to marry to get that,' replied Isabella with robust good sense. 'No man does!'

'No,' agreed Lady Carston, her head on one side as if considering. 'But he likes it well enough. So do I, if I'm completely honest. I thought I might – is it not shocking? – and I do. Which is just as well, after all. You don't necessarily have to be in love with someone to go to bed with them, you know, Lady Ashby. Imagine the revolution on the day more women realise that, and choose to act on it to fulfil their own desires instead of the desires of men! But seriously, he's a good friend. The best of friends. He wanted to help me; he knew how much it meant to me. If he has other motives – to make himself feel young, perhaps, and virile – I needn't be indiscreet enough to enquire into them.'

'Goodness,' said Isabella. 'The Duchess was right! We do have a great deal in common.' And leaning forward, she poured out her story, or most of it, into her companion's ears. She didn't feel it necessary to dwell on the half-formulated worries that had tormented her early this morning as she fell asleep; those really were private. And Cassandra's name, Leo's unrequited love for her, she withheld, as seemed only prudent under Lady Irlam's roof. But she shared the rest of it, including the strange nature of the bond she and the Captain shared.

'I see why Georgiana wanted us to talk,' said Her Ladyship when she was done. 'We are quite alike. We're using men for our own ends. They're good ends, or so we believe; ends that are necessary for both of us. But that's what we're doing. And enjoying it.'

'I don't like to think of it like that. But yes, I suppose we are.'

'You asked me what Carston gets out of our arrangement, but I could also ask...' she said, and trailed off delicately.

'It's plain to see!' Isabella protested.

'You just said to me that no man has any difficulty obtaining that.'

'Not like this,' she said with complete certainty. 'This is different, though indeed neither of us knew it would be.'

'I'm sure you're right. Yes, he is a lucky man. You have granted him an enormous favour, after all. When you are finished with him, he will be able in future to... explore his proclivities fully, as he might never otherwise have done. I expect there are places,' Lady Carston said thoughtfully.

Isabella expected that there were places, too. She'd been to one of them, although she hadn't really been looking; she wished now she'd paid more attention. Perhaps when she returned to London...

But she wasn't returning to London. She was going back to Yorkshire as she had promised, and she would stay there. A week or two, or a little more, and all this would be over, though it seemed much too soon as she thought of it now.

'You're right,' she said, and repeated, 'There's always a cost.'

23

Lord Irlam was worried about his cousin. He couldn't see that Cassandra's well-intentioned matchmaking schemes were working; as far as he could see, Leo was as besotted as ever, Lady Ashby was attracted to him but didn't seem to want to admit it to herself, and the weeks were going by, autumn was turning to winter, and no progress of any kind was being made.

'Why won't she admit she has a fancy for him, so they can just get married?' he asked Cassandra early one morning. 'People who can't stop glancing at each other and glancing away then glancing back at each other – did you see them last night, thinking they were being discreet? – ought to get married.'

She was lying with her head on his shoulder, and chuckled as she said, 'Like we did, you mean?'

'Exactly.'

'It's not enough, though, is it? People need to admit how they feel. Talk. Otherwise,' she said, trailing her hand idly across his chest, 'there are bound to be all sorts of misunderstandings. Being enormously attracted to each other, even having the odd illicit encounter as we did, is all very well, sir, but it's not enough by itself. It wasn't for us, and I presume it wasn't for Georgie and Gabriel.'

'I'd rather not think about my sister in that manner unless absolutely forced to do so, which I hope never to be again,' he said with dignity, half joking, half serious. 'Besides,' he added hastily as she showed incipient signs of arguing, 'we don't actually know if she cares for him. With Gabriel and Georgie, it was blindingly obvious – both Louisa and I could see that the poor fellow was suffering for love of her. But I can't read this girl and neither can you, so you can't say for sure if she'd give two pins for him beyond the fact that she clearly likes his looks well enough. You must admit that you don't have the least real idea how she feels about him, and nor does he, for that matter.'

Cassandra sighed and conceded that this was all too true. 'And I can't try to find out, either. If I reveal his feelings to her, I'd be betraying his confidence in you, and even if she isn't angry with him, she might take fright and run away, which is surely the last thing he wants, poor Leo.'

'Poor Leo indeed.'

'Is there truly nothing we can do? I'm thinking of all the trouble you had with Georgie when she met Gabriel, and how cleverly you handled it.'

'First of all,' he said, seizing her by her wrists and flipping her easily over so that she lay on her back, smiling up at him expectantly, 'I could only intervene in her affairs because I'm her brother and was her guardian, God help me. I have no authority over Leo and less over Lady Ashby. And secondly, I can't recall that anything I did actually worked. They had to sort themselves out in the end. And thirdly...'

'And thirdly...?' she asked, putting her arms about him and pulling him down for a kiss.

'Dashed if I can remember,' he said against her lips.

'All the same,' she said much later, 'we ought to think of something. We can't allow her to leave here. They might never see each other again!'

'We can't kidnap her and keep her prisoner,' said Hal reasonably. 'I dare say you'd like to, but we can't. We can't do anything at all. You said yourself – it's no use people being forced together, even obliged to marry by some clever trick, unless they talk afterwards. And even that wouldn't help if she doesn't care for him, and for all we know she might not.'

Cassandra sighed and admitted defeat. Or almost, for she was of a persistent character. 'I'm going to talk to Jane Carston. She's very shrewd; she might have some idea of what Lady Ashby feels about Leo.'

'No harm in that. But for God's sake be discreet, Cassie – the last thing we need is my Aunt Sophia getting wind of anything havey-cavey involving her son.'

'You're assuming she hasn't already. You know she's very far from stupid – she spent all those years looking after the boys; it must have sharpened her wits to an acute degree.'

Hal groaned and pulled a pillow over his face. 'Oh God, this family!' was his muffled response. 'There's never any end to it.'

24

Cassandra was not a woman to waste the day, and so as soon as she was up and dressed she set about separating Lady Carston from the rest of her guests with ruthless determination, and in a remarkably short space of time they were to be found tête-à-tête in Lady Irlam's private sitting room. Jane eyed her hostess rather warily – she wasn't entirely sure if Cassandra knew the rather curious particulars of her recent marriage, nor indeed whether she was aware of her delicate condition. She couldn't imagine why her hostess should so plainly desire this private interview. It wasn't very likely that she'd been drawn aside so that Cassandra could upbraid her for immorality; Lady Irlam didn't in the least appear to be that sort of person, and the way she lived her own life was none of her business. But one never knew.

She relaxed considerably when Cassandra said, 'Captain Winterton and Lady Ashby seem to be getting along famously.'

This wasn't really true; they certainly weren't spending a great deal of time together, or carrying on any obvious sort of a public courtship. Jane, who was in the know, had seen glances, the odd whispered word, perhaps a brush of a hand across a shoulder that might have been accidental but wasn't. Yet she wasn't sure any of it would have been enough to alert someone who was entirely ignorant of the situation.

'Do you suspect that your husband's cousin is developing a tendre for Lady Ashby?' she asked cautiously. Best to put it that way.

'I know Leo has strong feelings for her,' replied Cassandra bluntly. 'He told Hal so.'

'And you... disapprove of that?' Jane fenced. She wouldn't betray a confidence, a promise made to another woman.

'I don't disapprove of anything except people's feelings getting hurt.'

'You think that's likely?'

'I think it's inevitable.' They eyed each other warily, but neither was prepared to say more.

'Oh, you are admirably discreet!' said Cassandra with a smile at last. 'I cannot tell if you know things I do not, and I must not ask you to break a confidence, if indeed confidence has been reposed in you, which I expect it has by the conscious look on your face. But I think I know something that you do not, and I will tell you it: Leo is in love with her. He fell in love almost on sight, as I understand.'

'Oh Lord,' said Jane ruefully. 'I promise you she has no idea of it.'

'And if she became aware, what would she do? Have you the least idea?'

'She is entirely determined never to remarry,' said Jane. 'I think it very likely that she would leave here immediately and do her best never to set eyes on your cousin again.'

'You tell me of her determination, but what of her affections? Do you think it at all possible she cares for him more than she has admitted to herself?'

Jane rose to her feet and took a restless turn about the room. 'I don't look at this situation in the same way as you do, you know, Lady Irlam.'

'Cassandra.'

'Very well then, Cassandra. I must presume that as a member of Louisa's family, you are aware of my situation, at least in part, though we're not talking about that just now. I have never made any secret of the fact that I am an advocate of the rights of women. Men have plenty of rights, it seems to me, where we have almost none. And so I am sorry that your cousin should be hurt – I don't know him at all; from what I have seen of him, he appears to be an entirely admirable young gentleman. But he is also an adult. Men have been treating women much worse than Lady Ashby is treating him since the beginning of time, so will you think badly of me if I say that I cannot weep many tears when I see the balance being redressed a little?'

Cassandra sighed. 'Don't imagine that I am the standard-bearer for marriage in all its forms. And I cherish no naïve illusions about men in general, I assure you. You weren't in Brighton last summer, so you may not know my background; I'm an heiress, and my uncle was effectively keeping me prisoner while he attempted to force me to marry a friend of his so that they could divide up my fortune between them. This man assaulted me, and I was obliged to flee.'

'I am sorry,' said her companion. 'I didn't mean to imply that you were—'

'Of course you didn't. I'm not offended. What I meant to say was, I certainly don't believe that a woman should seize upon the opportunity to marry any man who shows an inclination to offer for her, and be grateful to him for it. If she doesn't care for him, I would be the last person to say that Lady Ashby should marry Leo just because he's in love with her. Why should his feelings take precedence over hers? Of course they should not. She is bound to him for nothing more than the decent treatment we all owe each other.'

'We are in agreement to that extent, then. I'm glad.'

'So am I. Therefore please believe me when I say that I'm not running around Hampshire making matches to gratify my own sense of self-importance. Nor am I swayed by a natural partiality for Leo, even though you're quite right, he is a perfectly lovely person. It was merely that my understanding of Lady Ashby's plans for her future made me a little melancholy. Not,' she hastened to add, 'because she has no plans to marry, but because it sounds like a sadly reduced life. To devote oneself to someone who is dead and out of reach, to live entirely looking backwards; to commit irrevocably to such a life at a cruelly young age...'

'I won't say I disagree, but it's her choice, and we must respect that. But I didn't answer your question, did I? I simply can't say if she really cares for him and does not know it. You are concerned, I take it, that she might be allowing her fixed intention to live her life in a certain set way to blind her to what is under her nose, and even perhaps to her own altered emotions?'

'Exactly,' said Cassandra eagerly. 'I fear that she will take her leave, if so, and only later realise what she has lost. And of course if that should happen, she will be far too proud to summon him to her side.'

'Especially since she has not the least idea of his true feelings because he daren't tell her. What a coil!'

'I wish there were something we could do.'

'I can't see what. Like you, I think, I am naturally inclined to act rather than do nothing. But it is such a delicate situation, and we would be so likely to do more harm than good.'

'We can't ask her, we've established that. I don't suppose...' She fell into a brown study for a moment or two. 'It would be immensely useful if she could be made jealous. If Leo were to flirt with someone, and she saw it, and found as a result that she cared for him, that might make her reflect and maybe alter her plans. It would be a start, at least.'

'I don't believe he has the least desire to flirt with anybody but her.'

'But if somebody were to make a dead set at him...'

'There is nobody here who is so disposed, or in any sense a possible candidate, unless indeed you choose to do it yourself, and I am sure you never would. It's one of the things I most particularly like about the party you have assembled. It's so restful. If you had been at Northriding Castle earlier this year when the Duke dropped the handkerchief...' She shuddered. 'My feelings of sister-hood were severely tried, I assure you.'

'I can very easily imagine what it must have been like. And of course I'm not going to flirt with him myself; everyone would imagine I'd run mad, Hal most of all. I'm not *that* keen to help Leo. No, I think we need to go to a ball, Jane. Or an assembly.'

'You can't assume that his mere appearance in public will be enough to inspire young women to throw their caps at Captain Winterton.'

Cassandra chuckled mischievously. 'Oh, can't I? You weren't with us in London. Word has got about of all the prizes he took; his estate is not so far from here and is well known to be substantial enough, and his family are well-established and highly esteemed here, quite apart from their connection with the Pendleburys. Why, I dare say he is easily the most eligible man in Hampshire at the present moment! If he was the object of some marked attentions in Town, how much greater will be the furore, do you think, here, where he was born? Oh, why did I not think of it before?'

'But will it work? She may not give a fig for any of it.'

'It may not, and she may not. But I have to do something.'

They felt themselves to be conspirators now, and shared further confidences: that Lady Carston was with child, which had been the entire purpose of her marriage, and that Cassandra was definitely not, and had no desire to be, or not at present. By the time they parted, they found that they had reached an excellent understanding, and in some sense, despite their superficial differences, each had recognised in the other a kindred spirit and a woman of action.

25

Cassandra carried out her investigations and discovered that there was a public assembly in the nearby market town in two days' time, on the evening of the full moon. Now she had merely to persuade her unsuspecting guests that they were all possessed of a powerful desire to go. Lady Carston had promised her support; she had agreed that the plan offered the only possible way of divining Lady Ashby's feelings for the Captain without alerting her to his (currently) hopeless passion. She had engaged furthermore to temper Lady Louisa's inevitable objections, or at least to persuade her to reduce the expression of them to manageable levels. There was no point asking Louisa to show enthusiasm for the project; if she did so, anyone even slightly acquainted with her would imagine that she was unwell, or even in imminent danger of losing her reason. It must be obvious that to drive for an hour over indifferent roads in order to attend a provincial assembly in what she would describe as the depths of winter so that she could watch a horde of unfashionable and badly dressed persons disporting themselves to the scraping of ill-tuned fiddles was her idea of torture.

Lady Irlam knew that her strongest ally was likely to be Mrs

Winterton. The genteel society in that part of Hampshire, whom Lady Louisa would characterise with aristocratic disdain as a parcel of rustics, were Sophia Winterton's neighbours and in many cases her friends from childhood, and it was not to be supposed that she would readily forgo the chance of meeting them on such an agreeable social occasion. Mrs Winterton was such a kind and pleasant lady, and one who had done so much for Hal and Bastian and all the Pendlebury children, that Cassandra calculated that if *she* expressed a strong wish to go, it was highly likely that her nephews would hurry to oblige her. As for Lady Ashby, Mr Welby and Mr Wainfleet, they were well-bred people who would surely acquiesce to anything that their hosts proposed, whatever private reservations they might cherish. The idea of Mr Wainfleet in particular summoning the courage to object must make her smile, it was so implausible.

She was proved right in every respect, and the matter was swiftly settled. Hal was plainly a little startled when the idea was first put to the company, and looked hard at Cassandra, as if suspecting his wife of having some devious and possibly dangerous plan in mind, but while his Aunt Sophia was exclaiming with honest pleasure at the idea, he could hardly pour cold water on all her happy expectation. Cassandra shot him a look that signified, *I am very grateful for your forbearance, and I will explain presently.*

When she made him aware of her scheme later that evening, he was doubtful but conceded that he couldn't think of anything that would serve as well. So it was agreed, and time would tell the upshot of it.

They would need three coaches for the expedition, as the persons attending from the Castle were ten in number, and Cassandra put a great deal of thought into the arrangement of her guests between the conveyances. She had every reason to know – she blushed pleasurably at the recollection – just exactly what could occur in a carriage in the darkness on the way home from a ball when two young people were strongly drawn to each other and their companions were asleep. But she reflected that the case was hardly the same; Leo's problem was far more complicated than mere lack of opportunity.

She had written everyone's names on pieces of paper and was moving them about between three larger cards that signified the carriages, and she soon discovered that it was quite ridiculously difficult to achieve a successful result. She would prefer to avoid an arrangement that put Lady Ashby along with Leo in a carriage with two other young men she barely knew, which was not a usual kind of thing to do to a lady and might easily make her uncomfortable, or alternatively put her with Leo and Mrs Winterton, which would have much the same effect given the nature of her secret. To place the pair with Hal and Cassandra themselves, on the other hand, would look enormously pointed and frankly odd, as if to say that they were two couples publicly recognised as such, which was sadly far from being true. The whole thing, which ought to be simple enough, was excessively complicated. She couldn't put all the ladies beside herself together, either, because they would never arrive at the assembly, or even leave for it, as they politely argued over who would take the seats of honour and who sit backwards in relative discomfort. Lady Carston was in an interesting condition, she now knew; Louisa and Lady Ashby were of higher rank; Mrs Winterton was older. It gave one the headache. There was also Tom Wainfleet to consider; he was so shy, it would be cruel to place him, unsupported, with ladies he might be disposed to be frightened of, which was all of them apart from Mrs Winterton, who was surely too motherly a figure to alarm even him.

In the end, Cassandra threw up her hands at the dispropor-tionate expenditure of time on the ridiculous little problem and regarded her little paper coaches with a certain measure of satisfaction. Tom would ride with Mrs Winterton, Lady Ashby and Leo, which admittedly was not ideal but could have been worse; Bastian and Matthew would ride with Lady Carston and Louisa, so that once again both the ladies could have the good seats, and she and Hal would ride alone. This would please Hal and – if she were honest – herself. A secret little smile curved her lips as she tied away her pieces of paper. They had rather a history, she and her husband, when it came to carriages in the dark.

26

Isabella had not been particularly surprised by the news that the party was to attend an assembly in a nearby town. This was a familiar, comforting sort of news that she hoped she would be able to share with her mama with little editing. When she had been living at Northriding Castle during the brief months of her marriage, the family had quite often gone to dances, both private and public, in their particular part of Yorkshire. It was in a sense expected of a noble family living in the countryside, if they did not wish to gain a reputation for being disagreeably high in the instep. For that matter, though the circumstances had been rather different, she had first met Ash and danced with him at such a public event, at the elegant new rooms in Harrogate when he had been recuperating from wounds taken in battle. He had been wearing regimentals, and had looked so handsome and distinguished; he had been presented to her an eligible partner by the master of ceremonies, had smiled down at her with silver eyes that should have been cold but yet were warm and full of life and spirit, they had begun talking and never stopped... She crushed the memory with a ruthlessness born of long practice.

She was a little uneasy when she realised that she must share a carriage with Leo, his mother, and the largely silent Mr Wainfleet, but again this roused no particular suspicion in her mind, as she could see that Lady Irlam had certain constraints upon her arrangement of her guests, given that all the ladies should be able to travel facing the horses, if this were possible.

After some reflection, Isabella chose to wear her finest gown: the dark blue one with the silver stars that she had first put on for the Duchess of Northriding's ball. That this was the occasion where she and Captain Winterton had first kissed was of no consequence at all. Many of her new gowns held such associations, or ones that were even more likely to bring a blush to her cheeks when she thought of them.

Conversation proceeded comfortably enough in the carriage, though Mr Wainfleet, to nobody's great surprise, took little part in it. If Captain Winterton felt ill at ease in the company of his mother and the woman whose bedchamber he was sneaking into nearly every night, he betrayed no sign of it that Isabella could discern. He chatted easily with his parent about the various people they might expect to see that evening, and assisted her in verbally sketching the most notable of them for the benefit of their companions. His mother, for her part, appeared to feel not the least constraint in Isabella's company. 'I hope we haven't overwhelmed you with description, Lady Ashby,' she said confidingly. 'I dare say you may not remember the half of it when you climb down from the carriage! But I always feel that it is agreeable to know a little about persons one is about to meet before one meets them. And you need not be uneasy that you shall be obliged to dance with anyone unsuitable or uncouth, for even if they were admitted, which would surprise me, I assure you that I should not allow it.'

Isabella thanked her, and murmured something to the effect that as a total stranger to the area she did not suppose her dance card would be full, which gave the Captain the opportunity, if not the obligation – had she intended it so? – to secure her hand for the second set. 'For I am sure that you will be obliged to first walk out with some gentleman of higher standing,' he said, 'and I would not wish to put anyone's nose out of joint.' His mother agreed that this was quite right, and there then arose a little awkwardness when Mr Wainfleet became aware that he too was obliged by social convention to solicit Lady Ashby's hand for one of the dances, even though he very plainly didn't want to, but this fence was successfully surmounted, to everyone's relief, just as they arrived at their destination, which was a large, respectable-looking half-timbered inn in the central square of the market town, with a more modern brick-built ballroom at its rear.

The party from Castle Irlam entered the crowded room together, the three carriages having in a pre-arranged manner kept pace with one another, and Isabella could not help but be aware, though good manners prevented her from betraying the least consciousness of it, of the little stir of interest that ran though the room as the company became aware of their arrival, and turned in unison to look at them. Lady Carston was at her side, and murmured in low, mischievous tones, 'One is reminded of the famous assembly at Meryton.'

'Good heavens,' responded Isabella quickly, 'I hope not! That would make us, surely, the party from Netherfield Park, and I have not the least desire to liken myself to Mrs Hurst or Miss Bingley, and I presume you do not either.'

'We have done better than the Bingleys, and have brought not two but four eligible young men with us,' put in Lady Louisa. 'How popular we must be! The Misses Bennet of Hampshire will be all aflutter, not to mention their mamas. Perhaps this evening will be amusing after all.'

Lady Carston shot her a look that mingled amusement and

reproof, and Lady Louisa replied drily, 'We have had this conversation before, Jane, and more than once. I have no power over anybody, least of all persons with whom I am unacquainted, to provoke them into behaving badly and making a spectacle of themselves. Like Mrs Bennet, Kitty and Lydia, they do so of their own accord. What harm if I merely observe their antics, and am entertained? Pray, how is it any different from reading the novel and laughing at it?'

'These people here tonight are real, not fictional, and the position of unmarried women in our society...' began Lady Carston with a sort of weary heat, but Isabella heard no more, since she was drawn into a flurry of introductions, and the blushing young baronet with whom she was to undertake the first set – gentlemen of higher rank who were both willing and able to dance being thin on the ground on this occasion – was duly presented to her. They took the floor together, and it was pleasant enough, though she could not help but wish him gone and Captain Winterton in his place, no doubt because they had often danced together previously and were accustomed to each other's steps. *He*, she noticed, was partnered with a most vivacious brunette in white muslin with whom he appeared already to share an excellent understanding; presumably, she was one of the many intimate family friends his mother had mentioned in the carriage.

The first set ended and they commenced upon their own dance, but Isabella did not find it as comfortable as she had anticipated, since she could not help but be conscious of many pairs of eyes on her, almost burning holes in her midnight silk, as the gossip-addicted part of the company – which appeared to be most of it – quite blatantly picked over who she was, what precisely she was doing at Castle Irlam, and what if anything the nature of the Captain's interest in her might be. Such attention did not make for ease and enjoyment, and Leo too appeared to be labouring under a certain constraint, presumably for the same reason, so that the few words they exchanged were unusually stilted.

Although common courtesy later obliged her to profess to her hostess that it had been a most enjoyable evening, Isabella did not in sober truth find it so. She was unaccountably out of sorts and looked forward to the moment when the last fiddle would scrape, the last curtsey drop, and it would be time to take their leave.

Lady Louisa's prediction that the gentlemen of the Irlam party would be in great demand was amply fulfilled. Gentlemen were often in short supply at public dances in any case, and unattached ladies might understandably be tired of dancing with the boys they had grown up with, danced with a thousand times before, and for the most part, knew far too well to find of any romantic interest. But the presence of four – *four!* – apparently unattached gentlemen, two of them familiar to some degree and two of them complete strangers, must stir all manner of speculation in the sharp minds and tender hearts of the young ladies present. They could not, of course, boldly offer themselves up as suitable partners to the Honourable Mr Pendlebury, Mr Welby, Mr Wainfleet or Captain Winterton, but their fond parents and devoted aunts could make the suggestion on their behalf, and did. These persons might experience a little awkwardness in proposing that their daughters, nieces, cousins and granddaughters should step out with one of the young gentlemen, but they overcame it bravely. Lady Irlam and particularly Mrs Winterton found themselves positively besieged by ladies and gentlemen of mature years who wished to proffer partners for all the young men of their party.

Isabella herself was not in such great demand, since a young widow – and one furthermore who had previously been married to the son of a duke – appeared to be an intimidating sort of a creature, neither the one thing nor the other, to the young gentlemen of Hampshire. She danced with Mr Wainfleet, as she had promised, and once each with the besieged Mr Pendlebury and Mr Welby, but few others were brave enough to approach her. And while she was glad that, as Mrs Winterton had guaranteed, she met with no unwelcome or uncivil attention, she did not particularly enjoy sitting at the side of the room amongst the matrons, where she supposed she belonged and would in future always be, watching Leo dance the soles out of his evening pumps with a succession of eager partners. He was, she thought, even more sought after than his cousin Bastian, though she could not have said whether it was because he was, as everybody must be well aware, a single man in possession of a good fortune (and a snug estate, just up the road), rather than a mere second son and younger brother, or because he was of a naturally friendly, open disposition and appeared more genuinely interested in the young ladies he took out than Mr Pendlebury, despite that gentleman's undeniable civility. It was, of course, none of her affair, and she should be glad, she supposed, to see that in the event of the Captain beginning to overcome his hopeless passion for his cousin's wife, there were many, many ladies who would be more than willing to console him and offer him a brighter future.

She might have hoped to take supper with Leo as her partner, but somehow matters did not fall out that way. It was not quite clear to her how it came about, but she found herself escorted into the separate supper room by Mr Wainfleet. She refused to believe that he had engineered this circumstance; apart from the fact that he did not have the social skill necessary to contrive such a thing, it was hard to imagine what purpose it could serve, since he had as little to say to her as ever, but merely pushed his food around his plate in awkward silence. And certainly *she* had not desired it, though it did undoubtedly offer her an excellent opportunity to observe Captain Winterton, at the next table, flirting outrageously – or being flirted with, it was hard to tell – with the young lady in white muslin who was, she had learned, a Miss Peters, and some kind of distant connection of his late father's. Isabella began to perceive that this young lady's vivacity was exaggerated, somehow false, and could easily come to grate on the nerves if one were obliged to spend a great deal of time in her company. Furthermore, her laugh was displeasingly shrill and so very frequent. But Leo did not appear to find it so. Not in the least. It was all a matter of taste, of course.

It was a long evening.

27

Captain Winterton found the assembly something of a trial.

It was not all bad. He was glad that his mother was enjoying herself and knew that part of her pleasure came from his presence. He had been at sea for so many years that she had still not entirely accustomed herself to his return, and she had missed him afresh while he was in London this past autumn. It was an innocent enough enjoyment, surely, for a woman widowed early and with just one dearly loved child, that child long absent in dangerous circumstances, to show him off to a gathering of her friends and say – though not out loud – 'Look at my grown boy! Is he not handsome and well-mannered?' He knew that he owed her that much and more.

He also knew that she was anxious to see him happily married, and here he began to feel uneasy. He had no idea, for he had recently avoided even the approach to such a conversation with an adroitness born of desperation, whether his mother had stopped to think for a moment that Lady Ashby might be a suitable wife for him. If the thought had so much as crossed her mind, it was very likely that she'd rejected it out of hand, he realised now, because surely she'd much rather he married a Hampshire girl, a young lady whose parents were her friends and neighbours, these people here tonight. It was only natural that she should want him to be bound more tightly than he currently was into the spider's web of intimate connections that tied her little rural society together. If she had even considered Isabella for a second as a prospective bride for him, she might easily have feared that marrying a woman from far-away Yorkshire would pull him away from her, so that she rarely saw him, which was the last thing she desired. And she was right to fear it, because if living out the rest of his life in the north was the only price he had to pay for winning Isabella as his wife, he would pay it in an instant, and gladly.

So he was not quite comfortable in his mind when he found himself in such demand as a dancing partner. His mother ruthlessly disposed of him among the daughters of her friends, and he tried to console himself that there was safety in numbers, but it was hard, when he would have liked to dance with his love for more than one paltry set. He could not help but contrast his emotions now with those he had experienced when he had first gone to London, when the girl in the blue gown had seemed like a distant memory that must always be out of reach, and when he had asked nothing more than to twirl about the floor with one young woman after another, not greatly caring which. That, of course, had been long weeks ago, before he had realised the extent of his feelings for Isabella, and before anything of an intimate nature had passed between them to bind him more tightly to her.

To see that Bastian, Matthew Welby and poor Tom Wainfleet were in much the same predicament as he was very little comfort. It was ironic, he thought as he squired one shy and silent damsel, that of the four gentlemen presumed so eligible none truly was, since

Bastian and Matthew presumably dreamed of a world where they might be dancing openly with each other, he would cheerfully consign this whole assembly to perdition for an hour alone with Isabella, and Tom Wainfleet was plainly suffering the torments of the damned, being forced to make some kind of stilted conversation with one young woman after another.

But they were all three of them better off than he was since nobody in their own party was genuinely trying to manipulate any of them into close contact with any particular young lady among so many. Whereas he soon began to suspect that amongst the crowd of damsels, his mother had one special candidate in mind as a bride for him: his distant cousin, Miss Peters. He found himself dancing with her twice, which occurred with no other lady, and which honour he had certainly not sought, and to set the seal on his suspicions, he discovered that she was, by some mysterious process entirely outside his control, his supper partner. When he realised this, he shot his dear mama a less than loving glance, which she met with a smile so implausibly innocent that it confirmed his belief that she had organised the whole thing.

He didn't like any part of this. If he had been on the lookout for a wife in a rational, dispassionate sort of a way – but did any man with warm blood in his veins ever do this? – he might have considered Susannah Peters. She was attractive, he supposed, if one cared for slim, dark women, which he didn't particularly. She was intelligent enough. She was a very distant sort of a cousin on his father's side. She appeared to find him excessively amusing these days, though he wasn't quite sure what he was saying that was so damn funny. But she wasn't Isabella.

The assembly ended at last, and back they went to their carriage. Tom Wainfleet seemed to have been stunned into silence by his experiences, Leo didn't feel much like talking himself, and

Isabella was very quiet too. His mother carried the conversation, with a constant flow of comments about the particulars of the evening in which Susannah Peters featured quite prominently. It was his own fault, he supposed; if he had not wanted her to match-make, he should have thought to speak with her about it in advance. But then he'd have had to lie to her, to say he had no thoughts of marriage just yet, which he didn't feel happy doing, and if he were honest feared he wouldn't be able to pull off. She was his mother. She knew him too well, or ought to.

The journey seemed longer returning than arriving, and it was a weary quartet – with the exception of Mrs Winterton, who appeared to have the boundless energy of a child who'd eaten too many sugared plums – that climbed down from the carriage at Castle Irlam just after midnight and entered the building with their companions from the other coaches. They stood together in the entrance hallway for a moment, shivering a little on the chilly stone-flagged floor, wishing each other goodnight, and Leo looked at Isabella in silent enquiry. Despite the stresses of the evening, he wanted – needed – to be in her arms. For a second he thought she meant to refuse him with a silent plea of tiredness, and then she gave a tiny, almost imperceptible nod. She wasn't smiling and her face was pale, but he chided himself that it was foolish to be appre-hensive. She had agreed to receive him, that was the main thing. There remained the constant need for discretion, and she, unlike Susannah Peters and her chattering friends, was not free to make sheep's eyes at him without fear of consequences.

The drowsy party climbed the stairs and parted to their sepa-rate chambers. Later, Leo would deeply regret his unspoken invita-tion, her acceptance and the events thus set in motion, but now he was conscious only of the familiar excitement and intense arousal that the anticipation of touching Isabella, kissing her, making love to her, always evoked in him. He undressed eagerly – he had no valet and needed none – and watched as the minute hand crept agonisingly slowly round his chamber clock until enough time had passed. Her maid would have left her long since and the Castle had fallen utterly quiet and still; at last, it was time.

28

NUMBER FIVE, NUMBER SEVEN AND NUMBER NINETEEN

Isabella had almost shaken her head when she had seen Leo's lifted eyebrow, the significance of which was quite plain to her, though, she hoped, to nobody else. She wasn't feeling particularly amorous that evening, and although there might be ladies who would be titillated by the idea of a man spending the evening paying public court to other women then coming in secret to her bed, she didn't seem to be one of them. She wasn't quite sure why she hadn't refused him when she easily could have done so. It wasn't as though he expected her to give herself to him, on this or any other occasion; it had been a question, not a demand. He never demanded anything of her. She knew that if she declared to him that number nineteen, the next item on her list, consisted of him reading her a chapter of a novel by Mr Scott or Madame D'Arblay, he would ask her, *Which chapter is your pleasure, ma'am?*

And yet that wasn't what she intended to require of him. Tired and out of humour as she was, the prospect of him coming to her chamber still ignited a treacherous little spark of desire inside her. She knew that when he lowered the latch and turned to face her, she would find a way to tell him what she needed from him. She always did.

It was the best part of an hour later when he came to her. He leaned back against the panelled door and said, 'I thought you might not wish to see me tonight. You must be tired, and it is very late. Are you sure...?'

'I have no cause to be tired,' she said, hearing the sharpness in her voice and instantly regretting it. 'I did not dance so very much.'

'I saw, and was so sorry,' he replied, crossing the room and sitting down beside her on the bed. He took her hand and held it loosely in his. 'You must know I would have danced every set with you if it had been possible. Of course it was not possible, but I would have hoped for two, and was bitterly disappointed when I could not take you in my arms again.'

'You could have asked me,' she said, hating the weakness in her voice.

'I could,' he conceded. 'My mother disposed of my person this evening according to her wishes and those of her friends, not mine, but that is a poor excuse, I am aware. My indulgence of her led me into a disregard of you, which was the last thing I wanted. Can you forgive me?'

'You don't owe me anything,' she said. 'There is certainly nothing to forgive; the idea is absurd. No doubt it was best that you did not single me out for any particular attention in so public a place. It would have raised speculation which must be unwelcome to both of us.'

He did not seem to be satisfied with this. Some demon of perversity prodded her on to add, before he could say anything else, 'On the contrary, I was glad to see you enjoying yourself.' This was a flat lie and Isabella was aware that it was as she said it.

'I wasn't enjoying myself.'

'You appeared to be.' She could feel a quarrel brewing, like the rumble of a distant storm, and knew that it would be entirely of her making. All at once she could not bear it – how many more nights would they have together? And she was wasting one. She said with a little break in her voice, 'I'm sorry. Let's not pull caps. Make love to me, Bear, and then we will part, and sleep, and tomorrow I will not be so out of reason cross with all the world.'

'I think you have some reason to be cross, with me if not with all the world. But you know I can deny you nothing. Is it to be number nineteen?' Clearly he'd been keeping count.

'It is.'

Perhaps it was unfortunate, what number nineteen was, she was later to think. There had been times in their past encounters when a sort of animalistic urgency had seized them both, and then the idea of him bending her over the bed and taking her from behind – at her command, always at her command – would have thrilled them both, left them breathless and sweaty and afterwards languorously sated. He pleasured her with his mouth and his fingers before he took her, with the intense concentration he always lavished on her, and she came; she came again when he held her tightly between his roughened hands and thrust into her with his own intense compulsion that always seemed to draw an equal response from her. Her body, at least, was satisfied. Their union was powerful, primal, but it left her shaken, a little tearful.

But tonight somehow this did not feel quite right; she could not see his face nor he hers, and it was too impersonal. Perhaps that was it: he could have been anybody, she could have been anybody, which after the events at the assembly was ill-timed. She wasn't sure why it should matter, but it did.

Maybe it shook him too, she could not know, maybe it made him incautious, but as they lay entwined afterwards, bodies touching, minds lost in their separate unknowable thoughts, he said,

'You didn't like to see me tonight, dancing with Susannah, then taking her in to supper.'

'I told you, I was happy to see you enjoying yourself. With Susannah.'

'And I told you, I wasn't. She's a cousin of sorts, and even if she hadn't been, I couldn't have spurned her publicly. She's less than nothing to me, but she doesn't deserve that. The fault was my mother's, not hers, and most of all mine for not finding a way to stop it.'

She said grudgingly, 'I don't actually know how you could have stopped it. I too have a mother, as I think you said to me once. It's very hard to say no to them when they are determined on something. I know this all too well.'

He kissed the top of her head. 'Thank you for understanding.' But his voice still showed constraint, he plainly had more to say, and a moment later he said it. 'It almost seemed to me, earlier and just now, that you were unhappy.'

She stiffened in instinctive rejection of the thought. 'Why should I be unhappy?'

'Perhaps you might think it in poor taste, that I avoided you all evening, if you thought I did, while all the while I knew, or hoped, that I would end up here, in your bed.' His voice was low and full of emotion she did not want to be forced to identify.

'I said it would have been unwise to show me too much attention in public.'

'You did, and it's true, I suppose. We do have to be careful. So if it wasn't that, if you knew I had little choice in how I behaved this evening, it seems to me that it must have been jealousy that was making you miserable. I must confess, I hope it was.'

Her heart was thumping now. 'Why would you hope such a ridiculous thing?'

'Because I love you.'

29

She jerked upright in the bed and stared at him. Leo was suddenly possessed by a sickening conviction that he was making a terrible mistake, but it was far too late to turn back now. 'I love you,' he repeated. 'If I could believe that you had feelings for me in turn, I would be the happiest man alive.'

'You don't love me. You don't.'

'I'm afraid I do. Desperately.'

'You don't. You're in love with your cousin's wife, with Cassandra.' It was a good name to hiss, and she hissed it with a great deal of force. 'You told me so yourself.'

'I lied.' She was looking at him in what appeared to be horror, her long hair wild and dishevelled about her naked shoulders. 'I lied because I already knew I loved you then, all those weeks, those months ago. I thought you'd wonder why I agreed to your scheme, once you came to reflect upon it. I felt... exposed. And so I lied to you.'

'You tricked me.' She seemed to be close to tears.

'I am sorry if I did. I can only say it didn't seem so to me. I felt as though I had no choice.'

'I'd never have started... this, if I had thought you cared for me.'

'I know you wouldn't. You'd have found somebody else, that popinjay... I couldn't bear it. I couldn't. It wasn't just that I didn't want anyone else laying so much as a finger on you – though of course I didn't – it was also my fear that some other man would use you, hurt you, let you down. I couldn't let that happen.'

Her face was shuttered, closed to him. 'You entered into this under false pretences. That's tricking me.'

'I suppose it is.' His voice was cracking and he didn't care. 'I won't apologise for loving you, though. Worshipping you. I can never regret that if I live to be a hundred. And tonight, when it seemed to me that you were jealous, it gave me just a whisper of hope that you might care for me too, at least a little. Was I wrong?'

'You have no right to ask me that question. It's not part of our agreement.'

'I know I don't. I'm not asking you out of vanity, I assure you. It matters more to me than anything I've ever asked anyone in my life. And you haven't answered me.'

'I don't love you,' she said. 'I don't. I can't. I can't love you or anyone. I love Ash. My husband Ash. I told you that from the first. I never tried to deceive you into thinking that anything else was possible for me.' She was weeping now.

An ugly silence fell between them. 'Then there's nothing more to be said.' He rose, and like an automaton, he climbed down from her bed, shoved his stiff arms into the sleeves of his dressing gown, and with clumsy fingers that did not feel like his own he fastened it and turned to leave her.

She said, tears still streaming down her face, 'It's over, then.' He wasn't sure if this was a question. If it was, it was a cruel, unnecessary one.

'I think that's best, don't you?'

He didn't wait for an answer. If she was expecting him to beg her to take him back into her bed, she would be disappointed. He knew he was capable of it, of begging; he knew that if she showed the slightest sign of wanting him to stay, he'd break and fall at her feet and implore her to give him another chance, to forget all he'd said and carry on for as long as she cared to. The power she had over him was not something that could so easily be shaken off. But he had just a little pride, enough to get him out of this room and back to his own, if she didn't say another word.

She didn't.

30

Isabella stared at the door as Leo closed it with painful care behind him. She was in a state of shock. She'd never expected such a declaration; she didn't know what she had wanted to provoke when she'd needled at him tonight, but not that, never that. She'd thought, if she'd thought at all, that he might admit that he was contemplating marriage at some point in the future, and Miss Peters, *Susannah*, was a prospect he was seriously considering. He'd have been well within his rights to say such a thing, and how could she have reacted? Even as she'd been saying what she'd said, motivated by some impulse she was unable to control, she'd known it was none of her business. He was free to do as he pleased; she had no claim on him.

But she was deliberately distracting herself, dwelling on such thoughts. They were all nonsense. He said he loved her. It was the very last thing she wanted.

At first, she hadn't been sure if she believed him. The idea that he was hopelessly enamoured of Lady Irlam was so firmly fixed in her mind that she found it almost impossible to rearrange herself to accept this new fact. She wouldn't. He was just saying it, surely, because he knew his love for Cassandra was hopeless. It must be plain to the meanest intelligence that Lord and Lady Irlam adored each other and were excessively happy in their marriage. Here he was, witnessing their closeness with pain, and at the same time there was a woman at hand who was prepared to take him into her bed, to couple within him in ways – there was no denying the truth of this, at least – that touched something deep inside him and brought him a species of pleasure he claimed he'd never known before. Of course, he might easily *want* to love her, which was a long way along the road to persuading himself that he did. He wasn't a man on whom deception sat easily, she knew that too. Concealing their liaison made him uncomfortable. How much more convenient, then, if no concealment were necessary.

But this was nonsense too. She couldn't forget the naked agony on his face as he'd left her just now. It reminded her horribly of the haunted expression Ash's dear countenance had carried when he kissed her a last goodbye in Brussels, to go to what he feared was his death, and proved to be so. She ought to know love when she saw it, and she'd seen it again tonight.

She hadn't asked for this.

She struggled sometimes to accustom herself to great or even small changes in her life, when they came unexpectedly; her mother had said that she had always been so, even as a tiny child, and she had come to realise over the past months that this inflexibility in herself had been one of the causes of her illness. It was one of the reasons she'd tried to take control with her list, and she had thought that it was working. She felt better.

Had felt better.

She felt terrible now. It must be awful, beyond awful, to make love to someone you adored, all the while unable to tell them how you felt. A parody of intimacy. So nearly everything you had ever dreamed of, but so cruelly not quite that. Constantly checking yourself as words trembled on your lips that must never been spoken. A vision of happiness dangled in front of your eyes and constantly snatched away.

Her mind was fluttering from one disjointed thought to another, like a wild bird trapped in a cage. She wasn't a cruel person. She'd never have done this to anyone willingly, least of all to Leo, who was so good and kind and endlessly considerate. She had been angry with him at first, had accused him of deceiving her, but now that she had a moment to consider she could see that he had had little choice. If you loved someone, of course you wouldn't want them exposing themselves to hurt or danger. You'd have to be a plaster saint to deny yourself the prospect of making love to the woman you yearned for when it was offered to you, and when you could advance many unselfish and credible reasons for going ahead with it, and picture so many dreadful things that might happen to her if you didn't. And Leo, despite his many noble qualities, was no saint.

And besides, he must have thought – she could see that he had thought – that there was always a chance that she might change her mind, might come to love him after all. If you had somehow developed the strength to refuse all the other temptations, how could you deny yourself that last and most seductive one? Women and men had changed their minds before. History was full of examples of it. Look at Gabriel, her own brother-in-law, who'd been famous throughout Yorkshire, and London society too, for his fixed intention never to marry, and yet was now the most loving and devoted of husbands. Leo hadn't tried to persuade her – he had never said a single word – because he would have thought that dishonest, and a betrayal of the spirit of their agreement. But he had hoped in secret. He had made that sufficiently and painfully clear tonight.

And there was no hope for him. She wished there could have

been. If she had known the slightest sliver of a desire to love again, to replace Ash with another, she'd have chosen Leo as the man to make that dangerous attempt with. She couldn't imagine anybody better. She cared for him, more deeply than she'd known and certainly more deeply than she'd imagined caring for the man her fancy had lighted on when she'd been looking about her for suitable candidates to be her lover. But it was not enough.

Not enough for her, and not enough for him either. Not to sustain a whole life together. She would wager that he thought now that he'd accept her as his wife on any terms, and that his love for her would be enough. But it couldn't be. Love had to be mutual to survive, and she could never love anyone the way she had loved Ash. She wished that she could tell Leo so, explain, make him see that the pain she'd unwittingly inflicted on him now would be as nothing to the bone-deep hurt of a lifetime of living with someone who could never care for him as he deserved.

And that wasn't by any means all. He had a fortune and an estate and a family name to hand down. He'd want children, need them, all men in his situation did, from princes of the blood to yeoman farmers. And she was horribly sure she could not give them to him. After all, she hadn't just been told so in the cruellest of terms by distinguished gentlemen with letters after their names. It was undeniably true that she and Ash had come together daily, more than that, over the course of their marriage, almost a year, and yet every month with weary, tedious regularity – she was like a clock that never needed to be wound – her courses would appear. She'd never been as much as a day late in all that time, and even when Ash had died, even in the depths of her illness, her unwelcome guest had arrived with cruel punctuality every month to mock her desperate wish that he'd put a child in her as a final act of love before he was irrevocably lost to her. She'd not wanted to believe the truth, had refused for a long time to do so, but the evidence had always been there.

So she was, in crude words, a terrible bargain. A cull ewe, to use the brutally honest farming term of her childhood. If he'd been a friend of hers, with whom she'd been able to share the word with no bark on it in the bluntest way possible, she'd have felt obliged to describe this woman he'd so unfortunately bound himself to as the very worst of choices: a woman who could never love him as much as he loved her, and who was barren besides. That would surely be how his family, his mother above all, would see her, if they knew everything. It was how she must see herself.

He'd had a lucky escape, though she supposed it would be a while before he realised it. There were, at any rate, as had been made crystal clear this evening, many, many young women who would be more than delighted to console him. Susannah Peters, for one.

So he'd live. She'd hurt him badly without ever intending to, and she was desperately sorry and wished she could take it back, but he would. One did not expire of love, or she would be dead and in her grave many months since. She would survive this too, though she was sad and tired and full of regret just now. She'd go home soon, to her parents, and for the first time, she looked forward to it. She had a sudden yearning for her mother's comfortable, comforting embrace. She couldn't rush away – it would be rude to her hosts and raise questions she'd much rather not have anyone contemplate – but in a few days, a week, she'd speak to them about how her removal might be managed. Perhaps Lady Carston and Lady Louisa were going back to Town and she could go with them. She had money and needed no chaperon; something could be contrived.

She tried to compose a letter in her head: *Dear Mama...*

No, she couldn't do it. Couldn't dissimulate, describe the

assembly and pretend the evening had been ordinary, and nor could she collect herself enough to talk of her plans to return home in a calm and rational manner. It was all far too raw to be set down as if it mattered little.

She turned her hot pillow over and punched it ruthlessly into shape, closing her eyes tightly and begging for blessed oblivion, but it was a long time before it was granted to her.

31

Leo didn't sleep, or barely did. It wasn't as though he was churning thoughts over in his head; once he knew beyond a shadow of a doubt that she didn't love him, there was really nothing else to say. To think. She hadn't deceived him. She'd never promised to love him, or even to open herself to the possibility of doing so. She'd always said she wouldn't, couldn't, that her love had been given to her dead husband and she had none left.

It was torture, but then it always had been, right from the start. He'd thought himself reconciled to that, with the ever-present knowledge hanging over him that one day soon it would be over. But the cruel hope was what had made it so much worse. He'd had a taste of it at the assembly, aware as he had been of her eyes on him as he danced with other ladies, and tried to fend off Susannah's flirtatious sallies over supper. If that had been all, he'd have dismissed it as a fantasy born of a desperate need for her affection, but when she raised the topic when they were alone together, a little flame of possibility had kindled in his heart, and he'd recklessly decided to tell her how he felt. He had only himself to blame.

He'd hurt her, and he was sorry, but he'd hurt himself far more. Now it was over, and even the self-indulgence of hope was denied to him.

He knew he ought to leave the Castle – make some excuse and go home, to nurse his misery where nobody could see – but he couldn't quite bring himself to do it. She would leave in a week or so, he'd made sure of that in his stupidity tonight, and it seemed cruelly possible that he'd never set eyes on her again as long as they both lived. Was he so lacking in self-respect that he'd stay here, struggling under the added burden of concealing his profound distress from his closest family, just so he could see a little of her, be in a damn room with her even if they didn't speak, or only exchanged the merest commonplaces? Apparently he was.

She didn't come down for breakfast – none of the ladies did, not even his mother, and he was glad of that at least, since he was in no mood to hear a single word more about last night's assembly and how very agreeable it had been. He ate with Bastian, Matthew and Tom Wainfleet, and none of them was likely to be reminiscing fondly about an evening they'd all endured rather than enjoyed.

He'd hoped last night wouldn't even be mentioned – he would have welcomed an entirely silent masculine meal – but it was not to be. Bastian said suddenly, 'Something horrible has just occurred to me.' They all looked at him enquiringly. 'I think it's reasonable to expect an unusually large number of calls from the ladies of the neighbourhood over the next few days.'

'Following up on their good work last night,' said Matthew with a grimace.

'Precisely. Enquiring about *your* prospects and the precise size and location of your estate, I shouldn't wonder,' said his lover sweetly.

'I'm penniless,' Matthew replied promptly. 'Notoriously so. The poorest man in Yorkshire. I dropped a few hints to that effect, in a subtle sort of a way – naturally – while I was dancing. Any woman who marries me will have to learn to shear sheep and churn butter.'

'Well,' said Bastian with a wicked grin, 'she'd do well to set up a hobby.'

Mr Wainfleet had plainly been cogitating over Mr Pendlebury's remark, for he said now, darting hunted glances about him as if expecting a battalion of ladies to burst into the room at any moment, seize him bodily and carry him off in triumph to the sacrificial altar, 'When d'you think they're likely to arrive? A fellow needs to be prepared.'

'Not till well after nuncheon, surely,' said Mr Pendlebury soothingly. 'You can go out. We can all go out. Let's do that. Leave Cassandra and my aunt to deal with them – obviously I mean Aunt Sophia, not Louisa. They don't care for Louisa, most of them – she's too satirical.'

'I *might* just stay if I could be guaranteed that Lady Carston would give them a lecture about the position of women in society and how marriage is a snare and a delusion,' said Matthew. 'It might almost be worth it to see their faces. But no, on reflection, it's too dangerous. One incautious word, Tom, or a smile in the wrong direction, and before you know it you'll be engaged to marry some girl you barely know, with no getting out of it. The whole hideous thing was Cassandra's idea, I distinctly heard her propose it, so I agree, let her suffer the consequences.'

'Let's play billiards till nuncheon, and go out shooting afterwards,' proposed Bastian. 'If it gets too cold, we can look in at the Queen's Head in the village, and sit snugly by the fire there till it's safe to come back.'

Leo wasn't sure he much relished the idea of spending the day in company, but his cousin was quite right; they'd be besieged by ladies again later in the afternoon, and that really would be unendurable. He'd pass the time in the way Bastian had suggested, and torment himself with mooning over Isabella in the evening. 'I'm in,' he said shortly.

32

Cassandra swiftly became aware that her plan to provoke Lady Ashby into jealousy and thence into realising her true feelings for Captain Winterton – assuming those feelings to be loving ones – had disastrously misfired. She did not so much as set eyes on Leo that day until the party gathered for dinner, since he made no appearance at nuncheon and was absent from the Castle for the rest of the afternoon, which was an ominous sign in itself, if one paused to think about it, but she did spend time with Isabella, who was looking pale, tired and perhaps even a little unwell. She found it impossible to divine precisely what had happened, but clearly something had, and it could scarcely be anything good. She might have consoled herself with the supposition that Lady Ashby had become aware of her own tender emotions and mistakenly believed them unrequited – such tangled romantic misunderstandings being all too common, in her own experience – had it not been for Leo's prolonged absence, which was unusual and surely boded ill.

As Bastian had predicted, the afternoon was enlivened by

several visits from ladies who had been at the assembly the night before; they came on the slenderest of pretexts or on none, and while some of them were well-bred enough to converse civilly and normally with their hostess, and with an animated Mrs Winterton and a rather subdued Lady Ashby, some shot obvious glances about the room, as if imagining that one of the young gentlemen might be concealed under a sofa or behind the heavy velvet curtains, and merely needed rooting out. A couple of them even ventured brazenly to enquire where the Countess's other charming guests might be, and would have entered into a discussion about precisely where Mr Welby's home was situated in Yorkshire and how large it was if Cassandra had given them the least encouragement. Presuming on the licence given by their remote family connection with the Wintertons, Mrs Peters – accompanied by her daughter Susannah, who was in high bloom and excellent spirits – was bold enough to ask where the dear Captain was that afternoon, as they had been so looking forward to seeing him again. 'It is so good to see him returned home after so long away, for we have missed him, have we not?' Mrs Peters gushed. 'I hope he intends to make his home permanently amongst us now and cease gadding about in London? I am sure we should be delighted to see more of him, would we not, Susannah?' Susannah assented with obvious sincerity that they would, and seemed to feel it necessary to ask again where dear Cousin Leo might be just now, and if his return could be imminent.

His mother made some smiling answer to all these rather pointed questions, even going so far as to agree enthusiastically with Mrs Peters that Susannah and her son had made a most handsome couple as they danced together last night, and as she spoke Cassandra surprised a brief expression of misery, rapidly suppressed, upon Lady Ashby's face. Once this round of visitors left, she was not astonished to hear Isabella say in a colourless voice that she found she had the headache and begged Lady Irlam to excuse her. Cassandra had the headache too, for that matter, but this deluge of guests was her own fault and she could not escape them without a display of gross incivility that would do her lasting damage in the county.

She was able to snatch a moment's conversation with Lady Carston as they waited to go in to dinner later; a lifted brow sufficed for that intelligent woman to respond, 'I have no more idea than you do, but it certainly does not look promising. Poor Lady A looks fit to drop; I'll try to converse with her and find out what is the matter, for plainly you cannot. If I discover anything and can't find a moment to speak with you afterwards, I'll send a note by Louisa's abigail.'

It was a large enough group of persons that some constraint between two of its members, which both were trying hard to conceal, made little impact on the general success of the evening. Lady Ashby and the Captain were both quiet, initiating no topics of conversation but responding suitably when addressed, but Cassandra thought that most of the party remained blissfully unaware of this fact, always excepting her husband, who was a great deal more perceptive than most people would give him credit for, and had already been concerned about his cousin for weeks.

Lady Carston did not approach her hostess before the party broke up – earlier than usual, for everyone was a trifle fatigued – but a note was brought to Cassandra's chamber as promised. It was not very informative, merely saying:

She did not tell me anything, but my impression that she is most unhappy was confirmed. She spoke of leaving the Castle quite shortly and how it might be managed. I did not feel able to ques-

tion her even a little, our acquaintance in reality being so very
slight and she plainly resolved not to speak. I am sorry I do not
have better news for you. J.

Cassandra showed the missive to Hal, who sighed and said, 'I'm
not surprised, though I am sorry. Leo spent the afternoon drinking
with Bastian, Matthew and Tom in the village, and Basty said he
was lifting his elbow more than he'd ever seen him do before; you
must have observed that Leo is pretty abstemious as a general rule.
My brother thought he was rather under the weather and out of
spirits, and mentioned it to me; I fobbed him off with some jest
about Leo not caring for all the attention last night, which God
knows is probably true enough.'

'I didn't know. Well, that sets the seal on it, I fear – they have
quarrelled in some fashion, do you not agree? It seems most likely
that he has declared his love at last and been rebuffed.'

'Must have done. Don't look so worried, Cass – you know it was
bound to happen soon enough, unless she changed her mind. It's
not in the least your fault, and you were only trying to help.'

She rumpled his dark locks affectionately. 'It's good of you to
say so. But I fear I may have provoked some argument that might
not otherwise have happened. They both look very sad.'

'I could cheerfully bang their silly heads together,' said her lord
robustly, seizing her hand and kissing it. 'We still don't have the
least idea how she feels about him, but I think you may be right
that her affections are engaged – she looks more glum-faced than a
falling-out with someone she doesn't care two pins for should call
for.'

'That may be true – in fact, I believe it is – but they are both
looking so miserable that there can't be any reason to hope for a
happy outcome. He has proposed, and been summarily rejected, I
am quite sure of it. How provoking it all is!'

'You must be right. Well, in any event, you've shot your bolt, Lady Irlam, and there's nothing more to be done. Some people can't be helped.'

His wife conceded that this was probably true, and found some measure of consolation in his strong embrace, as the Castle fell quiet, undisturbed by any nocturnal wanderings for once.

33

It was not possible for Leo to absent himself from the Castle for the whole of another day while he remained a guest there. He might resolve to be far distant from the blue saloon, generally used for receiving guests, during the hours in which morning calls were generally paid, but he found he simply didn't have the stamina for another afternoon spent trudging through muddy fields and then drinking in the village inn. Tom Wainfleet was too quiet for him, and Bastian and Matthew too cheerful, too damn young and bright-eyed and happy together. Everything irritated him. He felt as though a layer or two of his skin had been removed, and quite normal things – the bone-chilling cold, loud noises such as a startled bird bursting from the undergrowth, a dropped spoon at table – affected him in a manner he found frankly pathetic.

He hadn't spoken to her, nor she to him. Not really. The commonplaces exchanged in front of others did not count. To be close to her, and yet so at odds, was a torment he was not sure he could long endure. But if he left...

To set a cap upon the day, his mother cornered him while he was mooching miserably about the Castle late in the morning and dragged him into her sitting room – she had her own pleasant suite of rooms, decorated and furnished to her taste, that were always at her disposal – for a comfortable coze: words to strike horror into any son's guilty heart.

'What's the matter, Leo?' she asked once there, in tones that took him straight back to his boyhood. She had usually been able to soothe his petty worries then, but he knew she could not help him now. Nobody could.

There was little point in dissembling, though he had no intention of telling her everything. 'Is it so obvious?' he said, smiling bleakly.

'Of course it is. I'm your mother, for heaven's sake. I thought at first that you were out of humour because of the ridiculous fuss all those young ladies made over you at the assembly.' She had the gall to say this as though she'd had nothing to do with this occurrence and hadn't enjoyed every minute of it enormously. 'But I've realised it's more than that. What is it?'

'I have developed a... tendre for Lady Ashby. I had begun to think, to hope, that she might reciprocate my feelings in some measure.'

'She was watching you the other evening when you were dancing, though she tried not to show it,' agreed his mother complacently. 'I must admit it crossed my mind too.'

How had she had time to notice that when she'd been so busy matchmaking? It was a mystery he did not care to enquire too deeply into just now. 'I began to declare myself...' He could not truthfully say that he had asked Isabella to marry him, for she had not let him get that far. 'But she was horrified. She told me plainly what indeed I should have known already: that she is devoted to the memory of her dead husband, and never intends to marry again.'

'I'm sorry,' said his mother soberly. 'I could see, of course, that you were attracted to her immediately upon your arrival and hers.' Why 'of course'? She saw the thought cross his face – apparently, he was as easy to read as Isabella was, for his mother at least, which was unwelcome news – and she said, 'Naturally I can tell these things where you are concerned. But I had no idea it was so serious. And I suppose I thought you might consider her out of your reach, as the widow of a duke's son.'

'When did any man ever truly consider the woman he loved out of his reach?' said Leo bleakly. 'But, not that it matters in the least now, she isn't. Her parents are gentlefolk of a similar standing to ourselves; she merely married well. Much like your sister.'

'I had not known. She does not talk about herself a great deal, and I felt she would not welcome questioning she might consider vulgar.'

'I doubt that's true; she is very straightforward when one comes to know her. But she doesn't care to speak about her husband. They were not married a year before he fell at Waterloo, and was brought back to her in Brussels, mortally wounded, to die in her arms.'

'She has told you much, for one who does not talk about her husband,' remarked Mrs Winterton shrewdly. He was hardly going to tell her why, and so said nothing. 'She's seen terrible sights no woman of her age, or any age, should be obliged to see. I'm sure it's no wonder it should have affected her so deeply. It may take her a long time to recover from them. It's barely been eighteen months, after all.'

'I agree with you, Mama. But I have no option but to respect her decision. It is not my place to tell her that her feelings are somehow false. I don't believe they are, in fact, though I think you may be right that she is still in a state of shock. But many widows choose not to marry again, as you did.'

'I had a child to consider. And although I did have an offer or two – did you know that, Leo? – nothing that tempted me sufficiently to upturn my life and yours, and follow a man halfway across England. There were plenty of men, of course, who would have been quite willing to come and live in your house, at your expense, and have the running of it. But I'd never have wed one of those. Hal's father was my trustee, and wouldn't have let me marry such a man even if I'd been foolish enough to want to.'

'You don't regret it?' He was distracted from his misery for a moment.

She smiled at him. 'No. Not at all.'

'So you are counselling me to wait? Perhaps to try again in a year, two years?' It seemed very far off, but he could do it.

'I suppose I am. You should have told me, Leo. I wouldn't have encouraged poor Susannah to set her cap at you.'

'Just as long as you don't do it again, Mama. I didn't enjoy it. Though I know you did.'

She rose, came over to him, and took his hand. He squeezed hers in return, and they sat for a little while in silence.

After a while, she said, 'Do you mean to go home? You might find it easier, I'd have thought, not being here where her presence is a constant reminder to you.'

He sighed. 'I've thought of it. I feel it would be less painful, it is true. But then I consider that if I leave the Castle I do not know when, or if, I will ever see her again, and I find I do not have the strength to do it.' His unspoken addition was that Isabella would in any case surely be leaving soon enough herself. It was plain that being here was now making her deeply uncomfortable.

'You can go to see her in Yorkshire; you might make a plan to do it,' said his mother encouragingly. 'Perhaps next spring or summer.'

'I can. I will. But I still don't want to deprive myself of these last few days with her, difficult though they are.'

'You do not feel you could suggest a correspondence between you? She is no debutante; she can receive letters from male acquaintances without any particular appearance of impropriety, I believe. Perhaps it might be considered a little odd, but nothing more. She is her own mistress, or should be.'

She might be, but she was also his and always would be – as far as he was concerned, at least. Clearly, she no longer felt the same. 'I can try, but I doubt she'll agree. I would expect her to say that it would lead me to have false hope. Which it would.'

His mother agreed that this was probably true, and had no further suggestions to ameliorate his distress. He did not feel his situation to be greatly improved by their conversation; he was as unhappy as he had been, and now his mother, who loved him, shared in some part of his misery. There had been no relief in talking about it, or none that was apparent to him now. But he supposed he could console himself a little with the reflection that at least his mama's attempts to marry him off to one or other of the young ladies of Hampshire, and to Susannah Peters in particular, would now cease. That was something, but not much.

Leo would not have imagined that he could well be more unhappy than he currently was: a common belief among suffering humans, and, as he was soon to discover, a mistaken one.

34

Isabella was very anxious to leave Castle Irlam. The passage of time wasn't making it any easier to be in Leo's company, even if they barely spoke to each other. And she wondered how well he was concealing his distress at her continuing presence from his mother and his cousins; not well, she feared. If she could see that he was not at all in his normal state of mind, they surely must have noticed it too.

But when she was speaking to Lady Carston of her desire to go, she had experienced a sudden horrifying realisation that had almost overset her, and it took every shred of her self-possession to enable her to continue the conversation with any appearance of calmness. She had not been calm; she had been screaming internally.

When Leo had declared himself and she had formulated the design to depart as soon as possible, she'd known that not only courtesy towards her host and hostess constrained her movements. One did not – certainly she did not – plan to undertake a long and tedious journey halfway across England when one's courses were present, or soon expected. This was to be avoided if at all possible, for reasons that scarcely needed to be further considered. She'd had the vague sense for a while that her menses were impending, though now she stopped to think about it she could not feel their approach in her body as normally she did in a dozen little ways.

But they weren't. They were late. Several days late, in fact. While speaking to Jane, she had been frantically calculating dates in her mind, trying to make them fit. But they didn't. They couldn't.

She was with child.

She couldn't be, it was impossible. Unthinkable. But she was.

She wasted only a little time in attempting to persuade herself that she was merely late, a delay caused by the worries of the last few days. It wasn't true. Much as she might wish to believe it, she didn't see how it could be so. She'd never been late before, not even after Ash had died, not when she'd so desperately needed to persuade herself that she was carrying his child. If that appalling stress had not unsettled her monotonously ticking clock, it was hardly likely that this lesser upset would have done so.

It had never so much as occurred to her that she could find herself with child now. She'd had every reason to believe that that was quite impossible, or she'd never have allowed Leo to make love to her as completely and as frequently as she had.

There were many symptoms, she knew, that could indicate either condition: pregnancy or the ordinary approach of one's courses. She'd discussed all this with her mother once, long ago, when she was newly married and touchingly confident that she'd be in a delicate situation in a month or two and needed to prepare for it with some urgency, and then again later, a different and less happy sort of conversation, when it had become apparent that it wasn't going to be so easy for her. Her breasts were sore; they always were just before her menses. She was ravenously hungry, tired, a little tearful. None of this was unusual and could not be taken as proof of any kind. Did she feel a little unwell in the mornings, or was she merely convincing herself that she did? It was impossible to tell. But one thing was coldly certain – she didn't feel the horribly familiar dragging pain in the backs of her thighs and up into her belly that always preceded the arrival of her blood. It, and then the blood, should have come days ago, and there was not the least sign of anything.

She was in her chamber by now, and she jumped from her bed and stumbled to the mirror, pulling off her night-rail to stand naked in front of the glass. She looked at herself – did she appear any different? Would she, so soon? It was a ridiculous idea, surely. But she was almost sure that her nipples, and the areolae around them, were darker. Less pink, more brown. Bigger, even. She didn't normally look at herself that closely. Leo would know, she thought with a little hiccup of panicked laughter, but she could hardly ask him.

Perhaps this change was her imagination, there was no way to tell, but it didn't matter, because the truth was, she knew. She felt it, knew it in her body.

Oh God, how she wished she could talk or even write to her mother, or someone, about her situation, pour out her feelings and ask for advice. It would have been bitterly ironic if it weren't so serious. What a cruel, heartless twist of fate. All those months with Ash, trying. They'd not spoken of their failure – hers? His? – but it had been there between them all the same, growing with each month that passed. And so she had seen the doctors – secretly, without Ash's knowledge, hoping they could give her some remedy he needn't ever be aware of – and had been told that there was no hope. And now, when pregnancy wasn't happy news but a catastrophe, now when she'd thought it impossible in any case and so hadn't considered it at all... Now she was. There was no point wondering how it had happened – it was far too late for that, and the how of it was plain enough. The doctors had been wrong, pretending with masculine certainty that they had knowledge that in truth they did not possess. If they could have just been honest and said they didn't know, that these things were mysterious... Nature, she supposed, was cunning enough to find a way. Had it been the first night, the second time...? No point in any of that. Another distraction.

Her body, with a child in it. A child, good God, so desperately wanted once. A child she'd thought she never would have, had been resigned never to have. She had her hand on her belly, still looking at herself intently in the cheval glass, as she stood naked and cold – it was softly rounded, and it was easy enough to imagine it more rounded still. She was weeping, and as she became aware of it she chided herself for folly and clambered awkwardly back into bed, pulling her robe back on. No use catching pneumonia to add to all of her other worries.

She still wanted the child. Oh God, but she did. It wasn't – she'd realised this some while ago – just Ash's child that she had wanted, a son, an heir for Northriding. She'd wanted a child of her own to love, entirely regardless of everyone else's expectations. Those expectations had been a weight on her once, but she could have disregarded them much more easily if they hadn't chimed so closely with what she so deeply wanted for herself. A child, a baby of her own. Lady Carston had felt the same overpowering impulse, she knew, and she could fully understand it. Had been jealous, though she had suppressed the feeling as she suppressed so many unwelcome feelings, as they had talked on the subject. No need for jealousy now.

But she, unlike clever Jane, was in desperate straits. Unmarried. Reputation gone, when this came out, as it must. Carrying a nameless bastard.

She had, she thought, two choices only. It was another list: a very short one. She could tell Leo, and he would marry her. Of

course he would. That was number one. It was – she knew – the
obvious choice. Most people wouldn't consider it a choice at all, but
her only option, and she lucky to have it. It would be a great
betrayal of Ash, to set another in his place, and it was precisely the
opposite of what she had intended, going into this ridiculous
scheme of hers. Blanche had told her, she remembered now, that
Ash would have wanted her to marry again, to be happy. She could
see that that might be true. But he couldn't have wanted this. The
hideous irony that there might have been in truth no problem, that
she just hadn't been patient enough – or, much worse somehow,
that if there'd been a problem it had been Ash's and not hers – she
couldn't contemplate any of that now. Such dark, roiling thoughts
drew her towards the edge of an abyss that she'd struggled out of
with enormous difficulty and couldn't afford to fall into again. Not
now there was to be a child.

She had to think sensibly about her choices. One was marriage,
and betrayal. It horrified her, even though it was the conventional
and obvious path. Two was much chancier. She could go away
somewhere, when her condition was on the point of becoming
obvious – in two months' time, or three, or four, she wasn't an
expert, not yet – and set herself up as a widow, a recent widow, an
anonymous Mrs Somebody, a person of no importance at all, and
have her child. She'd have to tell her parents; that would be hard.
Horribly hard. But then, if she were lucky and clever, she could
reappear in Yorkshire, with a child she had adopted. Women
adopted babies. Widows did; spinsters, even. She could concoct
some plausible tale, if her parents helped her, which she was
almost sure they would. Eventually, perhaps grudgingly at first,
they would not be able to deny her this, however bewildered, hurt
and disapproving they might be when she broke it to them. She'd
have her child then, the child she'd never thought to hold. They'd
have the longed-for grandchild they had given up any hope of

having. This baby would be loved, wanted, cared for and well-provided-for. Her father's heir, and hers, whether it be boy or girl. She had money, a loving family – if any woman could pull off this difficult feat, she could.

But she'd be doing a terrible thing to Leo. A much worse thing than she'd done to him already. He'd have a child and never know it. Never be able to give a son or a daughter all the love he had to share, because she'd deliberately deprived him of that chance. His mother, though this could hardly be her chief concern, would never know her grandchild. It would be a wicked, cruel thing to perpetrate on him, this deception, and cruel to the child too, who would never know a father, by her selfish choice. She'd have to start with lies, and build a whole structure of more lies, one atop another. She would have to lie to her child when he or she asked who his or her father, his or her birth mother was. Deny her own blood. And what if one day the child suspected some part of the truth, and said, in justifiable anger, *Was my father a brute, a wicked man, that you fled from him and hid my very existence from him, and his from me? Because I cannot imagine any other reason why you would make such a dreadful choice.* She couldn't say yes. It would be the worst of all lies. He wasn't any of those things.

But if she married him, if she made that hard choice, what then?

What then?

35

The two largely sleepless nights that succeeded her discovery left Isabella still very uneasy and divided in her mind. She had given herself another day, imagining that her courses might magically come then and solve her dilemma for her, to her regret but also her relief, but they did not, and as the hours passed it had become clearer and clearer to her that she didn't really have a choice. All the world would say so, and in this case, all the world would be right. She had to tell Leo. Anything else would be unfair. He hadn't deserved such treatment from her. She couldn't lie to everyone, deceive him above all and one day deceive her child, their child, and still face herself afterwards.

She had to tell him. If Ash was looking down on her, she hoped he would be able to forgive her. She had to tell Leo, and to marry him.

To realise this was one thing, but it was not by any means easy to find a way to be alone with him. Not in the daytime. This was another irony. At night it would have been simple enough – she could have crept to his chamber as he had so often come to hers, but she didn't want to do that, didn't want to have any misunderstandings between them, not even for a moment or two, as to why she was there. He'd think she was coming to his bed to start again. Would he be glad or furious? She couldn't bear it, either way.

At last, she was reduced to an unpleasant stratagem: she required Lady Carston to pass a message to him, to tell him that she would be alone in a certain room at a certain hour, and very much wished to speak to him on an urgent matter. Luckily, she was a guest in a castle; there were many rooms in which one could in privacy tell one's recently spurned lover that one was carrying his child. Jane had raised an eyebrow when approached but nobly refrained from asking her anything at all, and she was grateful for the forbearance. Her composure was a very fragile thing.

He came at the hour she had appointed, to a small panelled Tudor sitting room that nobody ever appeared to use, down an obscure corridor that seemed to lead nowhere in particular, and stood in the doorway in silence, frowning a little as he looked at her. He was pale, holding himself under rigid control, as he had been ever since their estrangement, and she was aware that she must look much the same.

'I think you should sit down,' she said. She was sitting in a faded tapestry chair, her back very straight and her hands clasped in her lap.

'I can't imagine what you can have to say to me,' he replied as he obeyed her with every appearance of reluctance, his countenance set and grim. 'I cherished some brief hope that you might have changed your mind, or discovered that you were mistaken in your feelings, but that hope died when I saw your face. It is not such happy news, is it? Have you summoned me to tell me that you are leaving? You need not have troubled, for I had assumed as much, and wonder in truth that you are still here.'

'No,' she said. 'No, it's not that.' She felt an impulse to call him Bear, to recall the intimate moments they'd shared, but there was no point to any of that now. He was looking at her with a kind of weary patience, and she knew she must speak, before all her courage deserted her or before he rose and went away. 'I'm with child.'

He didn't appear to understand her, so she repeated it. 'I'm with child, Leo.'

He sat as one frozen. At last, he spoke. 'How can you know?'

It was a reasonable question, if a cold one, and she hadn't expected him to be pleased, after all. 'I'm late. I'm never late. I've never been late in my life. But I realised I am, and several days at that. I had lost track, not believing it to be possible. My courses are not coming; I'd know if they were. I know it is very soon, but I could not be mistaken. I feel... different.'

'You told me such a thing was quite impossible,' he said blankly.

'I thought it was. I was told it was. It was one of the worst moments of my life, when I heard that. And I believed that to be true, or I never would have...'

'I don't suppose you would. And good God, Isabella, nor would I!'

His words pierced her with sudden fierce pain, though she could not accuse him of cruelty. Of course he was horrified. How could he not be? She could not afford to regard it. 'I know you would not have done. I feel I should apologise to you, but indeed, indeed, I did not know.'

She could not hope to separate out the emotions that were warring on his face. 'Why are you telling me?'

She reared back as though she had been struck and tears started in her eyes, though she had with a great effort preserved her composure up till now. 'Who else should I tell? For heaven's sake, what kind of a question is that?'

He swore, and rose to his feet, coming over to her chair and dropping down awkwardly to kneel by her side. He took her hands in his, clasped them tightly and said urgently, 'That's not what I mean! Good God, I'm sorry, my dear Isabella! No, I meant... I meant to ask, to say, curse my clumsiness, I must assume you're telling me this because you are resolved to marry me. You don't think to go away, to... I don't know.'

'You haven't asked me to marry you,' she replied, suppressing a foolish desire to burst into sobs.

'I was about to, the other night,' he said in low tones. 'You know I was.'

She was a hopeless mess. 'I did think of going away,' she said with painful honesty. 'Not giving up the child, I could never contemplate that, but – not telling you. Doing it in secret, under an assumed name. Devising some ridiculous scheme by which I could later adopt it. Her. Him.' She saw the horror on his face and hastened to add, 'I couldn't do it. It wouldn't be fair to you, or to the child. To deny you both...'

'No, it wouldn't,' he said. A little silence fell between them. It wasn't pleasant. He broke it by saying drily, 'So, Isabella, Lady Ashby, will you marry me?'

'Yes.'

He was still holding her hand. She hadn't pulled away. He looked as though he wanted to speak, and at the same time didn't, but at last he said heavily, 'And then what?'

She was conscious of feeling cold; she was shivering. 'What do you mean?'

'I understand that we must marry. There is no point me saying again that this – your hand in marriage, you as my wife, I mean – is what I wanted, for you knew that, and it can be of no possible concern to you since you did not. Want it, I mean. Want me.' My God, how she had hurt him. 'But how shall we live?'

'Together, with our child when it arrives. How else?'

'Really? You will live with me, and share my bed, for all the years that may lie ahead of us, when you have told me in very plain terms that you cannot love me? That you can never love me?'

Her voice cracked as she said, 'What else would you have me do?'

He sighed, and in a dull tone said, 'Love me, as I love you, I suppose. Say you will try, at least. I think I could be content if you would say that you would at least try.'

'How can you try to love someone? Did you try to love me?' She was crying now, despite all her efforts to suppress it, and she thought he might be too, only her eyes were so blurred she could not see.

'No. You are saying, then, one loves, or one does not. And once again you make it very clear that you do not. I suppose you are right, and it is out of our control.'

She had known this interview would be difficult; she had not anticipated this. 'You won't marry me, then?' Was that what he was saying?

'Of course I will, I have said so. I must.'

'Then I don't understand.'

'I don't either. I had thought that nothing in this world could make me so happy as you agreeing to be my wife. I thought that if I could have you in my life and at my side, my God, with our dear child too, I would want for nothing else in this world. But I find it's not true.'

He took a deep, harsh breath and said, 'I'll marry you. I must obtain a licence in order to do so quickly, it will take a few days and a trip to London, but it may easily be arranged. And obviously it must be soon. But... but if you think you can never love me, if you are determined you will not, I'm not sure I can live with you afterwards.'

36

Leo hadn't meant to say it. He cursed himself a thousand times, but he couldn't get away from the essential truth of it. He was her servant and belonged to her utterly in a way that time could never break nor alter. He would obey her in everything, he'd have said he would, but it seemed, when he came to it, that he couldn't obey in this. He simply couldn't agree to live with her as man and wife if there was no possibility, not the tiniest glimmer of hope, that she might ever come to love him.

Even as he'd said it, he knew what he was giving up. Her, in his life, in his home, every day. In his bed. He knew the connection that burned between them well enough by now to be sure that bed would be part of it. A major part. She wasn't proposing a marriage of convenience, not in any conventional sense, and certainly not a marriage in name only. She'd give him her body. The bond between them was still alive, still powerful and electric and undiminished by their estrangement. He'd been aware of it, distressed as they both were, in that dusty, sad little room. A touch, a glance, and they'd have fallen on each other once again, though it would have solved precisely nothing. It was bitterly ironic that they no longer needed to be so careful, now that it was too late.

It didn't for so much as a moment occur to him to doubt her; she had no reason in the world to lie to him. She hadn't trapped him, far from it; she had trapped herself, to her evident horror. She wanted the baby, sure enough, that wasn't the problem – she just didn't want him along with it, not in the way he wanted her.

A child, her child, theirs. An everyday sort of miracle. More than that, after what she'd been told with such certainty by men who might have been supposed to know their business, but clearly did not. In other circumstances, it could have been some of the best news he had ever received, a moment he would remember for the rest of his life. He supposed that last part at least was still true. He wasn't likely to forget this dreadful day any time soon, when he had been offered a sort of twisted parody of everything he had ever dreamed of for himself.

But it wasn't enough. Not for him. He wished it were. It would be so much easier if he could accept it. He didn't enjoy doing this to himself. The prospect of marrying her then immediately separating, which was after all what he was proposing, was appalling to him. The idea of voluntarily denying himself the company of the woman he loved, of ensuring too that their innocent child grew up without him as a daily presence, was nothing less than horrible. Obscene, almost, and profoundly wrong. It wasn't that it would cause comment, even scandal – he didn't care about that, though he knew that others would, his mother included. But it would be pure misery. It was no way for anyone to live, married yet not. But spending every day at her side, holding her, kissing and touching her, without love, without any hope of love – that was a travesty too. He thought that for him that would be worse. Were those really his only choices? It appeared so.

He couldn't face her after this. He didn't want her to think he was deserting her, leaving her to confront this alone, because he would not do that – he had said he would marry her, and he meant to stand by that. This wasn't her fault, he wasn't blaming her – well, no, it was her fault, because she'd concocted this bizarre scheme, and this unwelcome outcome had always been a distinct possibility, whatever she had sincerely believed and convinced him to believe too. A man and a woman coupled; a woman conceived a child. There was hardly anything unusual about it. But he was an adult, and had agreed, so if there was blame to be apportioned it belonged to both of them. This must always be the case when two willing partners – and God knows they had both been that – made a child together. He'd marry her. But just now he didn't think he could stand to look at her. Because after all he still loved her, and it was unbearable.

He went to talk to Hal. He couldn't leave without telling him, although he couldn't face Cassandra or his mother, and after all, there was no great need for secrecy now. Everyone would know that they were marrying soon enough, and the haste with which they must do it was bound to result in speculation. He found Lord Irlam playing billiards with his brother, Matthew and Tom, but he didn't have to devise some ruse to take him aside, because one glimpse of his own face was enough to have Hal setting down his cue in haste and pulling him from the room to find some privacy.

His cousin had the sense to wait till they were alone to say, 'My God, Leo, what's the matter? Is there ill news – is it one of the boys? Georgie, her child? For pity's sake, tell me quickly!'

'No,' he hastened to say. 'Nothing like that. I'm sorry I made you think... No, it's this wretched business of mine. I can't be here, not now. I need to go up to London tomorrow, but I'll go home tonight. I have to.' He felt as though his tongue was swollen in his mouth, making it hard to speak, to form coherent sentences or even thoughts.

'What's happened now?' Hal asked with a certain measure of resignation.

'Lady Ashby...' It was ridiculous to call her that. 'Isabella... We quarrelled. I foolishly started to think, to hope, that she might care for me, and I declared myself to her, so stupid. But I was wrong. She doesn't love me, of course she doesn't.'

'I'm so sorry,' Hal said soberly. 'I really am, old fellow. I wish I could do something to help you.'

'Nobody can. But that's not all of it. She's with child, Hal. She just told me.'

His cousin swore, his face a picture of astonishment. 'Good God, man, I can't comprehend what you're telling me! You mean you... You mean she...?'

'I wanted to tell you, what we were doing and why, but I didn't want to betray her trust in me. It seems almost laughable now, and after all, there's no point explaining everything now. Yes, it's rather unfortunate in the circumstances,' he said with a bleak smile and considerable understatement. 'I'll marry her, of course. But I can't be with her just now. It's not that I'm angry – it's not her fault, or if it is it's as much mine too. But...' He broke off, fearing that he was perilously close to tears.

His cousin said rather grimly, 'I confess I didn't think she was the sort of woman to have a clandestine affair – nor you the sort of fellow, for that matter. But it's not the first time things have gone on under my nose and I ignorant as a schoolboy.'

'It wasn't like that, Hal. Please don't judge her when you don't know all. It made sense to her, my poor darling, what she was doing, and I could see it too, in a way. She's had a dreadful time of it, and I'd explain to you now if I could bear it. But I can't.'

Hal took him by the shoulders and shook him very gently. 'You really are in the devil of a fix. And even if I don't pretend to understand, I can help, actually. I can't do anything about your cursed situation, but I can go and fetch your licence for you.'

'There's no need…'

'I think there is. There's no doubt the clerks will see me quicker than they'd see you – privilege of rank, and we might as well take advantage of it. There'll be no trouble about getting the thing, you're both of age and it's all above board as far as they'll know. But to be frank with you, old fellow, looking at you, I'm not sure you're in a fit state to make it to London by yourself, and if you go to Doctors' Commons and present them with the face you're wearing at the moment, they'll smell some sort of rat and put you through stiff questions, which you don't seem to me to be in the right frame of mind to answer. Let me do this for you, Leo. It's the only thing in the world that I can do to aid you, and I want to.'

'Thank you,' he said gruffly. 'I shouldn't accept, but I will. Can you do something else for me? Spin some tale that will satisfy Cassandra and my mother and all the rest of them, something to do with a small emergency at Winter Manor, nothing too serious. Tell her, Isabella, that I'm going home to set things in motion, but that I'll be back as soon as everything has been arranged. I should tell my mother about my plans myself, but I can't face it, not just yet. When you get back, send for me, and I'll come. And we can tell everyone some damned romantic lie and be married.'

'You'll sort it out, you know. Cassandra and I did, Georgie and Gabriel did. We've had our bleak times, times when everything felt completely desperate. But we got through it.'

Leo was too bone-tired to argue. 'I hope you're right. I can't talk about it any more now. I'll pack, and go.' He made his way out of the room but turned in the doorway and said, 'Thank you. I can't tell you how much… But I do appreciate it, Hal.'

Hal waved a hand. 'No need for that. Be off with you. Take care. Drive my curricle, and Jem can bring it back.'

Leo threw his belongings into his bags all anyhow, and half an hour later he was tooling Hal's two-wheeler down the Castle's carriage drive with the imposing figure of Jem Oldcastle at his side. Jem was Hal's head groom and a great deal more than that, and besides was married to Cassandra's maid Kitty, who also happened to be Hal's old nurse. They'd known each other Leo's whole life, and at first he'd feared that Jem might make some comment on his sudden departure, or on his demeanour, which he was painfully aware was very far from normal, but his companion was blessedly silent for the whole of the short journey, letting him concentrate on handling the fresh pair of horses, and if he had any thoughts he kept them to himself on this occasion. 'Do you wish for me to bide here a while, Cap'n, or shall I take the greys straight back?' he asked when they reached Winter Manor and drew up outside the porch. 'His Lordship said I should take my orders from you.'

'Thank you, Jem, you can take them home. My cousin's going up to London tomorrow, so better you get back in good time in case he needs you.'

Jem made a noise that signified agreement, or at least understanding, and if it signified anything else besides Leo chose to ignore it. He jumped down, and Jem took his place. The elderly butler Lewis came out with the young footman Philip to take down Leo's bags, and a moment later the curricle was gone.

Perhaps there would be some comfort in being home, Leo thought as he made his way inside the panelled entrance hall, listening with half an ear to Lewis's talk of the doings of the house and estate. It didn't seem so at the moment, but perhaps being here with a little space and time to be alone and reflect would help. Although he'd have to tell everyone that he was soon to be married, and receive their congratulations, and that would be hard. But not yet, not today. His mother didn't know yet, and until she did he couldn't tell anyone else, it wouldn't be fair.

There were letters to deal with, waiting for him on his desk, though not many. Anything that looked urgent would have been sent on to the Castle. He'd been riding over here for a couple of hours every few days or so, though probably not as often as he should have in his obsession with Isabella, but it was winter now, and little was happening on the land. He didn't feel like reading business letters, or any kind of letters, but he wasn't sure what he did feel like doing. Nothing sensible. He sat in the comfortable room surrounded by his possessions and frowned at the lovingly detailed wooden model of his last ship, the frigate *Paris*, but he wasn't seeing it. He was imagining rushing back to her, and telling her he'd been foolish, and of course they'd live as man and wife, of course he'd take whatever she would give him. Even now he could do it. But it would be a mistake. He knew it would. He sighed, pulling the small pile of correspondence toward him and attempting to lose himself in it. At least here he could be miserable in peace.

37

Isabella didn't realise that Captain Winterton had left the Castle until dinnertime. He didn't appear at nuncheon, but that hardly surprised her. She was merely glad not to be obliged to face him over that meal, after the raw emotion of their interview. It had been bad enough before – it would be so much worse now. It wasn't as though she could blame him for his reaction, even though she hadn't expected it. She'd been selfish, she realised. Horribly selfish. She hadn't known he loved her until it was far too late – he'd lied to her about that, but she could understand why. He had been protecting himself, and she of all people could sympathise with the need for that. But there was no denying that her plan, which had seemed so clever and sophisticated when she first thought of it, had led inexorably to this catalogue of disasters.

They had no choice but to marry – well, he had a choice, he could repudiate her, turn his back and say that her child was nothing to do with him and she must deal with the consequences of her actions as she saw fit. She realised now the position she had so naively put herself in: not only had she no recourse to law to seek her unborn child's rights, unless she wished to see her reputation and that of her family torn to shreds and whispered over in every tavern in England and beyond; she had also laid herself open to blackmail for the rest of her life. But she knew Leo well enough to be sure that he'd never do anything of the kind. He was far too good, angry and hurt as he was. He'd marry her, whatever else happened.

He hadn't uttered one word of blame, either, and she could imagine many other men saying it was all her fault. That she'd been criminally irresponsible to believe on what seemed now like flimsy evidence that she was barren, and to convince him of it besides. (Her own father was a good man and a loving husband, but her mother still often found herself held responsible for things large and small that she'd been completely unaware of until that moment.) After all, it *was* her fault, all this – not the pregnancy, but the circumstances in which it had occurred. She had created them, with what she could not help but see now as breath-taking carelessness.

She was trying not to think about the life that lay ahead of her. She shouldn't object to it and wasn't sure why it filled her with unease, with a cold sort of dread. If she had shared her new secrets with Lady Carston – though she had not the least desire to do so – Isabella was sure that Jane would have congratulated her with ruthless practicality on how well things had worked out. She'd wanted sexual experiences for her own reasons – well, she'd got them. She'd wanted a child and thought it impossible – now she had the chance to be a mother, against all hope and against all the odds. How lucky her choice had been! The Captain would marry her, give her the protection of his name, and make no further demands on her. If the child in her belly proved to be a girl, and Captain Winterton wanted a son, as well he might, that too could be arranged in the fullness of time, if she agreed to it, and why would she not? She could imagine Lady Carston saying drily that the creation of this child appeared to have been at once distinctly agreeable and alarmingly easy for both parties – what could possibly prevent them from doing the same again? She'd made it very clear that she hadn't wanted a husband to replace Ash, a man to share every aspect of her life with – and if Leo could not bear to contemplate an ordinary sort of a marriage for excellent reasons of his own, well, why should she care? She could go back to Yorkshire, live with her parents as she had always intended, with the welcome addition of a child. A legitimate child, with a father and a secure future. There might be gossip about the absence of her husband, but Lady Carston – in exactly the same case herself – would tell her robustly to face it down. Many couples lived apart, for reasons that should be nobody's business but their own.

Why, then, was the idea not more attractive to her? She should be pleased, surely. Sorry she had hurt Leo, who did not deserve it, of course, but otherwise happy on her own account. There were no difficulties in her path now that she could not overcome. Why was she not soberly delighted? Because undeniably she wasn't.

Perhaps it was the shock – of the unexpected discovery of her condition, and of Leo's reaction to it. It must be that. Time would pass, the memory of Leo's pale, hurt face would fade, and she would gradually come to feel calmer, and look forward to the future with confidence and hope. She couldn't seem to feel either of those pleasant emotions at the moment, but surely they would come.

She spent the day doing nothing in particular in company with the other ladies, and if any of them were aware that there had been a further and more serious estrangement between Lady Ashby and the Captain – or if they so much as suspected anything at all about the earlier falling-out – they did not show the knowledge on their faces or betray it in their words or actions. Mrs Winterton was no less friendly to her than she had ever been, though perhaps a little subdued today. The hours passed slowly.

Lord Irlam drew Isabella aside before dinner, and said, 'I have something to tell you, ma'am.' She looked at him in sudden alarm, but did not speak, and he went on expressionlessly, 'My cousin Leo asked me to say that he has been obliged to return home this afternoon, but that all is in hand, and he will return in a day or so. There is no need to worry.' His face was a mask, and the message was cryptic, but surely he must know what it signified to say that everything was in hand. The pair were as close as brothers, she had realised, and in any case, the hurried wedding would be public knowledge soon enough, so there was no reason Leo should not have told his cousin. If he had, it was plain that he had not attempted to present the engagement as very cheerful news, a matter for celebration and congratulation, which argued, she thought, that he had simply revealed the stark truth about her unfortunate condition. The Earl did not reproach her for her conduct towards his cousin, but his manner could hardly be described as warm; she supposed it was no wonder. He must think she had treated Leo terribly, even that she had deliberately trapped him, which was so far from the truth – she could have no real idea precisely how much he knew, and certainly dared not ask. She murmured her thanks, and if she had thought to ask anything more so that she might understand him better, she had no opportunity, for he bowed punctiliously and moved away directly to engage his brother in conversation. Nothing occurred in the course of dinner or afterwards to enlighten her any further, and once again she slept badly.

When Isabella left her chamber late the next morning, she found the Castle strangely deserted of its other inhabitants. Although she would not have welcomed company in her present uncertain state of mind, it was all the same disconcerting to find everyone absent. If she had been a person who regularly gave way to wild imaginings, she might have thought that she was being shunned by her hosts and fellow guests; the idea crossed her mind, but she dismissed it as egregious folly. It must be pure coincidence, surely, that Lord Irlam had gone to London on business, his brother and friends were out shooting, Lady Carston was a little unwell – nothing serious, she was assured – and keeping to her chambers with Lady Louisa to tend to her, and Lady Irlam and Mrs Winterton had set out to visit an elderly dependant at the furthest limits of the estate. They couldn't *all* be avoiding her because they knew the truth and hated her. Impossible!

It was ridiculous to feel sorry for herself when she was perfectly comfortable; surrounded by luxury, in fact, with a well-stocked library at her disposal and well-trained servants to cater to her every whim. Isabella took up one of the novels that Lady Carston had recommended to her and which she'd missed because it had been published when she was unwell last Christmastime, and sat down to read it with determined attention. It would be a relief, if she could manage it, to lose herself in the doings of imaginary others for a little while. It was unlikely, she thought, that the dilemmas of fictional characters, however ingeniously devised by the very skilful lady author, could approach her own in intensity, or for that matter provoke her to dwelling any more than she was already on her own bizarre and unique situation. The book, if indeed she could concentrate on it, must offer an escape, which was just what she needed.

An hour or so passed, and Isabella, rather to her surprise, began to lose herself in the affairs of a wealthy young lady who was pleased to think herself a matchmaker with the right to meddle in the romantic lives of her acquaintance. She was so absorbed that when the door opened she started, and regarded the woman who entered the room with blank surprise for a moment.

It was not the housekeeper, Mrs Allen – she'd met her on her arrival – and it was not usual for female servants to wait on residents of such a house as this in the public rooms. A maid brought her breakfast to her chamber, but the downstairs portions of the Castle were the domain of the liveried footmen and the butler. This woman, who was tall, buxom and powerfully built, was a complete stranger to her, despite her respectable dress and air of assurance.

'I beg your pardon for disturbing you, my lady,' she said, curtseying correctly, 'but a message has arrived, and given the nature of it, I thought I'd better bring it to you myself rather than leave it to one of the footmen. I'm Lady Irlam's maid, ma'am, and was nurse to His Lordship and the other children once upon a time. I'm Kitty Oldcastle.'

This was all most odd, and Isabella felt a sudden pang of foreboding. She could hear that her voice was trembling when she said, 'I can't imagine what message could concern me... Is it bad news?'

'Yes, my lady, I'm sorry to say, from Winter Manor, and the groom was asked to seek you out most particularly, only he was a little bashful and found me instead, as was only natural, him being my own nephew. There's been an accident, seemingly, and I'm to ask you to come at once.'

38

'An accident? Involving Captain Winterton?'

'Yes, my lady. I'm not to let you think it's anything desperate, but apparently he's hurt and is asking for you in particular. I don't know any more than that. The groom's gone back in case he's needed there, to fetch a doctor and such, and Lady Irlam's carriage is being prepared for you now. I've sent for your pelisse and bonnet, as soon as I realised what was afoot, and all those footmen standing around like useless great lumps with no idea what to do. Will you go, my lady?'

She pressed her hands to her temples. 'He can speak, then? It's not...'

'I'm not sure exactly what's happened, my lady, though I don't believe he's at death's door, so don't you be thinking it. But he is asking for you and begs that you'll come, so he can't be all that badly hurt, can he? Will you go?' she asked again.

'Of course I will!' said Isabella, coming out of her trance with a start and jumping to her feet. 'Has his mother been sent for?'

'I believe so, but she's walked out through the park with Lady Irlam and nobody's sure exactly where they've got to, so it may take

a little while to find them, and then for them to get back once
they're found. I'm sure the carriage will be ready to take you now,
and your warm things brought down to wrap up in.'

Isabella allowed the woman to shepherd her out into the hall,
where a young maid was indeed waiting with her clothes. When
she came to put on her pelisse, she found that her hands were
shaking so much that she could not make them obey her, and Mrs
Oldcastle tutted in a motherly sort of way and buttoned it up for
her, and tied her bonnet ribbons securely besides. It was like being
at home just for a moment, with her mama. She thanked her for
her help with a tremulous smile and the woman said, 'I know it's a
shock, my lady, but you be strong and I'm sure all will be fine in the
end, you'll see.'

A moment later she was in the carriage, staring out of the
window as the wheels crunched out over the gravel drive. She'd
never been to Winter Manor and could not recall, if she had ever
known it, how far it was from the Castle – not too far, she hoped.
Her heart was racing and she felt light-headed, but Mrs Oldcastle
was right, she must be strong. He'd asked for her, he needed her,
and she was going to him. However much she had hurt him,
however angry he had been with her and still must be, he had
asked for her. She could only hope that didn't mean he was in a
truly desperate case, wanting to share some final communication
with her before... No, no, she couldn't think like that. She had too
much bitter experience of loss – she wouldn't give rein to her worst
fears and let herself imagine that Leo was going to be taken from
her just as Ash had been. Life couldn't be so unfair. Not again. It
couldn't.

Isabella closed her eyes and tried to still the fast, shallow
breathing that was making her dizzy, but an endless procession of
hideous scenes played themselves out across her mind – had he
fallen from his horse? Been shot by poachers somehow? – and she

opened them again, looking out with a sightless gaze at the bare trees and frosty, deserted fields as they rolled past. Could the coachman not go any faster?

Though in her agitation the journey seemed endless, it was in fact considerably less than an hour before the conveyance turned between two gateposts topped with pineapples and drew up outside a fine old house of soft pinkish brick with a white-stuccoed porch and two rows of regular sash windows. She had no eyes for any of its charms but was out of the carriage and at the door almost before the steps were let down. The Castle servant who had handed her down from the vehicle, or tried to, had to scramble to ply the doorknocker for her, and the elderly butler who answered his summons seemed a little taken aback to see them both. No doubt the shocking events of the morning had overset him. But when she asked breathlessly for Captain Winterton, unable to conceal her agitation, he merely bowed and opened a door for her, ushering her into a room off the hall and closing the door behind her.

She had expected, dreaded, a scene of frantic activity such as was all too familiar to her – a doctor, perhaps, hovering servants, disorder, distressing sights attendant on an accident, even blood. What she had not expected was to see Leo, to all appearances completely unharmed, though pale, sitting behind a desk and gazing at her in utter astonishment.

39

Isabella leaned back against the door, suddenly unsure if her legs would continue to support her. She had not the least idea what was going on, and nor, it seemed, did the Captain. He had risen instinctively to his feet upon seeing her, and said, 'Lady Ashby – Isabella! What are you doing here? I don't understand. Are you unwell?'

'There has been some inexplicable mistake,' she replied weakly. 'May I sit down?'

'Of course,' he said. His face was white and grim, but he was – she ran her eyes over his tall frame again to be sure of it – entirely unhurt. More than that, she realised as her wits returned with agonising slowness, he very plainly had not sent for her, nor had he expected her.

She sank into a chair that was set before his desk and said, 'I was told that you had been injured, that you had sent for me. I was told that there was a message...'

He looked at her, frowning. 'A message from me? I sent none. And as you can see, I am unharmed, there has been no accident or mishap of any kind. I don't understand this.'

'I assure you, nor do I.'

'Was it a written message you received?'

'No. I was told that one of your grooms had ridden over to the Castle in search of me, that you were hurt, but not so seriously that you were unable to ask for me. A carriage was put to and I came at once, in the gravest apprehension. But now I see that it was not true. I am so confused I can barely think straight.'

'You came alone?'

'Nobody else was present in the Castle. Lord Irlam has gone to London, Lady Irlam and your mother were out, Lady Carston is unwell and keeps to her chamber... It was Lady Irlam's abigail who gave me the message.'

'Kitty?'

'Yes, that was her name. A tall woman with curly brown hair. I'd never seen her before.'

'I think you have been tricked, Lady Ashby,' said the Captain slowly.

She put her hand to her forehead. 'That... How is that possible? Why would anyone do such a cruel thing?'

'I think it must have been Cassandra,' he said.

'Good God, for what purpose?'

His voice was dry and cold. 'When I left the Castle yesterday, I felt obliged to tell my cousin Hal of your condition. Of the... situation we find ourselves in. I could not abuse his hospitality by just departing in haste with no explanation, as I am sure you can appreciate. He knew I cared for you, of course – I'd told him that weeks ago, but until yesterday I had told him nothing more. When he knew all, he very kindly offered to go to London to obtain the licence on my behalf, and I accepted his offer. He must have told his wife at least part of it. And this is her response.' He saw her expression and said, 'I'm positive she didn't intend to be cruel – I expect she is matchmaking, trying to throw us together.'

'We are to be married as soon as it can be arranged. We have little choice in the matter, after all. If she knows that, which she surely does, why would she need to meddle further?'

'I expressed myself badly. I'm not sure there even is a word for what she is doing. I assume – no, I am sure – she knows that we are to be wed, but also is aware that things are not as they should be between us. Perhaps she thought if you believed me to be in danger, you might be brought to realise that you cared for me and would be sorry if you lost me. After all, she doesn't know you very well.'

That stung, as she supposed he meant it to. 'You mean it was all a deliberate deception? That everyone absented themselves on purpose, and by agreement, so that I was obliged to come alone? I can scarcely credit it!'

He shrugged. 'I cannot say if Lady Carston and my mother are privy to the scheme. Cassandra may have suggested an excursion without telling anyone the real reason behind it; that seems quite possible. I doubt she'd tell Bastian.' His smile was wintry, a little twisted. 'I am sorry you have been put to so much unnecessary trouble. But why did you come?'

She was astonished he could even ask. 'I was told you were in pain, I could not know how much, and asking for me. Of course I came!'

'You must have been in very great anxiety if you feared I had taken a mortal injury. You would be in such a terrible fix if I were to die before we can wed. You could have hoped, of course, that I might linger just long enough so that we could marry, then conveniently die; that would suit your purposes most admirably. I am almost sorry to disappoint you.'

She gazed at him without speaking, horribly wounded by his words. 'How can you say such foul things?' she whispered at last. 'I know I have hurt you, and I am truly sorry, but I do not think I deserve this. I am plainly unwelcome here, and I will go.' She rose, and made her way to the door, though sudden tears were almost blinding her, but when she reached it she turned and said fiercely, 'I wish with all my heart I did not have to marry you. You have said you love me, but anyone would be forgiven, if they heard you speak today, for thinking that you hate me. I wish I had the courage to refuse your understandably reluctant offer, believe me. But for the sake of our innocent child, I know I must not, despite my own feelings.'

He crossed the room to her side in a few long strides and took her by the shoulders, saying raggedly, 'I'm sorry too. Isabella, I am. I didn't mean it, not really. I knew it was a terrible thing to say even as the words were leaving my lips. But when I saw you here so unexpectedly, just for a moment I thought you'd come to tell me you'd realised you did feel something for me after all. And the disappointment made me an unconscionable brute. I gave in to that cruel impulse when I should not have done. But I could never hate you. Please don't think I do.'

She was still weeping hard, and looked up at him, silent save for the hiccupping sobs she was entirely unable to control. He uttered a muffled curse and took her in his arms, and she did not resist him, laying her head on his broad chest and bawling into his coat without restraint. He held her close and stroked her hair, murmuring inarticulate endearments. When she raised her head at last, she knew she must be a sorry spectacle indeed, but he did not remind her of it, but rather took his handkerchief and wiped away her tears with a tenderness that set fresh droplets spilling from her eyes again. 'I don't think I deserve to kiss you after my unforgive-able behaviour,' he said, 'but I would like to.'

'I don't know why you want to, Bear,' she sniffed, 'when I have treated you so badly.'

'If that is so, I redressed the balance a little just now, did I not?' he said. He was still holding her close and neither of them made any move to pull away. 'I'm so sorry. It seems we have the power to hurt each other very gravely, even without the well-meaning interference of others.'

She was still shaken, still not far from tears, and she found she was tired of talking. Talking just made things worse. It seemed a long time since she had been in his arms, and despite everything that had passed between them she was aware of the flare of dangerous excitement that always kindled whenever he touched her. She took his face between her hands and said, 'Do you still want to kiss me?' Perhaps he already regretted saying such a thing.

It seemed he did. He pushed his hand through his blond hair, disordering it, and answered sadly, 'My dear, I do, God knows I always do, but I beg you will put it down to a moment of weakness. I should not have said it, and I am sure it is best if we do no such thing. Kisses, with us, so often lead to caresses, and to love-making, do they not? And I am not yet grown so desperate for a pale shadow of the love I crave that I can contemplate such a thing.'

His words chilled her to the bone. 'You have been happy enough in the past to take what I offered you, without love. Are you really saying that you will marry me, but never touch me again?'

'I was deceiving myself before. It is perfectly true that you never promised to love me – you have always been honest, you said explicitly that it could never be. But I had hope, false hope, and now I have none. Don't think I blame you, Isabella, but do me the courtesy of admitting that you can see it is not the same, now that I know the painful truth.'

There was no answer she could make to that. She could see. And since she had repeatedly told him, told herself, told others even that she did not, could not, would not love him, she didn't know why his words, his coldness and his weary resignation, should hurt her so very deeply. The future that stretched before them was so bleak. But they neither of them had any choice, as he had said, and so she took refuge from dangerous emotion in practicalities.

'I should go back to the Castle,' she said, making him no direct answer, leaving his words hanging between them. 'It is most improper, that we should be alone together like this.' Even as she said it, she knew it was ridiculous, and she could not blame him when he reacted to her statement with a wintry smile.

'Will you come back with me?' she said when he did not speak.

'Do you want me to, Isabella?'

'Yes,' she said. 'I know it is hard for you – please believe me when I say that I do understand that – but I think we should go back directly and tell everyone that we are to be married. Lady Irlam knows already, plainly, and it is unfair, I think, to leave your mother in ignorance when others know. If she should hear by some mischance, she will be distressed and puzzled, and rightly so.'

'That's true, and I must tell her first, in private, before we announce it to others.'

'Of course you must.'

He did not question her further; perhaps he too thought they had reached some sort of unspoken truce, in which they dared not say more in case they wounded each other horribly again, or perhaps he was simply dazed by all that had happened, by the raw intensity of their encounter and the unwelcome truths that had been spoken. He sighed and said, 'You're right, we should go. I need to pack some clothes, if I am to return with you. Will you wait here for me? I won't be long.'

She let him go, and went across to an old, tarnished mirror that hung in one dark corner of the room, standing on tiptoe to tidy herself as best she might so that she could face the servants after her bout of weeping. It did not take long at all until she looked sufficiently respectable again, at least if she were not inspected too closely, though of course she was not, with his child inside her and her mind and heart in turmoil. She now appeared much less agitated, in fact, than she had been when she had arrived here, believing Leo to be hurt, perhaps very seriously. She hadn't been at Winter Manor very long – it seemed incredible. She was desperate for some solitude, and for the space to think, but she knew that he'd be back soon and there was the journey, alone together in a parody of intimacy, to be endured.

He returned in a few moments, looking immaculate, though perhaps a little weary. She was weary too, and in a sad state of confusion. Once again she resolved to speak of practical matters, as if walking on very thin ice above a yawning chasm. She thought he must feel much the same, for he made a greater business than he need of telling her that he had ordered the Pendlebury carriage to be brought up. When he had finished, she hurried into awkward speech. 'Leo, I do not know how I am to face Lady Irlam, after she played such a trick upon me – upon us. Will she not expect me to mention it? Or is it better I do not?'

'I was thinking about the matter while I changed,' he replied in the same spirit. 'It is undeniably a little awkward. I believe in the end you will be obliged to speak to her of it, but perhaps not today. We will have enough to do if we are to announce our betrothal, and perhaps it will do her no harm to wonder a little whether we mean to allude to her actions or not, and if so what we intend to say. And if you are angry – which would be understandable – it must certainly be better not to speak to her in the heat of it. You might say something you would later regret. Matters are difficult enough without that, it seems to me.'

Was she angry? She certainly had been when he had told her what he believed had happened, and she had acknowledged the truth of it – for if Lady Irlam's maid had deliberately lied to her, which undoubtedly she had, who else could have set her to do it but Cassandra herself? It did not seem to Isabella to be the sort of scheme a man would invent, and so she tended to absolve Lord Irlam from involvement; it was quite possible, since he had left for London early that morning, that he knew nothing at all about it. 'I might,' she said. 'I am not angry now, I don't think, but I can imagine I might become so again if we spoke of it. You're right – let her worry over it for a time. It will do her no harm.' The way they had both been deceived seemed almost unimportant now.

The butler came in then to tell his master that the carriage was at the door, and they departed in it. If any of the servants – Leo's, or the Pendlebury coachman and footman – thought it somewhat odd that a lady should arrive alone in extreme distress, and then go straight back to the Castle a short while later, accompanied now by Captain Winterton, who had only returned home himself less than a day ago, they did not betray any sign of it. They must, she supposed, imagine that they were witnessing the rumblings of a lovers' quarrel and reconciliation, and their subsequent marriage would serve to confirm this assumption. When her condition began to show, rather sooner after the wedding than it should, they might perhaps put two and two together and conclude that they held the key to the situation, and in a sense they would be right – but there was nothing she could do to prevent that, and just now she had far more pressing concerns to occupy her mind.

40

They agreed during the carriage ride that they would separate immediately on arrival at the Castle, and Leo would seek out his mother and tell her his news – he would not, he reassured his betrothed, divulge the secret of her delicate condition yet, though it seemed likely that when at last they did reveal it to Mrs Winterton they would also have to admit that they had anticipated their wedding vows by a few weeks. Let Isabella and his mother come to know each other a little better before that revelation was made, he said, and she could see the sense of it. A mother's natural partiality for her son might lead Mrs Winterton to blame *her* completely for the illicit relations that she had engaged in with Leo, and since she had in fact been the initiator of them, she could hardly say that this was unfair. It could scarcely be considered ideal that a mother-in-law's first impression of her only son's bride should be that she was some sort of unprincipled, promiscuous hussy. Isabella did not feel that she was any such thing, but again, it was not a conversation she cared to have at this point in her life and with this particular woman.

When they reached their destination, an apparently casual

enquiry by Leo to the butler confirmed that Lady Irlam and his mother had returned from their expedition and that his mother might be found alone in her sitting room; they exchanged significant glances, and Isabella went off to change. She would stay in her room, she decided, until Leo sought her out, since she certainly had no desire to encounter her hostess just now.

She summoned her maid, grateful as often before for her entirely incurious way of going about her duties, and changed her gown, then sat by the window, gazing out at the wintry landscape, where the lake showed grey as gunmetal under lowering skies, and the little temple folly stood out stark white against it. Now that she was alone, her mental and emotional turmoil could no longer be repressed, and she let the realisation wash over her.

She was in love with Leo.

After all her resolutions to be faithful to Ash in her own peculiar fashion for the rest of her life, after all her elaborate planning, she had fallen in love with the man she had taken to her bed. She had betrayed her dead husband at the first opportunity – not with her body, but with her heart. Was she really so weak that, despite all her vows to be unconventional and daring, she could not give her physical being to a man without persuading herself that she loved him? In her current confusion she could not say, but whether that was the cause of it or not scarcely mattered now: she felt what she felt. She loved him.

It had never for a second crossed her mind that she had the capacity to love again, and if anyone had suggested it to her she would have scorned the idea – had done so, with vehement tears, when Blanche mentioned it. And yet she loved him. Had loved him for some time, she now realised, and only today allowed herself to admit it. She'd been in love with Leo when he had declared his love for her, days ago, and she had been in love with him when he'd spurned her, here in the Castle – was it only yesterday?

It was true that nobody now alive would care that she had broken all her private vows of lifelong fidelity. There was no one to reproach her for it, not even in the slightest; she had Blanche's firm assurance, given of her own volition just a few weeks back, that she and Gabriel would be delighted if their sister-in-law found love again. Her own parents would be happy and relieved, even before they knew that they would have a grandchild after all. No, her distress was nothing at all to do with others; it was an intensely personal thing that she was now grappling with.

Isabella was deeply shaken. The need to come to terms with this revelation in her own mind was only one reason she hadn't said a word to Leo. There was another.

She was afraid he wouldn't believe her.

She had been so very adamant that she could never love again, and had so decisively rejected him when he had declared his love, that she was sure he'd struggle to accept this sudden change. Anybody would. Only yesterday he had almost begged her to concede that she would at least try to love him. And once again she had refused to budge, had not been able to move towards him even that much. If she now told him so unexpectedly that she loved him, had loved him for weeks, whyever should he credit it? Would he not think instead that she was lying, telling him what she knew he so desperately wanted to hear because she was frightened that he would abandon her and their child after they had married? Could he ever trust her, whatever she said, or must a doubt always linger in his mind, subtly poisoning their relations for years to come, possibly for their whole lives together?

How could she say it and make him believe it? She had not the least idea. It might, in fact, be impossible.

She wasn't sure she should say it. Not now, at any rate. They seemed to have reached some sort of temporary place of calm today, even though nothing had truly been resolved between them, after the trickery they had both been subjected to and the harsh words they had said to each other. Would it not perhaps be safer to bide her time, to tell him nothing until a little later? That seemed like cowardice, probably it was, but was it not perhaps also wisdom? Both things could be true. She could not tell, could no longer trust her own judgement where he was concerned. She was in utter turmoil.

Dear Mama, I'm in love, and what is more... She couldn't. She'd never so much as mentioned his name in any of her previous letters. She couldn't do it. She'd have to tell her something soon, but not today.

A short while later a maid came tapping at her door, sent by Leo with a message asking her to join him in his mother's private sitting room; she must presume he had shared the news with her and felt it was now time to receive her congratulations – whether genuine or feigned – and afterwards speak to everyone else. There was no point in waiting for Lord Irlam's return, as he would not be back until tomorrow or the next day, and then the wedding must be arranged with all possible haste.

She squared her shoulders and went downstairs.

41

Leo knew that Isabella was entirely right: his mother must be told without loss of time. But he didn't anticipate the interview with any pleasure, rather with something approaching dread. He knew his mama would assume that all was well between them now, despite his earlier unhappiness: that Isabella had come to care for him and told him so. This wasn't true, the truth was much more complicated, and he didn't want to share any part of it, but nor did he want to lie. If there was an obvious way through this thicket of half-truths, he couldn't imagine what it might be. He thought it best to say, with all the conviction he could muster, that he had persuaded Lady Ashby to accept his suit, but that she still had qualms about betraying her dead husband, as she had never previously thought of marrying again. It was a delicate matter, he would explain, and excessive celebration would be in poor taste while his bride's mind was still a little uneasy. He only hoped that his mother might not think to respond, *In that case, why not have a long engagement, to give her chance to accustom herself fully to the idea? There is no need for haste, surely?* He could have no answer to that, without revealing the guilty secret that he had promised to keep hidden for a while longer.

As he'd feared, it wasn't an easy conversation, on Leo's part at least. His mother was surprised to see him return to the Castle so quickly, and he was obliged to be vague about the so-called problem at home that he had left to tend to, until he realised that he could pretend to confess that it had all been a hum. Layers upon layers of disingenuity. He said, 'There was no emergency at the Manor, Mama – I asked Hal to say there was because I wanted to leave; I was finding it hard to be in Isabella's company when I thought she could never care for me. But she has relented – she came to see me, to say that she would marry me after all.' Of course – all this deception was making his head spin – he had no idea if Cassandra had revealed the nature of her stratagem to his mother, but he was gambling that she hadn't, that she would have been a little ashamed of it and thus kept it secret. To tell a loving mother that one had lied and said that her son was seriously injured, had involved a trusted family servant in the ruse – no, he did not believe Lady Irlam would admit such a thing unless she was obliged to do so.

It seemed he was right. His mama showed not the least sign of suspecting that Isabella's impetuous journey to Winter Manor had been motivated by anything other than a natural desire to speak to Leo and open her mind to him. She embraced him, and shed tears at his news – generous, happy tears. If she had doubts or fears, she wisely kept them to herself.

When he told her that Isabella was still somewhat unsure and prey to conflicting emotions, she was warmly sympathetic and understanding, which for some obscure reason made him feel terrible, as though he were taking advantage of her goodness. He hastily attempted to squash her suggestion that she speak to Isabella about the matter and attempt to allay her concerns. 'I think,' he said in sudden inspiration, 'that we must marry as soon as we can arrange it so that we can afterwards travel up to Yorkshire to tell her parents of our news. It is not fair that they should learn such a thing from a letter, when they have not the least idea, even, that Isabella has a suitor, much less that things have progressed so far between us. I do not believe that anyone in the world can help to set her mind at rest in such a circumstance other than her own mother.'

Mrs Winterton could only agree to this, as she could well imagine that Isabella was possessed by a desire to share her news with her parents, just as Leo had been. 'I only wish your dear father were here to share this happy news!' she said tearfully. This didn't make him feel any better, but he endured it. He called for a servant, and in a little while Isabella came into the room, looking pale and rather shy, and he was obliged to watch his mother embrace her fondly and wish her very happy. Obviously he would not have wanted her to do anything else, but it was still awkward, and he cut the private meeting short as soon as he decently could, saying that they should find the rest of the party and share their news with them too.

Isabella said all that was proper and sensible in response to his mother's congratulations, and if she was a little quiet in her replies, why, that was understandable. She must, surely, be thinking of another such occasion, only two or three years since – Leo was sure she was. Anyone possessed of a respectable level of sensibility must realise that such an event could never be one of unalloyed joy for her; he hoped that everyone would take account of this fact and assign his betrothed's rather subdued manner to it, rather than to any lack of enthusiasm for the match. He knew better, of course, but others need not suspect anything of the sort.

They found Cassandra with Lady Carston and Lady Louisa, taking tea before a roaring fire – Bastian, Matthew and Tom Wainfleet were known to be in the gun room, and so were sent for, and their prompt arrival dissipated the awkward little silence that had developed. Leo sat beside Isabella on one of the sofas, and took her hand in his before he addressed the assembled company. 'I have told my mother, and now I must tell you all, that Lady Ashby has done me the great honour of agreeing to be my wife. I hope you will congratulate us. It is to be a very quiet ceremony, and as soon as we can arrange it.' He hoped that this sober way of stating the news, and his restrained manner as he said it, would give everyone the hint that excessive exclamations of delight would not be welcome or appropriate. Most of all he hoped that the customary sly little allusions to how one or the other of those present had known the match was in the wind all along would not be forthcoming.

Lady Carston was the first to react. 'I do indeed congratulate you,' she said, calmly smiling. 'I am very happy for you both.' Lady Louisa murmured polite agreement, and Cassandra chimed in too, adding her felicitations in a friendly way that betrayed no consciousness of anything more, and for which Leo was grateful, and thought Isabella must be too.

Bastian said, 'I am very happy for you, old fellow, and sorry Hal is not here to congratulate you too. Or does he already know?'

Leo had not expected this, and his face betrayed the answer to one who knew him as well as his cousin did. 'Oh!' said Bastian. 'Has he gone to obtain a licence? That seems to me to be just the sort of thing Hal would do for you, now that I think of it.'

The Captain hardly knew what to say – if he admitted the truth of Bastian's supposition, his mother at least would surely wonder how Hal had known that such a thing was needed, several hours before Isabella had, as far as she knew, changed her mind and given her consent. But Cassandra, whether by design or accident, jumped in and diverted the conversation, asking about their plans after the wedding, and he hoped that the moment had passed. If his mother charged him with the discrepancy, he wished that it would be in private, and that he would think of some nonsense to divert her – perhaps that he had half-expected, half-hoped that Isabella was about to relent, and had confided as much in Hal, who had made his very generous offer, so that the lovers need not be parted by the necessity of Leo going to London for the licence. This didn't really make sense when examined properly – Hal was known to be both impetuous and very fond of his cousin, but even he, surely, would hesitate to undertake a long journey in an inhospitable season to procure an expensive item that might not, in fact, really be needed. Leo mopped his brow surreptitiously and wished all this could soon be over.

The party separated in order to dress for dinner, to Leo's enormous relief, and, no doubt, Isabella's too. Apart from the nasty moment with Bastian, nobody had said anything that was at all contentious, and though he supposed that dinner that evening would become a sort of celebration, he was now hopeful that it would pass off without incident. He anticipated too that there would be more difficult moments ahead – but he had not the energy to contemplate them just now. He was aware that he was using all this superficial noise to avoid contemplating his own deeper feelings, but he was resigned to have it so. What was the use of doing otherwise? He was not sure if Isabella realised that he still held fast to his resolve to marry her then immediately leave her; he had wanted to remind her of it a dozen times, in his study and then again during the awkward carriage ride, but he had not quite had the heart to do it in the aftermath of the distress he had already caused her. The fact that it was true and, as far as he could see, unavoidable, did not make it any the less cruel. He would take her to her parents, and endure another round of painful and unwarranted congratulations, and then he would leave her there and come home. He didn't want to do it, he dreaded doing it, but if he stayed with her, slept in the same bed with her, he knew he'd weaken, and for the sake of his own sanity he must not.

He'd come and see his child when he or she was born, would acknowledge the poor unfortunate creature and claim it for all the world to see, but then he'd go away again. There was no other choice for him. He'd meet them occasionally by cold arrangement as the lonely years passed, he supposed – the child whose daily presence was denied to him and the wife he loved to distraction but could not have. He could see already that it would be like living the rest of his life with an open wound. He expected that the situation he now only dimly imagined would be even worse in reality. The prospect of such fresh pain in the future on top of all the pain he was experiencing now was horrible to contemplate, but that was the situation they had made together. Why dwell on it now?

42

———————

They were permitted to be alone now – there was an irony in this that they both must be aware of. Leo drew his betrothed aside after dinner, and everyone pretended not to notice. He took her into the empty breakfast room and said, 'I must tell you something that has occurred to me. I was afraid my mother would wonder why we are so anxious to marry quickly; to allay her suspicions I found myself spinning her some tale, but as I uttered the words I realised that they were true. As soon as we are wed, we must go to Yorkshire, to tell your parents in person. Do you not think I am right?'

As she looked at him he could see that his words had struck home. 'Why... yes. Of course you are. I have been in such a daze... I knew I should write to them, but I did not know where to begin and so have not yet done so. They would think my letter so extraordinary, coming as such a surprise, and perhaps even be hurt by it, believing that I have been concealing things from them, as of course I have. It must be much better to go in person so that we can speak properly and any misunderstandings may be smoothed out, as they could not be by letter. My mother will cry, and I will apologise, and after a while, we may be comfortable again. And I must always have returned home by Christmas; they will expect me, as I have not told them otherwise. It will take days, you know, though, to get to Harrogate.'

'I do know, and that is why we must be married before we go. I am only sorry that you will find the journey extremely tiring at this season – I hope it may not do your health any lasting damage. We must make sure it does not. We will take it in easy stages, of course, so that you may rest as much as possible.'

Isabella blushed at this oblique reference to her condition but did not attempt to deny that the journey would not be an easy one. So that at least was agreed. They fell next to discussing what needed to be done before the ceremony – the rector of the local church must be approached and warned of what would soon be required of him, and Leo would have to go into Southampton or perhaps Portsmouth to acquire a ring; his servants would have to be told, too. They could not assume that Hal would return tomorrow, though he might, and so as things stood the wedding could not be any earlier than three days from now, and they must decide whether they would leave for Yorkshire directly once the ceremony was over, or spend a day or two at the Manor first. 'I think we should make an early start the next day,' Leo said. 'That way we can reach London that night, and put up at an hotel. The longer we delay at this season of the year, the worse the weather is likely to be.' *And the longer we delay, the harder it will be for me to leave you*, he thought but did not say.

'You're right,' Isabella agreed. 'And perhaps I can write a brief note to my parents, saying that I am coming home – Lord Irlam will frank it, I am sure, and it will go by the Mail and reach them before we do. That way my arrival will not be a complete surprise to them.'

'Are you worried that they will disapprove?' he asked abruptly. This was an added complication to go along with all the rest.

'No,' she said. 'No, I am sure they won't. But the more I reflect on it, the more I realise that they will be distressed and confused that I have told them nothing, not even referred to you in my letters, and so I confess that I am a little nervous at the prospect of telling them and seeing their immediate reaction. But I am sure it will all be resolved quickly enough when we are able to talk to them.'

Leo could indeed understand why Isabella's parents might feel all the emotions she had described and more. He was experiencing many of them himself. He realised – of course he did – why Lady Ashby, excessively anxious to conceal the existence of her list and everything to do with it, would with elaborate caution not so much have mentioned in her missives home the name of a certain captain who happened also to be a guest at Castle Irlam. In his experience of mothers, one did not, once one had reached the age of common sense, casually drop the name of an eligible member of the opposite sex into conversation without expecting to be taken up on it sharply and immediately. He would be willing to wager that Isabella had described, at least briefly, her other fellow guests, including Bastian, Matthew, and even poor Tom Wainfleet. There was such a thing as safety in numbers, and distraction. If her mother had responded with seemingly casual questions as to the appearance, disposition, age, income, family and situation of any or all of these young men, as she would have done if she was any sort of parent worthy of the name, Isabella could reply in a natural manner that made it perfectly clear that, just as she was not the slightest bit interested in any of them, they were not the least interested in her. Mentioning *him*, though, would have required a response at once less truthful and less easy to craft. He could see that quite clearly. That didn't mean it hurt any the less, apparently.

A charged little silence fell – they seemed to be a feature of this very long day. He said, 'I am sure you must be tired, and it will be a busy time ahead. Do you not think you should rest?'

'I believe I will,' she said. 'I certainly don't want to go back to sit with Lady Irlam and the others, and be an object of curiosity, even if it is well-meant.'

He wanted to take her in his arms and hold her, give her comfort, though he did not, that being closed off to him and likely only to make things worse for both of them. He loved her, and that meant he could see past his own hurt to feel hers. Even if she had loved him, which she did not, even if she were in this moment the happiest woman in England, which she was not, this time must be difficult for her; must throw up memories that made her uncomfortable, more than uncomfortable. The fact that she had been betrothed before, married before, and had lost her love in tragic circumstances, far too soon, must always be present in her mind. He took her hand, and pressed it, the only contact he would allow himself, saying, 'You will not have so very long to endure their unwanted attention. Just a few days, and then we will be gone.'

She said resolutely, surprising him, 'Yes. And after you have taken me to Harrogate, I assume you intend to leave me there, and come away. I cannot think you would be comfortable staying with me for long, or bringing me back to your home. Not after all you have said.'

She was still braver than he was. 'I am sorry, Isabella. I can see no other course of action open to me.'

'Naturally you cannot,' she said, and left him. He stood looking after her for a moment, then shook himself, and returned reluctantly to the company, to make Lady Ashby's excuses for going up to bed without saying goodnight.

43

Lord Irlam arrived home late the following evening, and although he did not emerge from his bedchamber until noon on the day after, he sent the licence he had obtained at such trouble to himself to his cousin immediately upon his arrival.

Isabella knew nothing of this – the first she heard of her host's return and his success in laying hands on the necessary licence was late the following morning, when the Captain found her alone, pacing slowly along the Castle's gallery of paintings, looking at them but not seeing them. She had not suddenly developed a passionate interest in art or in Lord Irlam's ancestors, handsome though most of them were; she was avoiding her fellow guests, and Cassandra in particular. She knew eventually that she would have to have a conversation with her hostess about her trickery, but she was unable to face it just now. There was simply no space in her head to think of what she might say. She felt the desire to blurt out her feelings to Leo growing so strong within her that it drove almost all other considerations from her mind, and made her very poor company indeed. It occupied and obsessed her thoughts. But at the same time, she still hesitated. After all the upsets of the last few days, she did not think she could endure it if he refused to believe her when she declared her love. They were to be married tomorrow, and surely it must be best to wait till after then to speak. How could she stand in front of the altar with him and speak those loaded words again if some fresh estrangement, some new rejection, should arise in the meantime? It would be too painful, and yet because of her circumstances, she would be obliged to go through with the wedding, whatever happened. As would he.

They agreed to hold the brief ceremony in the Pendleburys' private chapel in the late morning, then celebrate, for want of a better word, over a nuncheon at the Castle, after which they would leave together for Winter Manor for a night's stay. It was, as matters stood presently, a painful farce – a pretence at normality and joy when the reality was far different. They would be alone there throughout the afternoon and evening, and what needed to be said could be said then, in privacy. Isabella feared that come tomorrow she would find another weak reason to put it off – she dreaded so much to see disbelief, even disgust, written on his face – but she knew all the while that it was vital she was completely honest with Leo before they reached Harrogate, before he left her there, before a breach was opened up that might never be healed. It might already be too late; she might not be able to convince him that her feelings were genuine. But good God, she had to try.

The hours seemed to rush by, as they had not last time she was married. 'Last time she was married', a phrase she had never thought to say. Then, she had been nineteen and in a fever of impatience for the day to arrive, and the wait had felt long, though it had only been a few weeks. Now it was a much briefer time, and she wished it longer, or would, were it not for the secret of her condition. There was no time to order a special gown to wear, and she was glad of it. She would make do with one of her new day dresses. To be tricking herself out in finery like a virgin bride would be inappropriate. Last time she had worn... But no. She wouldn't even let it cross her mind. If she could get through tomorrow without thinking of that day in Harrogate, and Ash smiling down at her in his regimentals, loving her and confident she loved him, she would count it a small victory.

If she had been brave enough to tell Leo how she felt before, she'd be less apprehensive. She wished she'd done it, now. But it was too late. It would have to be afterwards.

She asked Lady Carston to be her supporter; she felt she needed one, and was not inclined to ask Cassandra. All too soon the next morning was upon her and she found herself waiting in her bedchamber, alone with Jane for a brief moment. 'Are you sure you really want to do this?' that lady said, regarding her with an uncomfortably penetrating gaze. 'This is not the time for confidences, but I can see you have been suffering, you are white as a sheet, and if you decide at the last moment you do not want to take this grave step, for whatever reason, I will stand your friend, you know, and help you if I can.'

'Thank you, you are very kind. But I am resolved to do it.'

'That wasn't exactly what I asked!'

'I know it wasn't. Well, the plain truth is, I have no choice. I must do this, and soon.'

'Oh dear,' said Lady Carston involuntarily, her expression one of sudden comprehension and almost comic dismay.

It seemed a long while since Isabella had laughed, but she could not repress a chuckle at that. 'Quite,' she said drily. 'But I want to, as well. Truly I do. It is just... a little complicated. But I have hopes that everything will resolve itself. I only need the courage to speak.'

'Good gracious, you mean he doesn't know?' hissed her companion. The door was opening; it was a maid, for they were being summoned.

She only had time to whisper, 'Oh, he knows *that!*' before they were proceeding together down the stairs, to where Lord Irlam, who was to give her away – there was after all nobody else suitable to do it at this most rushed of ceremonies – was waiting.

Just as they reached him, Jane said quietly, 'You don't lack courage. Never think that. You are brave enough for anything. And all will be well, I'm sure.' She was touched by her words and blinked away a sudden tear as she took Lord Irlam's arm and pasted on a smile. It was time.

44

The interior of the chapel at Castle Irlam was an extraordinary confection of chilly white marble and pale-yellow plaster, so cold on this frosty day on the cusp of winter that the small congregation could see their breath as they stood waiting between walls lined with monuments to generations of deceased Pendleburys.

The grandest tomb was that of Hal's grandfather – the Earl who'd gone on the Grand Tour at an impressionable age and never recovered from it. If there were any classical statues and putti left in Italy, it must be because he'd missed them inadvertently. His effigy lay garbed in flowing sculpted draperies, a stout Roman senator with attendant deities and nymphs, dominating one whole wall of the building. There hadn't been much room left for his son and daughter-in-law, and by contrast, their memorial was restrained, simple and affecting; presumably, Hal had chosen it himself, just one among a thousand tasks when he was dealing with the sudden heavy responsibilities that had come crashing down on him. Leo had been at sea then, ignorant of it all until later, and thus unable to help. As he had told Isabella once, the late Earl had been the closest thing to a father he'd known in his life, and despite everything he was glad to be married with him present in some sense. They were now a family made up entirely of women, young men and boys, Leo mused, and wondered if the various scrapes they had embroiled themselves in over the last few years – Leo himself, Hal, Georgie, Fred and the twins – would have played out differently if any of them had a father figure to advise them. There was no way of knowing; perhaps it would have made not the least difference. He'd be a father himself soon enough, and in theory at least head of a family, with all the responsibilities that brought and none of the compensations – it was a sobering thought. If he had any idea at all how to go about the business, and he hoped he did, he'd learned it from the late Earl.

Captain Leo Winterton stood waiting with Bastian at his side, surrounded by his family, as Isabella walked down the short aisle towards him. She had chosen for her wedding the dark green gown with the slashed sleeves – the one she'd been wearing the afternoon she'd revealed her scheme to him. She was wearing a spencer over it, but still he recognised it. That had been a day he would surely never be able to forget if he lived to be ninety. He didn't know if the choice was deliberate on her part, maybe it hadn't been, but he supposed that many of her gowns must carry associations for him now. And for her.

She'd left off the widow's cap today, of course, and she wore no bonnet, only a long veil of antique lace pinned to her bare head. She had dark green ribbons woven through her hair in an elaborate crown of plaits, but a few casual-seeming wispy honey-blonde tresses had been curled and left to fall either side of her face. She was pale, but she looked beautiful to him, as always. She did smile at him when she reached him, a little smile that seemed almost shy, if such a thing were possible after all that had passed between them. He did not smile back, but he took her hand.

It didn't take very long to be married, it seemed. Some of the words of the prayer book ceremony must hit home, and Leo was careful not to meet Isabella's eyes at several points, or Hal's, for that matter, given all his cousin knew. Leo didn't feel in the least like laughing just now, but he was afraid Hal might. 'Carnal lusts and appetites', that was a tricky moment, as was 'the procreation of children', and for that matter 'the gift of continence'. It was a little late for that.

Nobody declared an impediment. There was none. Isabella's dead husband did not appear, blood-boltered, dreadful, like Banquo's ghost, to halt the ceremony and claim her once again as irrevocably his. Leo realised now that he'd not thought about him much before, the late Lord Ashby, but then, they'd hardly ever discussed him – just once or twice, and then very briefly. He'd seen him, but never spoken to him, and had no idea what manner of man he'd been, except that he'd been greatly loved, and he supposed it didn't matter now, except to Isabella. God knows it still mattered a great deal to her.

She was very pale – paler now than she'd been when she first entered the chapel, he thought. He began to worry that she might swoon, faint into his arms, which would hardly be a good omen at one's wedding, but she did not, and in a little while they both pronounced the words that bound them together for life, or would have done if they had not already been tied by an older bond than that of the church. He kissed her at the end of it, and though her lips were cold, as was her white little face, it seemed to him that she clung to him for a second, and only moved away from him reluctantly to accept the congratulations of Hal, Lady Carston, Cassandra and all the rest. She was not enjoying this day, but enduring it, as was he.

She took his arm, and they walked out into the courtyard, surrounded by their guests and most of the Castle servants, and made their way across the cobbles back into the main house, where they would take wine in the great hall before the roaring fire, warming their chilled bones while the final preparations for their wedding breakfast were made.

Hal drew him aside. 'Congratulations, Leo,' he said. 'I wish you very happy. Sure you will be in the end, old fellow.'

Leo wished he could find a way to believe that. But it would not do to say as much. This was a wedding, not a wake. 'Thank you. And thank you for the licence and all the trouble you went to getting it. It was no small thing you did for me, and I am very sensible of it.'

'Nonsense,' his cousin replied, waving a hand airily. 'Consider it my wedding present. Let's have a toast to you, and to your bride!'

Leo drained his glass but refused to let his cousin refill it. This didn't seem the day to be getting foxed, not now and not later, and if he needed courage to face the future, he wouldn't find it in a bottle. Despite his abstinence, the meal and the toasts and speeches after it passed in a sort of blur of confused images, and he only came back to himself when he was climbing into the carriage after Isabella, and waving goodbye to his mama – who was weeping, though she'd assured him repeatedly that she wasn't in the least sad, but on the contrary very happy – and to his cousins and the rest of the company. They leaned forward and waved, but soon they were bowling down the avenue away from the Castle, and they sat back and looked at each other. Suddenly it seemed very quiet, and Leo thought he should say something, though he had no idea what it should be.

He'd found during the course of the day that he felt better when he was able to touch her, though it really shouldn't be the case and he could have no idea if she felt the same, and so, in need of comfort, he reached for her hand again, and said, 'Mrs Winterton...'

She made a curious little sound, between a choking laugh and a sob, and flung herself into his arms.

45

Isabella found the wedding ceremony difficult and was excessively glad when it was over. She wasn't able, after all, to avoid remembering Ash, and the day she'd married him, just two and a half years ago, and now – how greatly things had changed in so short a time – this memory felt like a terrible betrayal of Leo. The least he deserved, she thought, was that the woman standing beside him and marrying him was actually thinking about him while she did it, rather than another man. And so she tried to do so, but it was so hard, uttering those same words again as she'd believed she never would. In the early part of the service, she became possessed by an irrational terror that when she came to the point where she had to respond she'd say Ash's name instead of Leo's. The idea was so coldly horrifying, like standing on a cliff and being drawn to the edge despite terror of the dizzying drop, that she began to feel faint, the minister's words ringing oddly in her ears. But she bit hard on the inside of her lip till she tasted blood, and the small pain helped her conquer the fear, and she repeated the correct words without stumbling. She would never tell another soul of it, she swore to herself. Well, maybe her mother. Eventually. Never

Leo. It was possible, of course, that if all went awry later, as it so easily might, she'd never have the chance to tell him anything more.

Afterwards, she felt light-headed with relief, though she was careful not to show it, and it was perhaps this sudden giddiness that inspired her to confront Lady Irlam at last, while the company stood about and talked in casual groups in the hall. Cassandra had offered Isabella her congratulations, of course, along with everyone else, but they had had no private speech, and Lady Irlam must be conscious that her guest was avoiding her, and why. Enough of that; she approached her hostess with resolution, but before she could speak Cassandra took her hand, and pulled her swiftly aside into one of the recesses beside the great fireplace, where they could talk in some privacy.

'I'm sorry,' she said at once, her face troubled. 'I played a dreadful trick on you, and you are angry with me, which I entirely deserve, but I am so sorry. It was a cruel and thoughtless thing to do.'

'I was a little angry at first,' Isabella admitted. 'I was so very worried about Leo, and to think he had been hurt – it was an awful hour or so that you put me through. You must realise that.'

Cassandra grimaced in acknowledgement. 'I know. I did tell Kitty to play down the seriousness of his supposed accident, but I should have realised that you would still suffer from the gravest apprehension. In fact, I knew you would, and was counting on it, to make sure you would go. You'd hardly have gone dashing off to see him if you'd thought he'd bruised his knee or stubbed a toe. I am truly sorry, you know. It was very wrong of me. I don't ask you to forgive me, for I see no reason why you should.'

'It worked, I suppose,' said Isabella. 'If I hadn't been so shocked, I might never have realised that I cared for him. That was your aim, I take it? Or that was what Leo thought you must be about, at any rate. I had no idea at first what was going on, I was so confused, but he guessed straight away.'

'Yes,' said Lady Irlam. 'And I'm glad if it worked, because I want you both to be happy. And I have to say you neither of you appear to be overwhelmed with joy today. Forgive me – I shouldn't ask, it really is none of my business – but have you told him how you feel?'

Isabella swallowed. 'Not yet,' she confessed. And then with a stifled sob, she added, 'I'm afraid he won't believe me.'

Cassandra took her hand. 'Oh my dear!' she said. 'I do know how hard it is, to be married and yet have misunderstandings persisting between you. Everyone thinks that you must be so happy, and yet you're not, you're miserable, and it all feels like such a failure. But you don't need me to tell you that there is no other choice but to be honest, however hard it is.'

'You're right,' she said, returning Cassandra's pressure gratefully. 'I can only hope... But let's not speak of it any more, I beg, or I shall begin weeping.'

'Very well,' replied her hostess with swift comprehension. 'Shall I apologise some more, to give you a chance to compose yourself?' Isabella chuckled weakly and nodded.

'I am truly sorry. Your life is your own affair, and none of my business, and nor is Leo's. I'm like the heroine, if that's what she is, of that novel Lady Carston loves so much and has just made me read – I think she must have been making some sort of a point about my behaviour, and she was right. Don't encourage me by saying that it worked – I need to stop doing it regardless, or I shall quickly turn into the sort of horrid busybody everybody avoids. Is that better?'

'Yes, thank you, I think I can face people now. And there's no harm done, really,' Isabella said with a tiny smile. 'I do realise that you meant well.'

'You are very good to say so! Thank you. And please do tell Leo I am sorry, won't you, if there should be an opportunity? I have wronged both of you. And I wish you the very best of luck. I won't say more.'

There didn't seem to be anything else to say on the subject, and Isabella had no desire for any more extended confidences. She couldn't tell if Lord Irlam had told his wife of her delicate condition, which made the marriage a matter of such urgency, and on this matter, she preferred to remain in ignorance. She couldn't be angry with Leo, with her husband – for he was that now – for telling his cousin, or she'd be a rank hypocrite. She'd confided so much in the Duchess, in Georgie, after all, told her everything, and she hardly knew the woman. And she'd told Jane Carston too, without even the excuse of needing her help. She was tired of all these secrets, of wondering who knew what, and looked forward to a more straightforward life, if that were possible. Though for the rest of her existence, if the child survived and she did, she'd be telling all the world that her son or daughter was an eight-month babe, and hoping they believed her. Perhaps life would never be simple, and it was foolish to think that it would.

She had no more private speech with anyone while they remained at the Castle. When it came time to leave, Lady Carston embraced her tightly and wished her well, as did Cassandra and her new mother-in-law, who was weeping much as her own mother had wept that day in 1814, when she'd married for the first time and embarked on her new life. Lord Irlam shook her hand, and congratulated her, and if he had any private thoughts about her treatment of his cousin, he did not reveal them in his manner or on his face. He appeared to be an entirely uncomplicated young nobleman, but Isabella was beginning to realise that he wasn't quite that. Appearances could be deceptive, and she was not the only person who was more than she seemed. And these people she knew so little of were her family now.

She was glad to be alone with Leo at the end of all this, despite her anxiety over her impending confession and his reaction to it, having been aware of him as a quietly supportive presence throughout what she could only see as an ordeal. When he took her hand in the carriage, and spoke to her so gently, she let go of a little of the rigid control that had sustained her for so long and sought the comfort of his embrace.

She wasn't weeping, but she was trembling with suppressed emotion, and he must be aware of it. He held her, his arms strong about her, and she relaxed into his hold, her head on his shoulder. It had been a tiring day, and it was not over yet. He did not speak, and she was glad of it. This was not the place nor the time for the conversation they urgently needed to have. He seemed prepared to hold her for as long as she required, in spite of everything she had done to him and how she had made him suffer, and so in what she knew to be a childlike way she allowed herself to be soothed by him, and by the rocking motion of the carriage, and in a surprisingly short time they arrived at Winter Manor and pulled up before the porch. The lights inside the house were lit – dusk was falling already, so late in the year – and the old building looked warm and welcoming. She belonged in places like this, she thought, not in castles. If only she could make it right!

The servants had been waiting in the hall, or near it, and came spilling out to greet them in a confusion of handshakes and good wishes. Leo picked her up – it was plain that they expected it – and carried her across the threshold to the accompaniment of cheers. And then they were alone again, in a room she'd never seen before – but then last time all she'd seen was his study, and this was a sitting room. It was a charming room, another woman's room with all her much-loved possessions in it, and the sight of it made her heart ache. It was so much like her mother's chamber and spoke so strongly to her of a secure and happy life that she might never know if she could not now make herself understood and believed.

It was time – long past time, in truth – and as they stood regarding each other in the quiet, pleasant room where a fire crackled and popped, Isabella knew she must speak.

Leo was engaged in taking off his greatcoat, and she cast aside her warm shawl and set to unbuttoning her braided spencer. She crossed to the mirror above the fireplace but found that she was not tall enough to see herself in it in order to take off her veil. He saw her predicament and came to help her, pulling out the pins with deft fingers and setting them down carefully on the mantel. His gentleness brought a lump to her throat. When the veil was freed, he removed it and handed it to her wordlessly. She took it and set it aside with a shaky smile of thanks. 'It's very old and precious Alençon lace from before the Terror – I'm not sure that it is even made any longer. Lady Irlam found it in a trunk of your late aunt's belongings, and lent it to me, so I must see that it is returned to her.' She was babbling nervously; why was she talking such nonsense?

'I saw you speaking to her,' he said, apparently happy to accept the diversion. 'She was rather intense in her manner, and so it seemed to me that she was apologising to you, as well she might. Was I correct?'

'Yes,' she said. 'She did seem to be very sorry, and I accepted her apology. She asked me to tell you that she was aware she had wronged you too, and hoped you would forgive her, and I said I would.'

'It is not my place to refuse forgiveness, if you have given it. But you have cleared the air between you? It was good of you to be so gracious, I think.'

She shrugged, half-embarrassed, half-impatient, with him and with herself. 'We're none of us perfect, and I must believe she meant well, and did not intend any mischief. I choose to believe – I may be wrong, but if I am I'd rather not know it – that your cousin had not told her of my condition, and so she could not be aware of the full implications of what she was doing to me when she tricked me. Although I know you told him.'

He'd said as much in his hurt and fury when she had come to him in his study here, but still he looked anxious and a little ashamed when she mentioned it. 'Isabella, I must tell you that I am sorry—'

She cut him off ruthlessly. It was time. 'Don't apologise. I'm not angry. I have no reason at all to be angry with you. Quite the reverse is true. Leo, I need to tell you something of the greatest importance. Will you sit down and let me explain, while I still have the courage to do so?'

He could do no other than nod in agreement, his face even more troubled than it had been a moment ago. He sat on the comfortable-looking sofa before the fire, looking up at her, waiting. She considered sitting beside him, but it didn't seem enough for such a momentous occasion, so she crossed the carpet and sank down to kneel at his feet, her green skirts billowing about her. She took his hands between hers and drew in a deep breath.

'I realised something, last time we were together in this house,' she began. 'Please let me speak for a moment, while I try to tell you, though I fear I will make a sad hash of it. When I came rushing to your side, terrified that you had been badly hurt, that you might die, I was entirely overset and full of bitterest regret. I was thrown into confusion, all my certainties overturned, and then afterwards when we were so cruel to each other and hurt each other so much, I realised something that I should have realised long before. It was... a piercing sort of emotion, and very powerful. And unexpected. Completely unexpected.' He did not say a word, obedient to her wish, but he made a sudden restless movement, and she looked down, focusing on their clasped hands, not daring in that moment to look at his face for fear of what she might see. 'Among all my hurt and regret, I knew suddenly that I had been an utter fool, Bear, and that I loved you.'

His hands tightened on hers, and she gripped them back, hoping it was an auspicious sign and not mere shock that caused him to cling to her so. 'It hit me like a thunderbolt. I honestly had no idea of it. It wasn't just that I loved you then. It was more than that. I realised that love for you had been creeping up on me for a long time and I am such a fool I didn't notice it. I was so busy with my list, I didn't stop to think. My reasons for devising the list, for doing what I did, were all excellent, and I'm not ashamed of them – I needed to take back control of my life, and I have, though not at all in the way I intended. I loved Ash with all my heart, and I never meant to love again or believed I could. But I love you too, just as much. It's different, what I feel for you, but it's every bit as powerful and all-consuming. I didn't think such a thing was possible, but I know now that it is.'

Isabella broke off in frustration, afraid that her words were having little effect. She looked up at him now, daring to do so at last because it was so important that she knew what he was thinking, but she could not read anything in his face; his expression was forbidding and his thoughts were entirely closed to her.

'You realised this, days ago, and you said nothing?' he managed at last. She could not deceive herself that she could hear any softness in his voice.

'I was afraid you would not believe me.' It was the simple truth.

'I can certainly see why. You must admit your revelation is... highly convenient, for you and for your future.' His words dropped into the quiet room like cold stones that fell upon her heart and sank heavily into it. This was what she had been so frightened of. This was why she had delayed so long.

'I know it must appear so. I can't blame you for your surprise and your doubt. I know you must think that I am desperate for you not to leave me, desperate not to be exposed to the gossip and censure that a separation so soon after marriage must cause. Desperate, I suppose…' Her voice was cracking. 'Desperate not to have to tell my parents of all people that our marriage is a sham. It would be idle to deny that that would hurt me greatly. But not for the reason you think. Because it isn't a sham, Leo! I don't want it to be sham, I want it to be real!'

He had not pulled his hands away from her grasp; perhaps he had almost forgotten she was clinging to him. But she had not; the feel of his cold fingers under hers gave her a little courage, and she went on. 'I don't care about the rest of the world or what they think of me, not even my parents if it comes to that; I only care about you. I have been in silent agony over the last few days, knowing I must speak but not daring to do so. You have made it very clear that you mean to leave me very soon, and in all honesty, I cannot blame you for it or beg you to stay. I know you must protect yourself from further hurt at my hands.' She was weeping silently now, hot tears streaming down her face unregarded. She forced herself to go on. She could not expect or even want her tears to sway him; she needed to convince him that every word she spoke was true. 'I love you with all my heart, my dearest, but my great fear is that I have treated you so badly, and hurt you so much, that you will not believe me, or if you do in the end believe me, it is too late and you do not care any more.'

46

DAMN THE LIST!

Leo sat looking at her in stunned silence. At his wife. For a long moment, he was incredulous, and could not believe his own ears. She was – she could not be, but she was – telling him that she loved him. It couldn't be real. He'd called it up somehow, this fantasy, out of his enormous need for her. Or she was lying, as women sometimes were forced to, knowing how precarious her place in the world would be, and that of her unborn child, if he deserted her. He'd never thought her a liar – but she must be lying now.

But when she raised her eyes to his, the desperate anxiety and suspense in every lineament of her dear face told him that she was speaking nothing more or less than the truth. He'd always found her easy to read, and he could read her now. It was dazzling in its simplicity.

She loved him. She did.

He couldn't speak. He must, he needed to reassure her, but he couldn't. His heart was too full. He reached down with clumsy urgency and pulled her up into his arms. He set his hands either side of her face and held her there for a moment, and then from somewhere deep inside he found the ability to murmur with fierce intensity a few broken words. 'Isabella! Isabella, my love, my love, my dearest love!'

And the relief and comprehension that flooded her face and banished all the worry was the loveliest thing he'd ever seen. There was no more need for words after that, not for a long time. They kissed, both of them at last fully aware of all that was hidden beneath their physical passion and constant need for each other. They lay in each other's arms and kissed, sweet and deep and slow, and needed no more than that for a while.

At last, Isabella pulled back a little. She was lying in Leo's close embrace and they were both flushed and breathless, dizzy. She said, 'I'm sorry. So sorry I hurt you with my coldness when there was no need for it. I wish I could go back and alter that. I put you through so much unnecessary pain.' He shook his head in vehement denial, and she knew that in this moment he would forgive her anything. It was wonderful, but she must not take it for granted or abuse it. She had to try to make him understand her, in so far as she understood herself. 'Bear, I'm not like other people.'

All at once he was laughing as he looked up at her. 'My love, I know that well enough! I don't want you to be like other people. You're unique, and I adore you for it.'

'Yes, that's all very well, but... Stop laughing, and listen! I'm serious. I don't like change, and I can't cope with it. Sudden, unexpected events, like Ash's death, hit me very hard. I know they'd hit anyone hard – I'm not claiming some special sensitivity or sensibility, please don't think that. I'm not saying I'm superior to others, quite the reverse. I'm weak. I'm not strong like other people. I find it hard to move on, when tragedy strikes. I get stuck. That's what my illness was, in great part. I couldn't accept what happened – which was after all nothing that hasn't happened to thousands of other women in these years of war. People who have loved ones taken from them – as your mother did, as Lord Irlam and his siblings did, as my parents did when they lost one tiny infant or unborn child after another – they mourn, but eventually they pull themselves together and carry on with life, because they have no choice. I couldn't do that. My future was all planned out, and when those plans were broken into a thousand pieces, it broke me too.'

He was listening intently, and he stroked her hair back from her face with a loving hand, but he could see she hadn't finished, so he let her continue without interruption. 'And so I couldn't continue after Ash's death. I didn't want to, in fact. I clung to his memory like a drowning person clinging to a spar, and when people tried to talk to me, to make me see things differently, I wouldn't listen. Did you know that Blanche before she left told me that she hoped, as did Gabriel, that I would marry again and find happiness? That she believed that was what Ash would have wanted for me? I refused to hear her. I told myself it was because of my great love, and that nobody understood it or felt as deeply, but it wasn't really. It was all about me, and the way my mind is made.'

He did speak now. 'You're too hard on yourself. Your self-criticism might be just, perhaps, if ten years had passed. It's not been two, since you lost him. It's no time at all.'

'I know that's right, but I'd have been no different in ten years, or twenty, I promise you. I might say to you that I was afraid to love again, for fear of getting hurt, but it wouldn't be true, or not completely. Because that would be reasonable, if not very brave. And it wasn't that. I'm serious, Leo – I'm not like other people, and though I will try to be conscious of it, and fight against it, I don't think I can change my nature. I want you to be fully aware of what I am.'

'I love all that you are. I don't need you to change, nor should anyone, least of all me, ask you to. You are so very brave, and you don't know it. You took such risks, trying to take back your life. Who else would do that?'

'And that's another thing. I was afraid that you would think I had persuaded myself that I loved you, because in the end I was ashamed of what I'd done, after I realised the consequences of it, and it was easier to tell myself I must be in love rather than accept I gave my body freely to a stranger.'

'I don't think that. I do believe you, my love, and not just because I want to. I am a good judge of people – I have had to be. I know when I'm being lied to, and when I am not. There's no deception in you.'

'So you will know I am telling you the truth when I tell you that I'm not ashamed of anything I've done. I don't think that loving you justifies what I did, because in my mind it doesn't need justification. Lady Carston said to me once that the world will change when women admit to themselves that they don't have to be in love with men to go to bed with them. I disagree with her in part. I think lots of women *do* admit that already, if only in private, because they aren't yet in a position to choose the men they marry or take as their protectors. But she believes, as I do, that we deserve what most men have and we do not – the freedom to choose for ourselves what we do with our lives and our bodies, with love or without it. And I chose you, out of all the men in the world, Bear, and I'm so glad I did. But I also happen to love you – not because I should, not because it's convenient or morally right, or because we've made a child together. Just because I do, and always will.'

Naturally, these highly gratifying words obliged the Captain to kiss his bride again, but he realised that he too had a secret he must share, and now was the time. He said, 'My love, I must tell you something in my turn. It is not a great matter, perhaps, but I will feel easier in my mind when you know it.'

She looked at him questioningly, and he went on, 'I know that you believe I was first presented to you in London this autumn, by Georgie. But it's not true, you know. We had met before, though very briefly, and though I know I should have reminded you of it long since, I could never find the right moment.'

'How could that be?'

She had no notion of what he was about to reveal, and he continued with a little difficulty, 'I danced with you, just once, a wild country dance in a very crowded room. I wasn't properly introduced to you, and I didn't hear your name or realise that you were married until some time later. I must admit that I was greatly struck by you, and perhaps I have carried your image in my heart ever since – certainly in my memory. It was in Brussels, my dear. Late May last year. I recalled it, but for reasons I can fully appreciate, you did not. You can, I hope, see why I have hesitated to mention it.'

She stared at him, a little frown creasing her brows, and for a second he worried that he had distressed her; that the wound caused by Lord Ashby's death was still too fresh and always would be, coming to ambush their happiness and cloud their joy over and over again. He regretted speaking now, though he'd known he must. But then she said slowly, her frown clearing, 'I do remember... I wore blue, we were laughing together. Oh Leo, my dearest love, of course I see why you could not tell me! Nobody dares to speak of Brussels to me, or of Ash. Oh, but then... You saw him?'

He nodded, and then said, his voice low, 'I saw you together, and I could see that you were happy.' He couldn't manage any more than that.

She smiled at him through tears. 'We were, you know. Thank you for telling me. Perhaps later we can talk of it all, and of the strange coincidence that we were both there, and met. It's past and done, Leo, and it must no longer be a topic we avoid. It has no power to hurt us unless we let it, and I do not mean to let it. We have our future to look forward to. And my immediate future is not this sofa, but your bed.'

He laughed, his heart suddenly much lighter. 'I'm so glad, for I find myself in perfect agreement with you, madam. I'm going to carry you upstairs to bed – yes, in the middle of the afternoon, and I don't care who knows what I'm about. Are you not my wife? I made all sorts of promises today, and I intend to fulfil them. And along the way that list of yours is going to receive some serious attention, before I sleep in your arms for the first time, and wake to look at you, as I have longed to do.'

'Damn the list,' said Mrs Isabella Winterton, shockingly. But she smiled as she said it, and was smiling still when her husband picked her up and – with a little assistance in the awkward matter of opening doors – carried her out into the hall and up the stairs to his bedchamber. The only other coherent thing she said for a long while was, 'I'll want my dinner later, sir. If you mean to ravish me, or I to ravish you, or both, you needn't think you can get away without feeding me.'

'You shall have your dinner,' he said. 'But not for a good while yet, and it'll be on a tray, and taken in bed.' She had no objection to make, after that.

It was hours later, and Isabella rose, naked, to add logs to the fire, which had sunk low while she and Leo had been otherwise occupied. He lay and watched her in lazy appreciation, telling her that she'd exhausted him, and he was completely unable to move. It was true that she now had several items to cross off her list. The jewellery box that contained it, along with her trunk and all her other possessions, was no doubt sitting close at hand in her dressing room, wherever that might be. She had no inclination to explore the house just now, she told him; she wanted to get back to bed, to his arms. But having said that, she paused for a moment by the window. She'd gone to close the curtains against the winter night, but did not immediately do so. He watched the firelight play across her pale skin and strike glints of gold from her long hair, which at an earlier stage of the afternoon he'd unfastened from its plaits and ribbons with infinite care and tenderness, so that he could bury his face in it as he loved to do. Looking at her, perhaps he wasn't quite as tired as he'd thought... 'What's the matter, love?' he said. 'Don't think I'm not admiring the view, for I am, but I don't want you to catch cold. Come here, and let me warm you!'

She turned in all her naked glory, and said, 'I was just looking out for a moment. Leo, we won't be heading out to London tomorrow morning, and Yorkshire will have to wait a while. It's snowing!'

47

It was a little early in the year for really persistent snow in Hampshire, and so it didn't linger, but the white blanket lay thick for a day or two before it melted away, and it would be foolish, Captain Winterton said and his wife agreed, to brave the roads until they were clear. They were both perfectly content to stay indoors and wait; it was a little stolen honeymoon that they had not looked to have, and all the more welcome for it.

Isabella had written to her mother the day before her wedding, saying that she would be home soon; that she would not be travelling alone and that they were not to worry in the least for her safety. At Lord Irlam's insistence, she had told them that if there was the least sign of inclement weather they would halt somewhere comfortable and not attempt to proceed with her journey. If it snows, she said, you must not look to see us until it has passed. Weather-wise persons had been looking at the sky and muttering darkly for a day or two before the ceremony, but she and Leo had been distracted by their own affairs, and had not paid much heed, though Hal had on their behalf. The Earl had franked the letter, and it had gone off to the Mail coach, and they must assume that it would reach Yorkshire with as much speed as could be achieved in such circumstances. It might perhaps have been a slightly mysterious letter, with its mention of an unnamed companion or companions, and it was therefore one that would cause her parents to speculate wildly when they received it. But that was not a bad thing – they would be somewhat prepared for a surprise, if one ever could be, though they might not know what form it would take.

When the snow cleared and it was understood that travel was possible once more, the couple set off at first light one morning, and reached London and their hotel in Albemarle Street without too much difficulty. Lord Irlam's fine horses were at their disposal for this first part of the journey, although they would be obliged to hire their beasts in the normal way for the rest of their trip, and this would slow their progress up the Great North Road. They had not brought Isabella's maid, neither of them wishing to sit cooped up with her in the carriage for what would be a lengthy journey; they much preferred to be alone. They did not hurry, and Isabella found that she enjoyed the journey with Leo, sitting close to him in the carriage every day, talking idly of everything and nothing, and watching the changing landscape through the carriage windows as they travelled north, then stopping as the winter dusk drew in, eating together in their inn parlour by cosy candlelight, before retiring early to their chamber. Being undressed by him, undressing him. Lying in Leo's arms in a succession of deep feather beds. It did take several days to reach their destination, but she didn't mind in the least.

They arrived at Isabella's parents' house near Harrogate rather later in the day than they'd planned, having had a problem with one of their horses in the penultimate leg of their journey. The snow was still lying on the hills here, though the roads were relatively clear, and it was appreciably colder in the West Riding than it had been in Hampshire. She had directed the postilion where to go once they left the main road, and clutched Leo's hand somewhat tightly as they drew close. 'Are you nervous, love?' he asked her, and she admitted that she was a little, as was only natural. By now every hill, every tree and every turn of the stone walls that edged the winter fields was familiar to her. They were the same as they had always been, but she was very different.

They pulled up in front of the mellow stone house, and Leo jumped down to help Isabella alight, and then, squeezing her gloved hands comfortingly, he stepped aside to help the postilion to take down their luggage, and to pay the lad off and send him on his way with the horses. While he was thus engaged, the door was flung open, and Mr and Mrs Richmond came rushing out. At first, they were occupied in embracing their daughter and exclaiming over her, but as the boy set about disengaging the team, they turned to look at Leo with questioning faces. Isabella took his arm and drew him towards her parents, saying softly, 'Mama, Papa, I would like you to meet Captain Winterton. We have... I must tell you... This is Leo, and we are married!'

48

There was no denying that things were a little difficult for a while, and Isabella would not soon forget the hurt expression on her parents' faces when they realised all that she had kept from them, but their innate good manners and restraint carried them through it and inside the house. Everything seemed a little easier when they were sitting in the familiar old parlour with a glass of wine by a cheerful fire, the thick brocade curtains drawn against the cold.

Mrs Richmond said, 'I thought there was something a little peculiar about the tone of your recent letters, dear, but your father told me I was imagining it. Yes, you did, Peter. You mentioned such a quantity of young men, Isabella, and I was sure that one of them must be the cause of the strangeness, but I couldn't work out which. You seemed indifferent to all of them, or pretending to be so. And your name, sir,' she said almost accusingly to Leo, still somewhat stiff in her manner, 'she never mentioned at all. I didn't even know that you existed!'

Her mother was a little tearful, and Isabella hurried to say, 'I'm sorry! I knew I couldn't be natural if I referred to Leo, and that you would realise and question me, so I didn't say anything at all. And then things happened so quickly at the last, and it was far too late to break it to you gently!'

They'd discussed this beforehand, and Isabella had asked Leo to find some way to speak to her father alone so that she could have a heart-to-heart with her mother. There were things that fathers didn't need to know, she'd told her husband; he had smiled a little wryly, as if seeing a vision of his own future, but agreed all the same. The Captain set down his glass now and said, 'I know that all this has been a shock to you, ma'am, sir, but I hope at least that I will be able to demonstrate to you that I am perfectly able to support a wife and family, that my estate is well enough though it is not large, and that Isabella's marriage settlements will be all that you might desire for her. Shall we discuss it now, sir, so that I may set your mind at rest on such matters? I have brought papers for your perusal, including details of what I have invested in the Funds.'

'Yes,' said Isabella, 'that's an excellent idea! Mama, would you come and help me unpack? I am sure that Betty will have enough to do without waiting on me.'

In a moment or two, she was alone with her mother in her old bedchamber, and Mrs Richmond sank down into the comfortably shabby old chair by the window and gazed at her daughter, her gentle, anxious face a picture of confusion and several other conflicting emotions. 'I love him, Mama,' she said directly, jumping up onto the bed and hugging her knees as she had done when she was small. 'I love him and he loves me. That's all you need to know, really, in the end.'

'Why didn't you tell me?' her parent protested with some justice.

'I've been very foolish. I was so determined that I wouldn't marry again, so sure that I could never love anyone but Ash, that I refused to see that I was falling in love with him. I've loved him for weeks and weeks, and never knew it. Even when he declared himself to me, I wouldn't accept it. I told him I didn't love him and never would – I hurt him, Mama! If you had seen his face! And all along it wasn't true, and I've only recently realised it. I didn't want to tell you in a letter – can you understand that? I thought it better if you met him, so you can see how good and kind he is, and how much he loves me. I knew you'd only worry, if I wrote.'

'I would have worried. We both would. I'm still worried at the suddenness of it all. Is that why you married so quickly, without us even being present? So that you could travel to see us together?'

This idea obviously gave her mother some measure of comfort, and Isabella rather feebly wished she could accede to it; how much easier it would be, if she could say, *Yes, Mama, that is why*. But it wouldn't be honest, her mother wasn't stupid, and she wouldn't begin her married life with any more lies. The truth would have to come out soon enough, at least between mother and daughter.

'Not... entirely,' she said cautiously.

There was a little silence, as her mother looked her up and down, and she shifted uncomfortably under her gaze. It was written on her face, she knew. She might as well say it. 'I'm with child.' There. It was out.

Mrs Richmond looked at her, her mouth slightly open, anger kindling slowly but surely in her eyes. 'He took—'

'He didn't take anything. I made him. Well, no, that's not quite right,' she amended scrupulously. It certainly didn't sound right. She'd have to explain: maybe not the list, *definitely* not the list, but some part of it. The facts rather spoke for themselves, and could hardly be denied.

'I wanted a last time that I knew was a last time,' she said, as she had said once before. She glanced at her mother's horrified, uncomprehending face, and hurried on. 'I couldn't endure the way Ash was taken from me so cruelly, you know I couldn't, and I wanted to... control the memories, I suppose. To make new ones that didn't hurt so much. To feel as though I was in control of my life again. I thought I'd never marry or fall in love, I didn't want to, but... I was so lonely, Mama! And he is so kind and good. I won't have you blaming him, thinking he seduced me, because it isn't true! I knew I'd be coming back home soon, and that I'd be alone for ever after that. And so...'

Her mother was looking at her as though she were a stranger. 'But... You took him to bed. That's what you're telling me. This is what comes of going to that London – I always knew it was a terrible idea, and now look! You have been led astray by your fine new friends, I see now, and taken shocking advantage of! You must have been! I simply refuse to believe, Isabella Richmond, that you initiated... that!'

It was fairly obvious that somebody had. 'But I did, Mama, I swear it was all me... I can't speak of it! I'm sorry I've shocked you, but I've always been odd, you know it's true. Perhaps you can put it down to that, if it helps. But what I didn't know, Mama dear, was that he loved me then. He'd been meaning to ask for my hand, was biding his time because he knew I'd been hurt. He was going to woo me slowly. But of course when I... Poor Leo, he had no choice.' It would definitely be wise not to tell her mama that she had intended to try someone else if he had refused her. She'd have an apoplectic fit if she heard that.

Her mother's face was working in a curious way. 'Perhaps he did and perhaps he didn't! You have always been so very deter-mined!' Their eyes met, and suddenly they found themselves engulfed in helpless laughter. Mrs Richmond laughed till tears streamed down her face, and Isabella clutched at her bedpost till she felt weak, then flopped back among the pillows. 'He... he told me he was in love with someone else,' she gasped at last. 'He invented this whole ridiculous story... He thought it made sense at the time, he told me later, the dear idiot that he is. But I'm no better.'

Her mama was mopping her face. 'Oh, I am furious with you, but after all I'd say you deserve each other. And what's done is done, I suppose, whoever you say began it. At least you're safely married. How... how long?'

'I've just missed my courses once. They were due about two weeks ago, or a little more. I'm losing count, so much has happened. But I know, Mama. I can feel it. This time it's real, I promise you it is. Not like before. I never thought I could...'

Mrs Richmond rose then, and came to embrace her, and she found that she was crying in earnest now, sobbing into her mother's soft shoulder. 'My dear, my dear,' she whispered, and she was crying too. There was no need for words; her mother knew what she had suffered after Ash's death, and her pitiful delusion of carrying his child.

At length, her mama said raggedly, 'I'm happy for you, my love. Really I am. Despite the circumstances. You've been through so much, and now at last... It is very irregular, and most improper and wrong, but still, I must be glad, when I think of everything that you have endured, and all our worry over you... Oh, it's too much, I can't speak!'

This didn't help either of them to stop weeping, and it was only when she said, 'Mama, there is no need for Papa to know anything at all of this!' that they were able to stop. The speed of her mother's horrified agreement, and the comical expression on her countenance, set her laughing uncontrollably again, until she was obliged to hold her aching sides and struggle for her breath. It was a long while before they could compose themselves enough to wash their tear-stained faces and go downstairs to see how her father and Leo had been getting on in their absence. It was to be hoped that the very respectable nature of the Captain's fortune would have reassured Mr Richmond on worldly matters, at least.

They had a celebratory dinner, and all the servants, many of them people she'd known from the cradle, were brought in to toast the happy couple and wish them well. It was a happy evening in the end. Much later, Isabella lay in Leo's arms in her rose-papered childhood bedroom, surrounded by all that was dear and familiar, and sighed in contentment as she nestled into his chest. 'That's done,' she said, snuggling closer.

'We're lucky we arrived when we did, my dearest. It's meant to snow tomorrow,' he told her. 'A heavy fall this time, your father thinks. If it settles, and he believes it will, we'll be here for Christmas, I dare say.'

'Well, I don't mind if you don't. Do you?' She looked up at him, and he touched her face with a tenderness that made her eyes water a little. It was a wonder she had a tear left in her, but it seemed she did: one or two, at least.

'I don't. I don't mind anything if I can be with you.'

'I told Mama about my condition, Leo. I felt it only right.'

'I thought you might have done. Did she want to kill me?'

'Only for a second, until I explained that it was all my fault, and you were the innocent victim of my lust. Don't worry, I didn't mention the list.'

He chuckled. 'I should hope you didn't. Some things are private. What did she say?'

'She said a fair amount. She was quite shocked, naturally. But in the end, she forgave me, I think, and agreed that we should in no circumstances tell my papa!'

'By all means, let us not! Will he believe that his grandchild is an eight-month babe when he or she makes an early appearance, then?'

'He will believe,' she said with certainty, 'anything my mother tells him to believe!'

'Oh, he lives under the cat's foot, does he?' She nodded, smiling and running her hands suggestively over the thick hair of his chest. 'And am I to do the same?'

'I think so, Bear,' his wife told him, sitting up and straddling him, her hair wild about her shoulders and her breasts. 'Admit, sir, while you can still speak, that you would not have it any other way!'

While he could still speak, he did.

ACKNOWLEDGEMENTS

I wrote my first novel in my kitchen in lockdown. I'd never have developed the confidence to do it without the encouragement of all the complete strangers who commented so positively on my Heyer fanfic on AO3. But the real inspiration came from my good friends in the Georgette Heyer Readalong on X (formerly Twitter). I'm particularly grateful to Bea Dutton, who spent many hours of her precious time setting up and running the readalongs. I can't possibly name everyone – there are too many of us – but thank you all, amazing Dowagers, for your continuing support with this novel and far beyond it. Your friendship is very important to me.

Thank you to all of the reading community on X/Twitter, and now on Instagram.

I've been obsessed with Georgette Heyer's novels since I first read them when I was eleven. They have their faults, but they've provided solace and escape for millions of people in tough times, so thank you, Georgette, even though you would have absolutely hated this book.

Thanks also to my family for putting up with me while I wrote one novel and then another in quick succession. And then another four. Thanks for understanding when I just have to write another 127 words before lunch so I can stop on a nice round number.

My lovely work colleagues Amanda Preston, Louise Lamont, Hannah Schofield and Amy Strong have also been extremely supportive: thanks, Team LBA!

I am very lucky to have a superb agent in Diana Beaumont,

formerly of Marjacq and now DHH. She has believed in my writing from the first time she read it, and will always be my champion. Her editorial suggestions are brilliant, and she's just an all-round star. Thanks too to everyone else at Marjacq, including Catherine Pellegrino and Guy Herbert. I know better than most people how important the whole team at an agency is.

Many thanks to everyone at Boldwood, including Cecily Blench for the fantastic copyediting and Gary Jukes for the scrupulous proofreading, and to Team Boldwood as a whole for your amazing professionalism and unflagging enthusiasm: Amanda, Nia, Niamh, Claire, Ben and everyone else, not forgetting Rachel Lawston for the beautiful cover designs. And of course above all grateful thanks to my wonderful editor Rachel Faulkner-Willcocks, whose superb edits have made this a much better book, with much more heart. One of the many special things about Boldwood is the wonderful spirit of mutual support that the authors share, so I'd like to thank you all, particularly the amazingly talented Jane Dunn and Sarah Bennett, for your generosity and friendship.

Finally, if you're reading this because you've bought the book, or a previous one: THANK YOU!

ABOUT THE AUTHOR

Emma Orchard was born in Salford and studied English Literature at the universities of Edinburgh and York. She was a copy editor at Mills & Boon, where she met her husband in a classic enemies-to-lovers romance. Emma has worked in television and as a Literary Agent, and started writing in 2020.

Sign up to Emma Orchard's mailing list for news, competitions and updates on future books.

Follow Emma on social media here:

𝕏 x.com/EmmaOrchardB

⬚ instagram.com/emmaorchardbooks

ⓟ pinterest.com/EmmaOrchardRegency

ALSO BY EMMA ORCHARD

You're cordially invited to

The Scandal Sheet

The home of swoon-worthy historical romance from the Regency to the Victorian era!

Warning: may contain spice 🌶

Sign up to the newsletter
https://bit.ly/thescandalsheet

Boldwood

Boldwood Books is an award-winning fiction publishing company seeking out the best stories from around the world.

Find out more at www.boldwoodbooks.com

Join our reader community for brilliant books, competitions and offers!

Follow us
@BoldwoodBooks
@TheBoldBookClub

Sign up to our weekly
deals newsletter

https://bit.ly/BoldwoodBNewsletter

Printed in Great Britain
by Amazon

47042358R00169